Susan Donovan's novels have won accolades for being witty, sexy, and entertaining. A former newspaper reporter with journalism degrees from Northwestern University, Susan is a *New York Times* bestselling author whose novels have been translated into dozens of languages. Susan is a two-time RITA Award finalist and her novel *Take A Chance On Me* was named Best Contemporary Romance by *Romantic Times*. She lives in New Mexico with her assorted pets, and a view of the stunning mountains from her office. Follow her on Twitter @SDonovanAuthor and find her on Facebook at www.facebook.com/SusanDonovanFanPage.

Praise for Susan Donovan's enchanting romances:

'Susan Donovan will steal your heart' Christina Dodd, *New York Times* bestselling author

'Knows how to tell a story that will make your heart melt' *Night Owl Reviews*

'Manages to touch on several serious themes while skillfully telling a story that leaves the reader sighing at the romance' *Romantic Times*

'A captivating novel with dynamic storytelling and heartfelt emotions. Donovan's warm sense of humor and memorable characters are sure to ease their way into the hearts and minds of readers' *Debbie's Book Bag*

'Susan Donovan has brought action, myth, family, and love together to create a story that grabbed me from the first page and had me reading steadily until the end. That, for me, is the mark of a really good book, and one that I heartily recommend' *Smut Book Junkie*

'I love how Susan brings her characters to life. They are engaging and their story is one that will pull you in' *Harlequin Junkie*

'A sweet, warm-hearted romance . . . all you need for a great summer read' '

'Donovan's  klist

Moondance Beach
Susan Donovan

headline
ETERNAL

Published by arrangement with Signet Select,
a member of Penguin Group (USA) LLC.
A Penguin Random House Company.

First published in Great Britain in 2015
by HEADLINE ETERNAL
An imprint of HEADLINE PUBLISHING GROUP

1

Cataloguing in Publication Data is available from the British Library

ISBN 978 1 4722 1789 9

Offset in Times by Avon DataSet Ltd, Bidford-on-Avon, Warwickshire

Printed and bound by CPI Group (UK) Ltd, Croydon, CR0 4YY

*This book is dedicated to Grace Burrowes—
author, attorney, friend, banker, twenty-four-hour
airport chauffeur, dog rescuer, moving company,
and all-purpose fairy godmother. Thank you
for everything. You have been a blessing.*

The mermaid legend of Bayberry Island has managed to survive in a world hostile to myth and magic. As the tale goes, the mermaid has kept a vigil over her small Massachusetts island—halfway between Nantucket and Martha's Vineyard—for well over a century. Believers say that from her perch three blocks from the water's edge, she gently nudges inhabitants and visitors on their journeys toward the most elusive of all human needs: love.

The Great Mermaid's bronze form rises from a fountain and hovers sixteen feet in the air. From there she can observe a bustling Main Street, watch the busy marina, and gaze out to sea. From this lookout she has welcomed thousands upon thousands of sunrises, witnessed an equal number of evening shadows fall across the shops and houses, and shared in the joys and heartaches of the mortals below.

For those who believe, the question is not whether the mermaid is able to intervene in the affairs of the human heart. The only mystery is how, where, why, and for whom she extends her favor.

—Opening narration, *The Mermaid of Bayberry Island*, a documentary film by Nathaniel Ravelle

Chapter One

It was a recent June evening on Bayberry Island. Shop lights flickered. The old-fashioned gas streetlamps cast a warm glow over the bricks of Fountain Square. A crescent moon peeked over the horizon. And right on schedule, the last passenger ferry of the day made its unhurried approach toward the public dock.

Suddenly, the front door of the tavern flew open, spilling light, music, and laughter onto the boardwalk. A voice carried on the breeze.

"Get outta here, you bunch of good-for-nothings, or I'll call the police! I'll call the mayor, too!"

The mayor of Bayberry Island ignored the empty threat and lurched toward the door of the Rusty Scupper Tavern. At his elbow was his son, the off-duty police chief.

"Go right ahead!" Frasier Flynn made eye contact with most of the crowded barroom. "This place is a dive, anyway! You'll be hard-pressed to ever find me here again!" When the mayor tried to swat at a piece of party streamer snagged in his thick white hair, he only smacked himself in the eye. The regulars roared with laughter. "All right, then. See you tomorrow."

"Thanks for putting up with us, Rusty." Police Chief Clancy Flynn looked over his shoulder while stuffing his father's large body through the exit.

"It was an honor." The bartender smiled at Clancy and wiped confetti off the bar. "It's not every year the big kahuna turns seventy. Am I right?"

"I told you no one's allowed to use that word!" Frasier's head might have been out the door, but his ears were keen, and his bellow carried back into the noisy establishment. "And that includes any variation of 'seven' or 'tee.' I don't even want to hear that you've got a seven a.m. tee time!'"

" 'Night, Rusty." Ashton Louis Wallace III smiled politely and placed a large tip on the bar. It was no mystery why he looked rumpled that evening. Not only had Rusty poured him half a dozen Sam Adams Summer Ales in the span of two hours, but Ash was a proud papa of a baby not yet sleeping through the night and was long overdue for a boys' night out. His wife, Rowan, had no complaints—in fact, she'd coordinated her father's birthday outing.

Nat Ravelle was the last of the four-man entourage to make his exit. The California ex-pat and husband of Rowan's best friend, Annie, gulped down what was left of his fourth martini before he passed through the door with his good friends. "Later, dudes!"

The group began a slow stroll along the waterfront, heading south toward Main Street. Frasier held his face into the sea breeze and gazed out over the boat slips.

"Nothing better than a night out with the finest young men on Bayberry Island."

"Thank you, Frasier." Even alcohol couldn't dull Ash's finely tuned manners. As Clancy had learned the last couple of years, his brother-in-law might have come from Boston Brahmin money, but he was as down-to-earth as anyone he'd ever known.

"We're short one man, however. And that's just not right."

Clancy braced himself, aware that his father was preparing to orate about his prodigal son, Clancy's older brother, Duncan. Before Frasier got started, he nearly tripped stepping onto the boardwalk. Clancy grabbed him. "How about we get you home in one piece, Da?"

His father grumbled, throwing an arm over his boy's shoulder as they strolled. "Now, let me tell you how things were back in the days of ol' Rutherford Flynn, my great-grandfather, the brilliant immigrant entrepreneur who first tamed this wild and stormy island . . ." Frasier gestured grandly at the bistros, Internet cafés, and lobster-roll stands that surrounded the public dock. "Now, mind you, this was way before there were planes and diesel ferry boats and frozen custard on a damn *stick*! Did you know that the men of Bayberry Island lived and worked as a single unit? By God, they were together on the fishing boats all day and in the pub together at night. It was a sacred brotherhood!"

"Wouldn't want to be downwind from that bunch," Nat said.

Ash chuckled. "That's an awful lot of fishin' 'n' drinkin'. Bet their wives weren't thrilled."

Frasier raised a cautionary finger and scowled at his companions. "Bayberry men were rough around the edges, I'll give you that, but they were civilized. There was always a hot bath waitin' for 'em when they got home . . ." Frasier's voice had grown progressively louder, and he now pointed skyward, a sure sign that he was reaching a rhetorical climax of some sort. "And after a good scrub, they made certain their women thanked the Lord for being born!"

The wild pontificating had caused Frasier to list to port. Nat propped him up from the other side, and Clancy nodded his thanks to his friend.

"Let's keep moving, Da. We're almost there."

"No. I need to say something." Frasier planted his tree-trunk legs on the boardwalk and refused to budge. "We need to get together more often. I miss this. All of us together—it's how it should be."

Ash patted his father-in-law on the back. "We see you nearly every day, Frasier. And since your official birthday party isn't for another week, there's plenty more celebrating to come."

"Oh, hell, Ash! You know what I mean." Frasier sniffed as his gaze followed the movement of wispy night clouds. "Duncan should be here. He might be a Navy SEAL, but he is also one of us, a son of this island—*my* son."

The group remained quiet for a moment, the younger men exchanging glances. Eventually, Clancy cleared his throat. "Duncan's not ready for a pub crawl, Da. He'll be home as soon as he's discharged for outpatient therapy."

"Nonsense." Frasier leveled his gaze, his cheeks red from the alcohol and the oncoming rush of sentiment. "That boy is strong as a bull shark, and one day real soon he'll be healthy enough to get himself shipped out to some far corner of the world, the way he always does. Dammit, we all know why Duncan didn't come home in time for my birthday. For the last sixteen years that boy's only come home a few days each year, always during festival week, and never a day more. His absence tonight has nothing to do with his injuries!"

Though the annual Mermaid Festival was still two months away, a fair number of tourists strolled along the boardwalk on this breezy June night, and all of them had noticed a rather tipsy mayor holding court in front of Talbot's Nautical Antiques Shoppe.

"Why don't we talk about it at your place, Da?"

"This needs to be said right here, right now." Frasier lowered his chin and scowled. "Duncan isn't here tonight because this would be too messy for him. He doesn't want anything holding him to Bayberry—no entanglements, no celebrations, not even his own damn family. He never has. And that's the God's truth."

Since that was an accurate description of his big brother, Clancy didn't disagree. He gently nudged his father forward.

"What makes a man put down roots?" Frasier stopped again, this time shaking off the assistance of both Clancy and Nat. It took him a moment to stabilize. "Come on now, boys. You know the answer to this one, so let's hear it!"

"Family," Clancy said.

"Ha!" Frasier slapped his son on the back. "For you, yes, because you are loyal to the bone. And it sure helped that your woman came to Bayberry to claim you, which was awfully nice of Evelyn, I must say, and I'll have to remember to thank her when I see her tomorrow."

Frasier directed his gaze to Ash, then Nat. "Come on, fellas. What's the one thing that can make a man stay put no matter how determined he is to leave?"

When neither answered, Frasier let go with a belly

laugh. "By God, you two are the poster boys for this particular affliction, so spit it out!"

They glanced at each other, then said in tandem, "Love."

"Aha! You got it! *Love* makes a man stay. Love makes a man do all kinds of stuff he wouldn't otherwise have half a mind to do."

Frasier tapped a finger into Nat Ravelle's chest. "Look at you, boyo. Three Christmases ago you flew in from Los Angeles with plans to produce a TV show. But you met Annie, quit your job, married her, and now you live here year-round."

"Guilty as charged," Nat said with a grin. "And marrying Annabeth Parker was the best thing I ever did."

"And you!" Frasier pointed at Ashton Louis Wallace III. "You blue-eyed, blue-blooded bastard! You showed up here with visions of bulldozers and dollar signs dancing in your Harvard head, and what happened? You met Rowan, stopped the island from being destroyed by development, and changed the course of Bayberry history — for the better. You're a goddamned hero! And how did all that come about?"

A slow smile spread over Ash's face. "I fell in love with your daughter."

"Now we're cookin' with gas!"

"Come on, Da. It's late."

"It's never too late." With that cryptic comment, Frasier spun on his heels and marched off down the middle of Main Street. Clancy followed. Ash ran ahead.

"Hold up, Frasier." Ash began a backward jog, stiff-arming his father-in-law. "You've had a lot to drink. Maybe it's time to — "

"I've been holding my liquor since Kennedy was in

the White House. Now, step aside, son." The mayor continued his charge, changing direction and heading directly toward Fountain Square. His loud arrival disturbed
the couples canoodling on the benches surrounding the
mermaid fountain. They all stared, clearly annoyed by
the invasion.

One man stood up, placing a protective hand on his
woman's shoulder. "What's the deal, Gramps? You're
ruining the mood."

"As of right now, this attraction is closed."

"Really?" The tourist couldn't have been more than
twenty-five, and he sure wasn't going to miss a chance to
impress his girlfriend. He took a few aggressive steps
toward Frasier. "This is public property. You can't just
show up and—"

Clancy slipped between his father and the chest-
puffer, pulling his badge from the pocket of his off-duty
jeans. "I'm sorry, sir. The mayor is correct. This is official
city business, but Fountain Square will be open again in
a few moments. Thank you for your cooperation."

They didn't look happy about it, but the tourists shuffled away, some glancing over their shoulders with dis-
dain. The girlfriend slapped her protector on the arm.
"What were you thinking? That old man could have
been a psycho killer!"

Clancy waited for the tourists to disappear beyond
the hedge of bayberry shrubs and turned to ask his father what he was up to. But Frasier had already wandered off. He now stood with his back to the others,
staring up at the bronze mermaid, his large hands gripping the edges of the engraved historical marker at her
feet.

"What the hell's he doing?" Nat whispered.

"I have no idea," Clancy said.

"Is he all right?" Ash made a step toward Frasier, but Clancy touched his shoulder.

"Give him a minute."

The men watched in disbelief as Frasier tentatively reached up, then cradled the mermaid's hand in his own. They saw his wide shoulders soften. They heard him speak several sentences—but the combination of the fountain spray, faint music from town, and the ever-present hiss of the ocean drowned out most of his words. Clancy could have sworn he heard the name "Duncan," however. And the name "Mona."

Whoa.

"I thought Frasier hated the mermaid."

Clancy shrugged in response to Ash's comment. "I don't know what he thinks of her. All I know is he hates Ma's obsession with the Mermaid Society and claims the group was the main reason they separated. He's always saying her friends are nut jobs, but as far as the mermaid herself goes, I can't really say how he feels."

Ash leaned closer to Clancy. "Does he . . . ? I mean, do you think it's possible . . . ? Could your father believe in the legend?"

Clancy didn't answer right away. Eventually, he shook his head. "I think the chances of that are mighty slim."

"But he's holding the mermaid's hand," Ash insisted, gesturing toward Frasier like Clancy couldn't see for himself. "Is he asking to be guided to true love? Is he asking for himself or on behalf of someone else?"

"Like I said—I got no flippin' idea." Clancy abruptly turned to face his brother-in-law. "And what about you, *Ashley*? Do you believe in the legend?"

"Me?" Ash touched his button-down shirt and laughed uncomfortably. "Of course not. There's . . . Well, obviously, Rowan and I named Serena after the mermaid—*wait*! What I meant to say was we named our daughter after your great-great-grandmother. And the statue was built in her image, right? I didn't mean to imply Serena was an actual merrrr—" Ash squeezed his eyes tight for an instant, collecting himself. When he opened them again, his gaze shot toward Nat, who was frozen in an open-jawed stare.

"And you, Ravelle? Do you believe in the legend?"

Nat made a clicking sound with his tongue and rolled his eyes. "Dude. Seriously. Just because I met Annie by falling down in front of her shop doesn't mean I believe in the mermaid. I mean, fate? Sure. Why not? But I think I'll leave the mermaid legend for my documentary." He tossed the question back to Clancy. "What about you? You're a Flynn—do you believe?"

Just then Frasier let the mermaid's hand slip from his, stepped back from the statue, and turned toward the group. His eyes held more than sentiment—Frasier looked stunned. His skin shimmered under the lights. Fountain spray had misted his hair and face, plastering the soggy paper streamer to the side of his neck. And for just a moment, Clancy wondered if his father had been crying.

Of course he hadn't. Clancy had never seen his da cry.

"Let's go." Frasier swiped the back of his hand across his wet cheeks. "It's late, and you made me drink too much. For God's sake, I'm seventy years old."

At that instant, a large figure moved silently from the shadows toward the streetlamp. It was a man with two bags slung over his shoulder, and he seemed to be walk-ing a bit unsteadily. Probably another inebriated tourist, Clancy thought, but until he was sure, he would keep his hand on his service weapon.

Just then, a deep voice said, "That old sea hag's not gonna help you, Da."

Frasier's head snapped to attention. Clancy's heart rose into his throat. And his brother stepped into the light.

They all rushed toward Duncan, but he kept them at a straight-armed distance. "Hold up. I'm not very steady." He dropped the duffel and a hanging bag to the bricks before he hugged them one at a time—Da first, then Clancy, Ash, and Nat.

Ash reached out for both his bags. "Let me get these." As Duncan handed over his duffel, he clearly favored his right leg over his left. It had been about six weeks since they last visited him at Walter Reed, and at that time he hadn't even mastered using a walker. He had come a long way.

"Damn, you're doing great, son." Frasier's voice cracked. "Thanks, Da."

"You might want to use a cane," Nat suggested. "You know, to be on the safe—"

Duncan's glare sliced off the rest of Nat's sentence.

"Except you don't need a cane, right?"

"Right," Duncan said.

Frasier made a quick call, and an island taxi swooped in to get them. They tossed Duncan's bags in the trunk and watched him cautiously lower himself into the back-seat with Frasier. Clancy and the others said they would continue walking home.

As the taxi drove off toward Shoreline Road, Nat said, "I thought he was going to bite my head off."

"My God," Ash said. "He dragged those heavy bags all the way from the ferry. That is one tough bastard."

Clancy sighed. "You don't know the half of it."

Chapter Two

Duncan Flynn didn't need to open his eyes to know where he was or how soon darkness would ease into dawn. His birthplace was many things, but subtle was not one of them.

He heard the breath of the surf and the chime of sailboat halyards down at the new marina. He felt expensive cotton sheets cool against his skin. And right on schedule, nature's alarm clock began to chime—the mellow baseline of their local horned owl combined with the never-ending twittering of a northern mockingbird perched on a turret outside the open window.

After only a week, that little fucker was really starting to get on his nerves.

With eyes still closed, from his fancy third-floor guest suite at the Safe Haven Bed and Breakfast, Duncan decided to deduce the time, right down to the minute. It was one of many contests he would have with himself that day, just one more measure of his progress. Was he getting quicker? Stronger? More observant? As it turned out, the game was too easy that morning. It had to be a Saturday between zero five fifty and zero five sixty, because Mellie's freshly baked berry scones were about to come out of the oven the way they did every Saturday morning. The scent had already migrated up to his third-floor suite. He could almost feel the dense pastry dissolve in his mouth and taste the explosion of buttery sweetness on his tongue.

He laughed at his own ridiculousness. Had all these months of recuperation turned him into a freakin' poet? What was next—musing on how the scent of "sea spray" had slipped through the window curtains and filled his nostrils?

Not hardly.

He was no poet. He was a U.S. Navy lieutenant, a language and demolition specialist with SEAL Team 2, and he lived in the brutally real world, where exceptional men died and "sea spray" was just a flowery term for a mix of suspended salt particulates and microscopic organic matter so corrosive it would wreak havoc with planes, ships, aircraft carriers, and every other piece of equipment it touched. It was a time bomb that cost the Pentagon billions every year.

But, oh boy, they sure loved that shit around here! Bayberry Island's only local beer was made by the Sea Spray Microbrewery. There was a small, family-friendly state park on the South Shore called Sea Spray Beach, plus a "See" Spray Sunglass Boutique, a Sea Spray Day Spa, and, of course, a Sea Spray Automated Car Wash. The expression had just the right amount of fluffy delusion about it, Duncan thought, ranking right up there with "Great Mermaid," and "true love."

Duncan stretched his arms toward the ceiling, clasped his fingers, and tucked them behind his head. He took a deep breath and focused on his lower body, cautiously stretching both legs beneath the sheets, judging how much stiffness he would be working with that day. He alternated pointing his toes and flexing his calves twenty-five times on each leg, a gentle warm-up that would please his newest physical therapist, no doubt. Then he lifted his left leg five inches off the bed, held it, and slowly set it down. He did it again. And again. And he'd do it a hundred times more by the end of the day.

Pain radiated in all directions from his left hip. It cut across his abdomen, sliced down to his ankle, and shot up the side of his body to pierce his skull. No surprise there. He was used to it. In fact, some variety of pain had been his standard operating procedure since his first day of BUD/S training a decade ago. He understood physical pain. It was a no-nonsense function of cause and effect, and he'd learned that it could be contained and controlled—maybe not completely and maybe not every moment, but he could handle physical pain.

Just by staying the course.

But the guilt? That was something else entirely. It was a spiteful shape-shifter that lay in wait for him, crouched inside a dark cave in his brain, infinitely patient. Guilt lay coiled in silence, ready to strike the instant his eyes closed, or his guard dropped, or his breath deepened ... and just like that, an explosion would crack open the sky, flaming debris would fly, and the jeep would pin him to the ground as his friends screamed in agony. There he would stay, facedown in grit, blood pooling in his mouth while he flailed, nails bleeding as he tried to get free, useless, trapped by the weight of his failure, unable to free himself until it was too late.

By the time Duncan had reached them, they were dead. He'd failed them all. He had promised to have their backs and he had lied.

He woke with a start, his throat raw and his hair wet with sweat. He scanned the overly bright room, and it took him a moment to piece it together. He wasn't on board the MH-60 headed to the field hospital. He wasn't on the C-17 taking him from Afghanistan to Germany. He wasn't in the recovery room at Landstuhl or the re-hab floor at Walter Reed. The light that hit his eyes also spilled over fancy upholstered furniture, an attached marble bathroom, fresh flowers on the fireplace mantel, a dining nook, expensive linens, and a huge painting of . . . *that damn mermaid.*

Duncan groaned, propping himself against the fancy tufted headboard. He willed his pulse to slow. A quick check of his cell phone revealed it was almost seven thirty—hence the nightmare. He had fallen back asleep for at least two hours, which he should never do. Morning nightmares tended to be the most vicious.

Duncan looked down at himself. His legs and arms trembled with weakness and fear. His T-shirt was soaked through with perspiration. He couldn't let anyone see him like this and knew he had to pull himself together. After a few moments, he slowly draped his legs over the side of the king-sized bed.

His eyes automatically flashed to the painting again. She called to him from above the mantel. Like a well-sexed woman waiting for her lover to return to bed, she lay stretched out on her stomach, cheek resting on folded arms, making sure he noticed her. All that wild dark hair floating in a halo around her head. Those sleepy eyes.

That sexy dip of the small of her back before it curved into her—*mermaid tail*.

"Oh, for God's sake, Flynn," he mumbled to himself. He steadied his feet on the shiny wood floor and was about to push himself to a stand when he froze.

Duncan snatched the large feather from the nightstand and twirled the stiff vane between his fingers, examining his mother's latest gift. The tail feather was that of an adult osprey, this particular specimen measuring about ten inches long and two inches at its widest, dominated by alternating black and white stripes. Duncan stroked his fingers upward along the downy softness. He'd seen many of these through the years, dropped on Bayberry Island beaches or snagged in the dune grass by winds. But this particular feather was obviously a product of one of the tourist shops on Main Street. Its natural beauty was accessorized with a strand of elaborately knotted black and white string dotted with multicolored glass beads, which trailed from the vane like the tail of a kite.

It was pretty enough, he supposed, but his mother shouldn't have spent her money on something like this. Duncan sighed, figuring he'd get around to putting it on the bookshelf, along with the rest of the week's haul—a shellacked starfish, a necklace made of tiny shells and stones, and chunks of sea glass in blues and greens.

Duncan stood. Slowly. Carefully. He focused on the even distribution of his weight and took the thirteen steps required to reach the head, intentionally keeping his eyes away from the painting. With unwavering concentration and one deliberate movement after the next, he managed to shower, shave, and throw on a clean pair of shorts and a T-shirt. He refused to dwell on the fact that it took forty minutes of precise concentration to perform basic tasks that once took no more than five mindless minutes of his time. He couldn't go there. All he could do was push himself harder than he did yesterday. Work longer. Trust that tomorrow would be better than today and that it would be even better the day after that. If he wanted to get back to active duty, this thought process was his only option.

And returning to duty was the only thing that mattered.

Just as he set foot back in the bedroom, Duncan heard a knock at the door.

"Are you decent?"

The feather wasn't enough?

He shook his head as he went to the door. Apparently, it didn't matter how many times he told his mother that he was injured, not the sick kid he used to be, and he was capable of going downstairs to feed himself. She hadn't listened. In the week he'd been home, not once had he been allowed to go down to the kitchen and grab a bowl of Cheerios like the nonpatient he was. And if it wasn't his mother at the door with a tray, it was his sister, Rowan, or Mellie, the family's longtime housekeeper and cook. Even Clancy's wife, Evelyn, felt compelled to fib about how she happened to be in the neighborhood during the lunch hour and thought he might enjoy some of her homemade black bean and quinoa salad, which, for the record, he hadn't.

Duncan was under siege, and his enemy was a legion of relentlessly fussy females.

"Good morning!" His mother was a gray-haired, arthritic lady of sixty-nine years who barely came up to

Duncan's shoulders. Mona Flynn had no business carrying a loaded-down serving tray like a waitress at a Shri-
ner's convention.

Duncan snatched it from her immediately. "Ma—"

"Oh, now, hush. The exercise is good for me. Mellie
made both blueberry and strawberry, and I know those
are your favorites so I brought you one of each, along
with three scrambled eggs, bacon, orange juice, fried potatoes ..."

While Mona recited the menu, Duncan placed the
tray on the small round table by the windows. He pulled
out a chair and motioned for her to sit. Though he hadn't
uttered another word of complaint, his mother continued to justify her visit.

"I just want you to eat right. The next time you go to
Boston for your follow-up, I want the surgeon to be
shocked at your progress and call the bigwigs in Virginia
with the good news."

Duncan prepared a cup of coffee for his mother, adding a swift pour of cream and one packet of sugar, the
way she liked it. He handed it to her, then immediately
poured himself a cup—black.

"So don't forget that tonight is your father's birthday
dinner."

It was a good thing Duncan had just chomped down
on a crisp piece of bacon, because he was sorely tempted
to blurt out a question along the lines of: *You two aren't
going to be in the same room together, are you?*

His mother laughed, obviously seeing the unspoken
question in her son's eyes. "Go ahead. Eat. And yes, I'll
be there. Frasier is seventy. We're having a family celebration. And though your father and I are separated, I've
been married to the crusty old bastard for forty-five

years, so by God I deserve a slice of roast beef and a piece of birthday cake."

"Good eggs, Ma."

"And while everyone is assembled in one place, we'll go over the family's plans for festival week, in particular divvying up jobs at the clambake and going over menu items for the annual barbecue. Since you happen to be home this year, you'll be expected to help out."

"*Really* good eggs."

"I'll tell Mellie. She sprinkled chives on them—did you notice?" Mona took a sip of her coffee and glanced around the suite. "Are you comfortable?"

"I am." And he was. Just as he had been comfortable the previous six mornings she'd asked him that question.

"Dinner starts at seven in the main dining room. They aren't serving to the public tonight, so it will be just us— Clancy, Evelyn, and little Christina; plus Rowan, Ash, and Serena. Then your father, me, Annie, and Nat, and of course Mellie, who might try to convince Adelena to join us."

Duncan stopped chewing. Almost unconsciously, he found himself turning toward the giant mermaid painting above the fireplace mantel, the work of Mellie's daughter, Adelena. With its swirls of blues and greens, flashes of pinks and yellows, those mysterious mermaid eyes, the dark hair scattered with the current, and a boat-load of soft, warm, bare female flesh, the painting was so powerful that it made him vaguely uncomfortable, almost as if she were insisting that he look at her, teasing him, pulling him in . . .

Enough. Today was the day he got rid of that damn painting. He'd find a storage closet or throw it in the attic—anywhere but here.

"You know she's incredibly famous now."

"Huh?" He turned to his mother in surprise. He had forgotten she was even in the room with him. "Yeah. So I hear."

"She bought old Harry Rosterveen's land a few years ago, sixteen acres on the North Shore. She named it Moondance Beach, which I think is very romantic. Did you know she's a full-time island resident these days?"

Moondance Beach? Why must everything on this island be turned into a fairy tale? Adelena must be as delusional as the rest of them. "Yep. Clancy told me."

"She lived in Harry's old shack for a year or so, then built a glass and cedar fortress out there. It's her painting studio, too. Beautiful, but too modern for my tastes. I've only caught a glimpse of him downstairs."

"I see."

"And heaven knows why she needs all that room. She's all alone in that big house, quiet as a mouse. Doesn't socialize much. Lena's always been such an odd bird."

Duncan nodded, digging into the hash browns. He remembered her. Imelda Silva's daughter had been a scrawny, black-haired little girl who used to follow him around the island during his high school years. He had a vague memory of how she would sometimes keep him company back when he was sick. They would play Chinese checkers. She would read him stories and draw him pictures. She'd been a harmless enough kid.

"What do you have planned today?"

Duncan glanced up from his rapidly clearing plate and dabbed his mouth with a cloth napkin. "Same ol', same ol', Ma. The physical therapist comes this afternoon. I've got some studying to do."

Mona produced a stiff smile and fiddled with her coffee cup. He couldn't fool her. Though he was taking on-line Pashto, Persian, and Arabic refresher courses, Ma knew that his "studying" also included writing letters to the families of his dead teammates.

"How many more do you have left?"

"Two."

"Have you done Justin's yet?"

Duncan shook his head and gazed out toward Safe Haven Beach, already dotted with tourists. Justin's would be the last. Though each of the men in that insertion team had been like brothers to him, Justin Jaramillo was the closest friend he'd ever had in his life. They'd met the first week of prep at Great Lakes and leaned on each other through the multiphase agony that was BUD/S training and the year that followed, eventually being assigned to SEAL Team 2 together.

Each letter had been excruciating to write. In every instance, he took great care to describe the man who was their son, brother, husband, and even father, and how he had lived and died with the utmost courage and dedication. But with Justin's family, what could he say that hadn't already been said? Nestor and Beth Jaramillo had been Duncan's West Coast family when he was training at Coronado. They'd treated him like he was one of their own. The day the grieving parents had flown all the way to DC to visit Duncan at the rehab unit of Walter Reed was the hardest day of his life. He'd held them as they'd cried for their boy.

"I'm working my way up to that one, Ma," Duncan said.

"Son?"

Duncan turned toward his mother. He saw worry carved into her face.

"I was just wondering . . . Have you given any thought to . . . you know . . . ? There are so many things a man with your expertise and training could do. Maybe the foreign service. Or national security. I was watching this new TV show about CIA operatives the other night—"

"Stop." Duncan pushed himself from the table. He wanted to jump from the chair and put some distance between himself and his mother, but that was too tall an order. It infuriated him that his brain flashed with intention and his body flowed like cold pea soup. It was as if the tether connecting his mind to his body had been cut—his thoughts raced and his legs stumbled.

He would never accept that the honed and perfected body he'd once commanded was gone. He would fight to regain what was rightfully his until his last breath.

At that moment, he fought just to push himself to a stand. He took a moment to stare out at the ocean and stretch his arms. The last thing he wanted to do was be ugly to his mother, but he just couldn't talk about it anymore. She didn't listen. How many times had he told her? He *would* regain his strength. He *would* return to active duty. He *would* once again do the only job he was meant to do.

"I'm sorry, Duncan. I ask too many questions."

"No, Ma. It's okay." Duncan took a few measured steps her way. He placed a hand on her bony shoulder, startled by the feel of her, fragile and tiny under his big hand. He bent down and placed a soft kiss on her wispy hair. "I apologize for snapping at you. I have no right to take out my frustrations on you like that." He patted her back. "Thank you for the feather."

"The what?"

Since he was already up and walking, Duncan fetched

the feather from the nightstand and laughed as he placed it on the shelf. This was their little game, and they'd been playing it since he was about ten, when the gifts had started appearing by his sickbed—little pieces of nature brought inside for the frail boy who often couldn't go outside to experience the world for himself.

"It's nice," Duncan said, turning away from the bookshelf and smiling at his mother. "Is it from Annie's shop?"

"I have no idea." Mona crossed her arms over her chest and scowled. "I did not bring that feather to you. The gifts are not from me and they never have been."

Duncan rolled his head around on his neck, working out the kinks. "Let's change the subject."

Mona rose from her chair and came to Duncan, reaching up to stroke the side of his face. "I have always told you the truth about that, my dear boy. You're just not willing to hear it."

He sighed and pulled her to him, hugging her slight figure close. "Whatever you say, Ma."

Duncan felt a sharp jab in his ribs. "Ow!"

His mother glared up into her son's eyes, a good fourteen inches above her own, her brow lined with seriousness. "You're not paying attention to what I'm telling you."

"Ma ..."

"Sit back down, Duncan." She pointed to the dining chair by the window. Duncan went. Once Mona was satisfied with his compliance, she peered into his eyes. "Those little presents began when you were in fourth grade, I think, back when the fishery was still running. At first I thought it was your father."

"Da?" Duncan laughed. Frasier wasn't at all the type.

Mona shrugged. "You're right. It wasn't him. We were

still talking to each other back then, so I asked. Besides, more than once the gifts showed up while your father was on the mainland for business."

Duncan leaned back into the chair, puzzled by the seriousness in his mother's face. This made no sense. Of course she was the source of all these presents! Hundreds of anonymous offerings had been made over the years. Who the hell else *but* his mother could be devoted to him like that?

Mona continued to shake her head. "Mellie denied it, too. Besides, I remember that some little trinket or other was delivered to your room when she was in Nantucket Hospital with the flu. We know it wasn't Clancy, who couldn't keep a secret even back then—every thought in his head was broadcast on his face. And Rowan wasn't your biggest fan, as you might recall. She tended to keep her distance."

Duncan nodded. It was true. His little sister had been scared of him, and he didn't blame her. He would snap at her and call her names. She didn't deserve any of it, of course, but he hadn't known what to do with all the rage he felt inside. For four long years—from age eight to twelve—Duncan was often confined to his room while the world went on without him. That made him intensely jealous of Clancy and Rowan, normal kids who got to run and play and sail and swim whenever they liked, while he was forced to watch the days crawl by from his sickbed. Duncan despised the hospital stays in Boston and all the doctors with their fake smiles. He hated the inhalers and the medicines. He was ashamed of his own weakness, ashamed that for whatever reason he wasn't strong enough to fight off the asthma and repeated attacks of bronchitis. But more than anything, Duncan was terrified that he would be stuck in his bed, in his room, forever.

He'd been a spiteful little bastard back then.

Mona kissed his forehead, her face drawn tight with concern, maybe even pity. "You will be fine, son. You will recover from your injuries, and you will be happy again, no matter what career you choose."

He felt his shoulders stiffen.

"Now, that said, I don't want you hiding up here thinking you're back to your boyhood. Because you're not. You know that, right?"

Duncan managed to smile at his mother, though he wasn't pleased that she'd brought up the proverbial elephant in the sickroom. The similarities between then and now were obvious, but he'd really hoped to avoid talking about it. He wanted to focus his energy on getting the hell off the island and returning to duty, not dredging up ancient history that couldn't be changed and didn't matter anymore. "Of course I do," he said. "And I'm glad to hear you do, too."

Mona began to gather the dishes and cups, but Duncan gently pushed her aside and took over the chore. As his hands kept busy, his mind latched on to the nagging loose end in their conversation.

"So who is it, then? Seriously, Ma. Who could be leaving me all this crap, then and now?"

Mona's eyes sparkled. Her grin became so open and joyous that she looked like a little girl. "Do you remember what I always used to tell you?"

Duncan squeezed his eyes shut. He shook his head, as if he could will the conversation in another direction—any other direction. He'd rather talk about fucking *sea spray*. "Please, Ma. Don't start—"

"Maybe it's the Great Mermaid, leading you to your one true love!" Mona hooted with laughter, grabbed the tray, and headed toward the door. "You're still a young man. There's still time to open yourself to receive the mermaid's gifts, you know."

"Don't hold your breath."

"Remember, your father's dinner is at six," she called out over her shoulder, still chuckling. "Wear long pants and maybe a nice blue shirt—it brings out your eyes. And don't be late."

Duncan stared out the bedroom door long after his mother had vanished down the hallway. A blue shirt? Who the hell cared what color shirt he wore?

Suddenly, he felt the hairs on the back of his neck stand to attention. He turned to look right into those haunting—and somehow familiar—mermaid eyes. They cut right though him. Did she know something he didn't?

Why? he wondered. *Why is everything around here about goddamn mermaids?*

Adelena Silva emerged from the surf, morning sunlight warming her skin. She squeezed water from her hair, then let it fall in a black ribbon over her bare shoulder. She continued up the beach, taking pleasure in the easy strength of her stride, the silken sand between her toes. The knowledge that she was equally at home in water and on land never failed to delight her.

Lena felt a wave of gratitude wash over her, and she closed her eyes for an instant. She thanked the tides for delivering her to this place and time. She gave thanks for her mother's love and tenacity. She acknowledged the blessing of her talent and reminded herself that it was art that had paid for her happiness. Art had allowed her to serve as caretaker of Moondance Beach, a place where land, sand, and sea converged, which was all she'd ever wanted.

Lena opened her eyes, smiled to herself, and whispered into the wind, "Thank you for bringing Duncan home alive."

She grabbed the towel from a piece of driftwood and wrapped her naked body in warm cotton. Lena slipped into a pair of flip-flops and climbed the wooden access stairs, crossed the dune, and went into her backyard. What stretched before her wasn't one of the carefully manicured lawns of the South Shore. Her acreage was windswept and wild, pathways of sandy soil snaking through saw grass, cinnamon fern, bayberry, heather thistle, and blue iris. Beech, pine, and oak trees hunkered low to the ground, stunted by the ocean winds. And at the top of the rise, facing the beach, was her home and studio.

Lena's mother had recently asked if she didn't get lonely "rattling around" in such a big place. Lena couldn't help but laugh, since she'd lost track of the number of times she'd tried to convince her to share her new home with her. Imelda Silva always dismissed the idea.

"Stop worrying about me, *menina*. Maybe it's time for you to start caring for a family of your own."

"Maybe it's time for you to retire."

The last time they'd had this conversation, they'd been seated on the first-floor deck in the early evening, watching the sunset and enjoying a bit of her mother's favorite sherry. They got together for dinner about once a week, and Lena enjoyed spending time in the kitchen with her mother and talking until dark—even if nothing was ever resolved.

"You know I can't leave Rowan and Ash now that the baby has come. Serena is attached to me, and Rowan needs me."

"Be reasonable, *Mãe*. You've hardly had a day off since you came to this island twenty-four years ago. You deserve to enjoy yourself."

"I do enjoy myself! I enjoy working. Keeping busy makes me happy. If I retire, I will dry up and blow away. What will be my purpose?"

Lena had sighed as she'd placed a hand over her mother's. "Your purpose would be to relax and share in my success. We could travel. We could even go back to the Azores if you'd like."

That got her mother's attention. She shot Lena her trademark stink-eye, an expression reserved for things related to her mother's place of birth, Lena's Portuguese-American father, and his family in Rhode Island, where Lena had been born. In other words—anything having to do with the past she had left behind.

Her mother shook her head and turned down the corners of her mouth. "You know there is nothing for us over there. We are Americans. We are *Bayberry Islanders*."

The evening ended with the usual kisses on the cheek and a stalemate. Lena watched her mother drive off toward Shoreline Road, glad she had kept her snarkier comments to herself. Her mother didn't need to hear that Rowan and Ash could afford to replace her a hundred times over at the Safe Haven. She would have been hurt, since she considered herself a member of the family, not the bed-and-breakfast's director of housekeeping and head cook. Lena knew the Flynns considered her family, too, and had since the night Imelda Silva and her seven-year-old child had shown up on the mansion's doorstep just as hail had begun pounding down.

"Would you by any chance need a housekeeper?" her mother had asked that night so long ago. And the rest was fate.

Lena shook her head to clear away the memory. She stepped into the mudroom off the back of her sunny kitchen, happy to spend another day "rattling around" in her oceanfront retreat. She didn't care what people said—the size was not excessive and it certainly wasn't for show. Lena required high ceilings and elbow room for her canvases. She needed lots of natural light and huge windows to observe the sea and sky. And being alone did not mean she was lonely—she got more than enough socializing during the gallery receptions, art shows, and media appearances that took up a full week of every month. At the end of each trip, she was relieved to trade the noisy, wine-sipping crowds of Los Angeles, Chicago, New York, or Boston and return to her sanctuary by the sea.

A long, hot shower washed the sand from her hair and skin. She threw on a sundress, grabbed her second cup of coffee, and headed to the upstairs studio to greet the work of the day. The space spanned about two thousand square feet, which was most of the second floor, and the studio's entire south-facing wall and most of the ceiling was constructed of "smart glass," window panels with built-in tinting. With just the tap of a button on a remote control, Lena could optimize or block the light, whichever was needed, no matter the season or time of day.

She worked barefoot that morning, her preferred state for all but the most brutally cold North Atlantic winter days. She'd learned long ago that if she wanted to stay focused, her feet needed to be in contact with the wood floor as she painted. It centered her to be bound to an earth element while her mind and spirit drifted away to the sea.

Lena clicked on the studio's speaker system, and the delicate sounds of Debussy danced in the sunbeams. She stood before her most recent commission and stepped into the world she had created—a voluptuous creature sunning herself as waves crashed against a rocky shore, her blond curls and curvy flesh glowing with life, her eyes flirty and laughing. It didn't take long for Lena to detect an error in the play of light and shadow, of air and water. She loaded a fantail brush with a dab of sienna and a hint of crimson, then set about darkening the value of water-slicked mermaid scales.

Here's how she saw it: if a Seattle dot-com genius shelled out a half million dollars so that she could portray herself as a sunbathing sea nymph—and if Lena's distinctive signature would be at the bottom-left corner—then *Rhonda on the Rocks* would be technically perfect.

Lena accepted two such "vanity" commissions each year without a twinge of shame. Why shouldn't she strike while mermaid-themed works were hot? The art world was fickle, and the fine-art economy testy, and she knew she had been extremely fortunate that her passion had any kind of sustained commercial value. Almost all of her friends from art school were bartending or bill-collecting to fund their painting habit. Lena was an anomaly—a working, wealthy painter, and she did not take her good fortune lightly. With the help of her business manager, Sanders Garrett, she was secure in knowing that every penny of outrageous profit from these vanity commissions would go toward paying off the

Moondance Beach mortgage. At this rate, it would take only another five years before she would be free to do whatever she pleased for the rest of her life, without regard to the vagaries of Wall Street or the temper tantrums of art critics. All that from taking on two commissions per year. The rest of her paintings could sell for a fraction of the price, and she would have no worries.

When she had completed the finishing touches, Lena selected a delicate rigger brush and cradled it between her thumb and fingers. She had raised her left hand to sign the finished painting with her stylized "A.S." when suddenly, the colorful glass beads of her bracelet caught the light. They sparkled against the elaborately knotted black and white twine encircling her wrist.

The simple beauty of it made Lena smile.

Chapter Three

Twenty-four years ago ...

Lena Silva was seven years old the night she arrived at the Safe Haven, and her brain hurt just trying to piece together all the sudden changes that had taken place in her life. The most dramatic difference was in her own mother.

Back home in Rhode Island, Mama had never said much and had mumbled when spoken to. She'd let Daddy's mother and his sisters be in charge. Lena had heard her mother's real voice and real laugh only when the two of them were alone. She would sing Lena to sleep with her Portuguese songs, or she'd try to read aloud from the storybooks Lena brought home from school. More often than not, Lena ended up reading to her mother, who would fall asleep next to her in the small bed.

Sometimes, when it was just the two of them like that, her mother would talk about maps and little towns Lena had never heard of, and weather, and the ocean. Or she'd tell fairy tales. Some of Lena's favorites were about how her family had always made a living from the sea, respected it, and understood its magic and mystery.

"Grandmother doesn't believe in things like that," Lena had pointed out.

Her mother nodded. "If a person's spirit is too small to believe in the magic of the ocean, they will never be comfortable with its power."

How suddenly things turned upside down! When Lena's daddy left, her mother instantly seemed taller. Her voice was steadier than it used to be, even at home with Daddy's family. Her mother now looked straight ahead instead of down, and she looked people in the eye. Her mother sang for no reason and whenever she felt like it. She smiled almost all the time.

It made no sense to Lena. Her grandmother and aunties were so sad Daddy left that they yelled and cried. They even told her mother that she was the reason he left. They called her a witch.

"He would never have abandoned us if you hadn't put a spell on him. You drove him out, you evil harpy!" Grandmother then pointed at Lena with a shaking finger. "And you—you are nothing but the spawn of a witch!"

Lena had been so frightened by the words that she'd cried. Her mother had later explained that people sometimes said cruel and untrue things when they were overwhelmed with sadness and anger. Her mother said to stay as far away from her grandmother as possible.

A few weeks after all the crying and yelling and mean talk started, Lena's grandmother pulled her aside and told her that her daddy went to a place called Brazil and was never coming back.

"Is Brazil the same as heaven?" Lena had asked.

Her grandmother assured her it was not. Then she told her to pay attention because she had something important to tell her. "Your mother is from a family of sorceresses in the Azores, and they shipped her to America to marry the kind of decent, upstanding man she could never get at home."

The story confused Lena. It hurt her heart.

Maybe it was Lena's fault Daddy left. Maybe, as Grandmother said, there was something wrong with her.

Just days later, Lena's mother came to school early to get her. She had their suitcases waiting in a taxi. They got on a bus and then a ferry. While they were out on the water, it began to rain very hard and Lena got sick. But soon they landed and walked in the dark and the rain down a road until they reached something called the Safe Haven.

Lena's first morning there was difficult. First she met the father, who patted her head at breakfast. He was a tall man with red cheeks who smiled a lot and got very loud when he laughed. Then she met a girl close to her own age named Rowan and a boy named Clancy. And now the mother of this new family was walking them up two flights of stairs, and Lena clutched at her mother's leg the whole way. Who else would she be forced to meet today? How many people lived in this big old place, anyway? The mother led them down a hallway, heading toward a big sunny window and a closed door on the left.

Lena noticed the door was made of heavy old wood with big black hinges, and the doorknob was a greenish metal carved with a fancy pattern. Everything in this place was big and fancy—but too old to be pretty. And everything was salty, too, like the sea air, and the rooms were so big that they echoed. She didn't like it. She worried there were ghosts around every corner.

The door opened. Lena hid behind her mother as a sharp medicine smell came from the room and spilled into the hallway.

"Imelda and Adelena, this is our oldest child, Duncan. He's Rowan and Clancy's big brother. Duncan, please say hello to Mrs. Silva and her daughter, Adelena. Mrs. Silva will be helping us around the house now."

Clutching at the fabric of her mother's cotton dress, Lena dared take a peek. A gasp escaped her lips.

The boy wasn't anybody's "big" brother! Clancy was a lot bigger than this kid. He was skinny, and his skin looked too white. His hair, as dark as Lena's, was cut close to his head. Immediately, she felt so very sorry for him, because she understood something was wrong with him. He was sick.

And then the boy looked up from his puzzle. Lena felt his eyes like a hot bee sting in her chest. His eyes were deep blue and sad, trapped inside dark circles. But they were on fire from the inside. His eyes were filled with a kind of light she didn't know the name for. She decided the boy might be sick, but something inside him was powerfully alive.

Without thinking, Lena slipped out from behind her mother and stood in the middle of the bedroom. She fiddled with her hair as she glanced around at the bedside table covered in books, pencils, and markers. A nearby desk had a mini music player with headphones, a Game Boy, and the family's computer. She saw papers and sports magazines scattered on the floor and movies for the VCR player stacked against the wall. There was a tissue box sitting on top of his Boston Red Sox comforter, and a little machine whirring in the corner, blowing out air. She wondered why one little boy needed all this stuff.

"Hi," she said. "You can call me Lena."

The boy lifted his chin, then looked away, as if he didn't know what to say to her. Maybe he didn't get a lot of visitors.

"What's wrong with you?"

"Adelena!" She felt her mother's hand on her shoulder.

"It's all right," the other mother said.

The boy turned back to her. "I'm sick, Sherlock. How old are you, anyway?"

"Seven."

The boy rolled his eyes. "Great."

"Duncan. Be polite."

"How old are you?" Lena asked.

"Ten." He sighed, tossed the puzzle from his lap, and collapsed down onto his pillow. Without another word, he flipped on his side to face the wall, his back to Lena.

The visit was over.

The women ushered Lena out into the hallway again. She couldn't help it—before she turned the corner, she looked back. The boy had already sat up and turned around. He had been watching her. And when their eyes met, Lena felt that hot sting again.

Was it her imagination? Or did the sick and sad boy tip his head and grin?

Chapter Four

"Good morning, Lieutenant Flynn! How's it going? Ready to get to work?"

His home-based physical therapist out of Nantucket was newly minted from the program at Northeastern, extremely efficient, and probably the perkiest person Duncan had ever encountered. Brandy was five feet tall and one hundred pounds of positivity, and though other patients might enjoy having Tigger as a physical therapist, she gave him a nasty headache.

Brandy had barely made it through the threshold of the bed-and-breakfast fitness center before she began clicking on her tablet and asking questions. "Are you icing regularly? Taking your medication as prescribed? Hitting your daily exercise goals?"

He smiled at her from his perch on the weight bench, forearms resting on his knees. "Good afternoon. The answer is yes, no, and no."

Brandy glanced up from her tablet with huge eyes. Her index finger hovered over the screen. "Yes *and* no?"

"Right. Yes, I ice down at least twice a day, and no, I stopped taking pain meds last week ago. And I've been doing about four times as many reps as I'm supposed to, plus my own training regimen."

"But—" She frantically scrolled through his digital chart, becoming flustered. Within seconds she had bounced over and sat down next to him on the bench. "You can't do that, Lieutenant. You'll hurt yourself."

Duncan didn't want to yank the girl's chain. She was only doing her job. But he knew exactly how to get back into shape, and it sure as hell wasn't five sets of thirty leg raises, resistance bands, and three trips up and down a flight of stairs per day. "I'm already doing it."

Her mouth pulled tight and she placed a hand over her heart, covering the PIN OAK PHYSICAL THERAPY logo embroidered on her polo shirt. "I'm supposed to make sure you follow the doctor's rehabilitation orders. That's what your benefits are paying me for. If you insist on pushing yourself too hard, you could destroy everything the surgeons have put back together. You could end up back in the OR or in a residential rehabilitation facility. Is that what you want?"

"I know my limits."

"You're doing yourself harm." She waved her hands around in frustration. "Prescriptions help control the pain so it doesn't control you. If you are too uncomfortable, you won't do your exercises."

"That's not a problem, Brandy."

"Ha!" She jumped up from the weight bench and shoved her hands in the pockets of her uniform shorts. Clearly, Duncan's lack of compliance had upset her. "How many surgeries have you had since you were airlifted out of that battle in Afghanistan?"

"You can call me Duncan. It was an ambush. And I've had eleven surgeries."

"That's correct. I've seen your chart. You were a mess. Burns on your left side from under your arm to your thigh. Surgeons rebuilt your hip, put screws and pins in your broken femur, and fixed your knee—and despite all those injuries, you somehow managed to lift a damn jeep off your ass and crawl into the fire to try to save your friends. I don't need to tell you how lucky you are to be alive."

Duncan nodded. "I agree. You do not need to tell me."

Brandy began bouncing on her heels in frustration. "So you're shooting for a dozen surgeries? Is that it? You're trying for an even number or something?"

Duncan weighed his response. He didn't want to alienate his physical therapist, because her opinion would eventually end up on Captain Sinclair's desk. Duncan had requested and been approved for outpatient rehab in conjunction with regular doctor visits, and it was essential that her reports eventually showed he was following orders, was in optimal physical condition, and was fit to return to his preinjury duties.

That said, Brandy needed a reality check.

"You're doing a fine job, and I appreciate your dedication." Duncan stared her down until she stopped bouncing on her heels. "You understand how the human body works, but I know how *my* body works. Have you ever had a SEAL as a client before?"

She crossed her arms over her chest and pursed her lips. "Well, no. Not really."

He chuckled at her answer—she either had or she hadn't. "If not, then you cannot possibly understand that for a guy like me, those pain meds were way worse than the pain itself. I can handle pain. The concept of mind over matter is at the heart of my training. But if my mind is dead from narcotics, it doesn't matter if I burn through a whole case of your resistance bands—I will never heal."

She shook her head. "I've had other patients say that, but most go back to taking their prescriptions because they can't cope."

"Those other patients are not U.S. Navy SEALs."

By that time of day Duncan had warmed up on the stationary bicycle, stretched out on the yoga mat, and was moving pretty easily. So he decided to put on a good show for ol' Brandy. He stood from the weight bench without pushing or steadying himself with his hands, and as he had hoped, the physical therapist's eyes widened in surprise. He stood straight and tall in front of her, hands at his sides. She would not see how unsteady he really was.

"Okay. Wow. You're a lot stronger than just a few days ago."

"Because I've been pushing myself."

Brandy looked up at him and scowled. "You're a very stubborn person."

That made Duncan laugh. "So I've been told."

"All right." She raised her hands in surrender. "Walk me through whatever it is you've been doing to yourself. At least let me make sure you're doing it with correct form and—"

Duncan's eyebrows shot up.

"Not that your form would be anything but perfect."

Forty-five minutes later, Duncan had taken Brandy through his own version of physical therapy. She didn't lecture him during his stretching, weight lifting, and scaled-down grinder calisthenics, but she went nuts watching him ruck up the back stairs of the Safe Haven.

"You can't do that." She began springing up and down on her heels as Duncan strapped on a rucksack filled with forty pounds of rocks. "You're going to kill yourself."

On the third trip, Duncan nearly blacked out and had to catch himself by gripping the banister, but he made sure it didn't look like a big deal.

"Are you okay?" she asked, getting right up in his face.

"Of course. I'll be doing fifty round-trips by the end of the summer."

"You're the worst patient I've ever had."

"I'm an all-or-nothing guy."

Brandy's expression turned serious. "Look, Lieutenant. You're a human being who's been through hell, and you're pushing yourself awfully hard. I don't care how many steel plates and bolts you've got inside you— you're not the freakin' Terminator. Keep that in mind."

Frasier was twenty minutes late to his own party, which shocked no one. Mellie, Evelyn, Rowan, and Annie had taken great care to make the dining table fancy. They'd sprinkled glitter on the white tablecloth, wrapped little ribbons around the stems of the wineglasses, and arranged a pretty floral thing in the middle of the table.

Duncan watched everyone running in circles, busy and laughing. He decided to ask his sister if he could help, since he was the only person sitting around doing nothing.

"Sure!" Rowan grabbed a stack of white cloth napkins off the sideboard and told him to start folding.

He looked at the pile. "How?"

"I don't care. Do you know how to make a French pleat or a standing fan?"

"Those are yoga positions, right?"

"Goofball." She kissed him on the forehead and walked off.

In the Navy, Duncan had learned to fold undershirts and U.S. flags and to create razor-sharp hospital corners on bedsheets, but the topic of dinner napkins had been overlooked. So he decided to create neat trifold napkin packets, like mini flags, the ends tucked in to the fold. As he finished one after another, he observed the organized mayhem going on around him, fascinated by how the pieces of his family fit together. If he asked anyone on the island to give a name to the collection of individuals at the Safe Haven that night, they would answer, "The Flynns." They would give that answer knowing there were as many McGuinnesses, Wallaces, Parkers, Ravelles, and Silvas as there were Flynns in the room. And if he asked them if they were all locals, they would answer "yes," even though some of them came from California, Maine, Connecticut, Boston, and Portugal via Rhode Island.

Duncan wondered why that was. He wondered how Bayberry Island could claim people like that, act as an umbrella over whoever and whatever anyone happened to be, and offer them a home.

He realized it was ironic that he had been born and raised on the island—a Flynn, no less—but didn't consider Bayberry his home. He didn't consider anywhere "home." He couldn't wait to be on his way.

" 'Sup?" Clancy smacked Duncan on the back as he walked by the table.

"Hi, Uncle Duncle!" Clancy's five-year-old adopted daughter hopped by on one foot, performing what was known as "the tee-tee dance." Christina's bladder must have been the size of a raisin, but Duncan had to admit that his niece was pretty damn cute.

"It's Dun-*can*. Not Dun-*cull*, you little stinker."

"Good luck with that one," Clancy said, following Christina to the half bath off the large formal dining room.

As Duncan went back to his napkins, he moved his attention to Annie and Nat. They were so affectionate with each other, giving little kisses for no reason, whispering private jokes, teasing each other. Duncan had known Annie all his life, and he liked her husband just fine. Nat was finishing final edits on a documentary about the mermaid legend. He'd been working on the film for three years, and all anyone could talk about was whether he'd get a spot at a film festival. Duncan could tell Annie was proud of the guy. It was obvious by the way she looked at him while he talked about his work. For just an instant, Duncan wondered what it would be like to have a good woman at his side, sharing in his achievements like that.

And his struggles.

Rowan swooped in, jiggling baby Serena on her hip. "How's it going?"

Duncan held up a napkin.

"Nice," she said. "But I was kind of hoping for swans. Are swans out of the question?"

"Swans are always out of the question."

Rowan laughed as she handed him the baby. "Here," she said, securing the squirming bundle in Duncan's lap and tossing the pacifier on the tabletop. She began fishing around inside the front pocket of her apron, eventually pulling out a strange-looking ring of hard, bumpy plastic. "Just talk to her; make silly noises. If she gets fussy, give her the teething ring."

Mystery solved.

Rowan grabbed the stack of napkins and placed one at each plate, adding the silverware as she went. As with most everything his sister did, the job was done quickly and well.

As she worked, Rowan chatted about Serena, the tourist season, the research institute, and a few other things. Duncan didn't pay close attention to her words. He simply observed his sister. Motherhood agreed with her. She was still smart, funny, and pretty, but she seemed softer around the edges. Some of her signature snark had been smoothed out, too, probably the result of being worshipped by Ash and letting him lift the weight of the world off her shoulders. Rowan deserved every bit of the happiness she'd found, Duncan knew. She'd gone through hell a few years back, when her smarmy Wall Street boyfriend swindled what was left of the family's money, earning him a prison sentence and sending Rowan back to the island to run the crumbling Safe Haven Bed and Breakfast—which she'd done out of sheer guilt. Things were different now. Ash's money had revived the Flynn family's ancestral home, and they operated the B and B during high season only because they enjoyed it.

True, when Duncan had first met Ash two years before, he'd found him a little heavy on the starch. But he had mellowed out, too. He'd gone from being a high-stakes real-estate consultant to the chairman of a marine-life foundation and research center, an enterprise that had brought an infusion of money and people to Bayberry for something other than the Mermaid Festival, which was good for everyone. And Ash had helped make another contribution—Serena Flynn-Wallace.

That fascinating creature was now tucked in Duncan's lap, staring up at him with big baby eyes fringed in wet baby eyelashes. Duncan couldn't help but smile at the contrasts he saw in that chubby face. Nine-month-old Serena possessed the purest and most unspoiled human skin he'd ever seen, but she stared at him with unblinking judgment. Her expression reminded him of the Navy's BUD/s Hell Week instructors at Coronado, whose only goal was to make him beg to "DOR"—request to drop out of the grueling SEAL training. Who knew? Maybe Serena was tough enough to be the girl who finally broke the Naval Special Warfare Combatant gender barrier, becoming the first female SEAL in the nation's history.

He bent down, inhaled the baby smell of his niece's neck, and whispered in her ear, "You'd never DOR— would you, sweetie?"

Serena raked the teething ring across his cheek.

"Whatcha talking about over there?" Rowan asked.

Duncan laughed. "I think we're bonding."

His sister gave him a sideways glance and smiled.

"You're a natural, Duncan. I hope one day you have a little one of your own. I think you'd be a really good dad."

And just like that, Duncan's mood went from cheerful to foul. "For God's sake, Row."

"Well, it's true!" Rowan shrugged. "Don't be mad. I'm just telling you what I see. You're really good with her, and with Christina, too. It's a compliment, Duncan. I'm not getting on your case. I'm telling you you're doing a good job."

"Well, thanks."

At that moment, Christina came running back into

the dining room, scrambled up the rungs of Duncan's chair, and began cooing and giggling to Serena, who cooed and giggled right back. Duncan felt like a human version of the monkey bars.

"Da's car is coming up the drive!"

Almost simultaneous to Clancy's announcement, Mona and Mellie burst through the kitchen swinging doors bearing two large serving trays, one holding Frasier's favorite eye-of-round roast beef—cooked medium—and another featuring a selection of broiled seafood. Annie, Nat, and Evelyn came right behind, placing serving dishes on the sideboard and filling water glasses. Rowan hurried around the table, making one last pass to make sure every place setting was in order.

Ash grabbed Serena and Clancy grabbed Christina, and everyone stood behind their chairs, waiting for the family patriarch, the guest of honor, to walk in the house and through the dining room doors, which were thrown open in welcome.

Nat craned his neck so that he could see past the velvet drapes to the drive. He reared back and whispered, "Ohhhh, shit."

"What the—" Annie gasped, peeking around Nat's shoulder.

"We're going to need another plate," Ash said dryly. "And maybe a SWAT team."

Duncan watched in disbelief as his father tiptoed into the room, a senior-citizen blonde on his arm and a shit-eating grin on his face.

Apparently, his father had thought it was a good idea to bring a date to his family birthday party, and he'd picked a real doozy. Duncan recognized his companion as Sally, the woman who was the leader of the Bayberry

Island Fairy Brigade and his mother's archenemy. Duncan had always thought she looked like a taller version of Dolly Parton.

At the far end of the table, Duncan's mother remained poised and smiling, though the veins in her neck looked close to popping.

"Sally," Mona said flatly. "What a thoroughly unexpected pleasure."

Sally's face broke out in red hivelike blotches.

"Oh, Da." Rowan slithered down into her chair with Serena in her arms. The disappointment in his sister's face was awful to see.

"I *told* you not to bring me here!" Sally hit Frasier with her sparkly purse. "Dammit! You promised me nobody would care!"

Duncan assessed the mood of the room. Yes, it was safe to say everyone cared. In fact, Annie and Evelyn were shocked. Ash was embarrassed. Nat tried not to gawk. Mellie kept shaking her head and muttering what were likely Portuguese curse words.

"Who's that lady with Granda?" Christina yelled out, pointing. Evelyn shushed her.

"All right, everyone. Let's just keep things in perspective." The police chief held out his hands in appeasement. It reminded Duncan of his three-day visit two years ago, when he'd watched his little brother coax a knife from an intoxicated festivalgoer. In fact, Duncan wouldn't be the least bit surprised to hear his brother say something like, "Hand over the bimbo before someone gets hurt."

Mona's deep sigh broke the silence. "I'll get Sally a plate."

That was Duncan's cue. "Bringing a date to a family

celebration is piss-poor decision-making, Da. It's disrespectful to your wife, children, grandchildren, friends, and Sally as well. I think the honorable thing would be to go and to take Sally with you."

"Dunkle just said *piss*!"

"Sssshhhhh!" Evelyn hissed.

"I think I've had enough awkwardness for one night." Sally turned to go.

"I'll drive you."

Sally shot Frasier a nasty glance. "I'd rather walk. In the pitch-dark. In a freakin' blizzard."

And with that, Sally slammed the Safe Haven's massive front door and was gone. Frasier stood about five feet from the dining table, seeing for the first time all the effort his family had gone to in his honor, eyeing the mound of roast beef that was front and center. A wave of sadness crossed his face.

"Don't worry," Mellie said. "I'll send a Baggie of leftovers to your apartment."

"I'm . . . I'm sorry." Frasier didn't know where to look, so he stared out the windows while he summoned the courage to explain himself. "It was my birthday, and I just thought . . ." He looked at Mona. "I didn't think you'd be here."

"I'm your wife."

"Well, I mean, because we're separated, I didn't think you'd want to spend time with me."

"I've already spent half a century with you. That's counting everything—forty-five years of marriage, four years of dating, and even that year you were dating me *and* Sally at the same time."

"Oh boy," Nat muttered.

"Mona!" Frasier looked around at his children, grandchildren, friends, and finally Mellie, who gave him the evil eye. "That was forever ago, and I've already apologized a hundred times. I was a stupid college boy, and I thought juggling two girls made me a big man. You know she meant nothing to me—she was just an island girl and you were my college sweetheart. I chose you."

Mona crumpled her trifolded napkin and tossed it to her empty plate. "And yet here you are on your seventieth birthday, Frasier, still dating the same Sally, who's now the head of the fairies! You couldn't have insulted me more if you tried. Maybe you *did* try!"

Duncan wasn't privy to all the details, but he knew the Fairy Brigade and the Mermaid Society were mortal enemies. Apparently, Sally had once been a mermaid but had split off and started her own group after some kind of smackdown with Mona. Years later, when island landowners had to decide whether to sell to developers or preserve the island's quaint-but-broke status quo, Sally and Mona went to battle on opposite sides of the issue. Duncan had missed most of it, but Clancy had told him it had been ugly at times.

Duncan reached into the pocket of his pants to check his cell phone. Six thirty. This party was just getting started.

"But we've been separated for nearly three years!" Frasier glanced around the table again in search of support, but didn't find it. He stepped closer to the table, now standing right behind Christina. "Mona, you won't talk to me. You avoid me. You won't answer my phone calls. I see you in person about twice a year, and even then I don't know what is going on in your head. What am I supposed to do?"

Clancy made a move toward his father, but Frasier stopped him.

"I don't need a police escort," he snapped, turning away.

Everyone stayed silent, listening to the slam of Frasier's car door, the whine of the engine, and the sound of him driving far too fast down the Safe Haven drive.

Mona sat down, and everyone else did as well. The only sound in the room was Serena gnawing on her plastic teething ring.

Then Annie accidentally knocked a fork onto the wood floor, and the sound shattered the silence.

"Pass the meat," Christina said. "It's time to eat."

So that's what they did. They ate—scallops, cod, lobster, and clams. A rice pilaf. Roast beef and twice-baked potatoes. Asparagus. Fruit salad and several kinds of homemade breads. They had some wine. Then they had some more. And within twenty minutes the discomfort had faded and the laughter had returned. Even Mona had bounced back. But in the midst of the revelry Clancy flashed occasional glances Duncan's way, a silent acknowledgment that the two of them *had to do something about Da.*

Coffee and tea were served. The dessert was a personalized cake Mellie had decorated just for the birthday boy and then hastily edited. The cake top was nothing but a multicolored smear of icing, the only letters visible being *H-A-P-P-Y.*

Duncan excused himself, saying he didn't care for dessert and needed to rest. He received nine simultaneous inquiries about whether he was okay. He assured everyone he was, then went around the table to kiss his mother, sister, Annie, Mellie, Christina, and baby Serena, who gave him another drill-sergeant stare, and then he headed for the main staircase.

Duncan was lying. He was bone-tired. It had been a long day, the most physically and mentally demanding day he'd had since the ambush eight months earlier. Today had been complicated, too. He had been blindsided by emotions, feelings that hit hard and lingered with him even now. He wasn't used to that. He'd felt tenderness for his nieces, happiness for his sister, protectiveness for his mother, and maybe even a little jealousy seeing how close Annie and Nat were, along with Rowan and Ash, and Clancy and Evelyn. He almost felt like a crasher at a committed-couples convention.

And then there was his da. What an insensitive dickhead he could be! And yet . . . Duncan was sad for him, too. Frasier seemed lost without Ma. That didn't excuse his stupidity, but it might help explain it.

Clancy had been right—they would definitely have to do something about their father.

Wait.

Duncan was halfway up the first flight of wide oak stairs when it hit him: this was why he didn't like staying too long on the island. His family was a mess. Relationships—every single one he'd ever seen or been a part of—were difficult and complicated. Relationships had never been his strong suit and never would be.

Just then he heard the front door open and an unfamiliar female voice float over the hum of conversation and laughter.

"Hello, everybody! I hope you don't mind that I stopped by."

"Lena!" Rowan yelled.

"You showed up!" Annie said.

"It's really great to see you. Welcome." That was Clancy.

Then Mellie's voice sounded alive with pleasure and surprise. "You made it, *menina!* Come! Sit down and have some cake!"

"Would you like coffee?" Evie asked.

Duncan froze on the step. He rested his palm on the highly polished railing, sliding it back and forth on the smooth wood, unable to decide. He knew he should go downstairs and say hello. It would be the decent thing to do. He hadn't seen Mellie's daughter since . . . God, since right after high school.

But he was too tired to be decent. So instead, he lowered his chin, looked down through the stair railings into the dining room doorway, and spied the outline of a shapely female leg ending in a frilly little sandal. That must be her.

"You missed Duncan by minutes!" Mona said. "I know he would have enjoyed seeing you again after all this time. I can go get him."

"No, please. Let him rest. I can't stay, but I wanted to stop by and say . . ." The voice trailed off. Clearly, she'd just noticed the guest of honor was nowhere to be seen.

That voice. He had never heard it before, not the adult version of it, anyway. It was slightly husky but feminine. Soft, but clear enough to carry right up the staircase, brush along the back of his neck, and settle in his ears.

An image flashed in his mind. Dark, heavy-lidded eyes, swaying black hair, a knowing half smile, and the sweet, soft terrain of the female torso—lounging on the sea floor, waiting for her lover to return.

Duncan's legs felt weak, but he made it up both flights of stairs and down the hall without taking a rest. He read for a while. His eyes wandered to the painting. He turned on the TV. His gaze traveled along her shape. He turned off the lights. He still envisioned her in his mind's eye.

And then, unbelievable as it seemed, he was with her.

Her touch was silky soft and hot on his skin, her mouth wet and greedy upon his. Damn, it had been so long since he'd held a woman in his arms. But this? This was different. Duncan knew instinctively that she wasn't just a woman. She was his *woman. For the first time in his life, his touch had become a devoted caress, and his need originated in love.*

He rolled with her, her body sliding along his, her arms around his neck, his hands all over her hips and thighs and ass. He couldn't get enough. He wanted so much more. She laughed, and his whole being rose up to meet the husky, feminine sound. Where were they? In the sea? In a field of wildflowers? In a bed protected by an endless blanket of stars? Somehow he knew they were all those places and none of them, that the only important thing was that they were together, and ahhh . . . Her hot little mouth had just moved down the front of his body and she wrapped him up in a silky embrace. It was almost too much to bear. Such an outpouring of giving. Teasing licks and sucks that drove him to the edge. Duncan grabbed long and thick sections of her dark hair in his hand, fascinated at how it spilled between his fingers. The pleasure expanded; the need increased. He could not wait another second.

He was inside her, his eyes locked on hers, and it was like nothing he'd ever known. She was his. She had always been his, and he could not enter her deep enough. This beautiful woman closed her eyes and cried his name. Yes, he wanted this for her. Yes, she was falling apart beneath him, breaking free, flying so high that her only tether was her love for him and his love for her. He climaxed with her, and the instant was so beautiful, it danced on the edge of pain. He wanted to call out her name as he emptied his soul into hers, but his tongue caught . . . The words weren't there. He didn't know them.

Her name! What was her name? Who was this woman? As hard as he tried, his brain remained mired in mud, spinning its wheels. And that's when she slipped through his embrace and disappeared, carried away like an osprey feather on a wave, like smoke on the wind.

Duncan jolted awake with a gasp and flipped on the light. He touched his fingers to his face and found tears rolling down his cheeks. Tears. *Un-fucking-believable.* The last time he had cried was seventh grade.

He dropped his head into his hands. How was it that this particular nightmare had cracked him more than the ones filled with bombs and blood and death? Why did he feel this particular loss so deeply? Why was there so much grief?

He did not understand the symbolism of the dream, but he had enough sense to know that he had just allowed something precious to slip through his fingers. The sadness he felt was loss. Regret.

Duncan stretched, then carefully walked toward the fireplace, knowing what had to be done. He reached high and lifted the gilded frame over his head, carried it out into the hallway, then flipped the painting around before he leaned it against the wall.

Tomorrow morning, after he'd gotten some rest and pulled himself together, he would find a place for it in the attic. Way off in a corner somewhere. Away from him.

He went back to bed, and in the morning when he woke he found that another trinket had been left for him while he slept. It was a garden-variety rock the size of a book of matches and the color of dirt. He held it in his palm, seeing that it was unremarkable in every way except for one.

Its edges had been worn away by water, sand, and the passing of time, carving it into the shape of a heart.

"Well, I'll be damned!" Rusty waved the group inside the tavern, his face lit up with surprise. "It's our very own Navy Lieutenant Duncan Flynn! We wondered when you'd make an appearance."

"Good to see you, Rusty."

While Rusty wiped down a table for five by the marina-side windows, Duncan shook hands and got slapped on the back more times than he cared to count. He handled the questions about his injuries and the raid with as much grace as he could muster, but Clancy wasn't pleased with his performance.

"Come on, now," he whispered as they approached the table. "These are our locals, and you're a hero to them."

Duncan did his best to tamp down the rage he suddenly felt. "Clancy," he said, pulling out a chair and sitting next to his brother, "I am no one's hero."

Once Nat, Ash, and Frasier were seated, Rusty came by with Frasier's usual Guinness on tap, a martini for Nat, and a Sam Adams for Ash, who scowled when it got placed in front of him. Maybe Ash needed a couple more weeks before he was ready for another night on the town.

Rusty slid an ice water over to Clancy, who was on duty, and then looked at Duncan with anticipation.

"What can I get the man of the hour? It's on the house, whatever it is."

"That's awful kind of you, Rusty, but I'm not drinking much these days. I think an ice tea would do the trick."

"You got it, son." Rusty placed his hand on Duncan's shoulder before he hustled off.

The men didn't say anything for a moment, and Frasier looked out the window like a grumpy kid who'd just been dragged into the principal's office. As previously discussed, Clancy would be taking the lead in dressing down his father tonight. They decided it was the only option since Nat was too buddy-buddy with Frasier; Ash was too polite and respectful; and Duncan was too straightforward to be effective.

"I don't want to talk about it," Frasier said, still looking out the window.

"Here you go!" Rusty arrived, setting the ice tea glass on a coaster. "You boys let me know what else you need, all right?"

"Da." Clancy waited until Rusty was out of earshot. "We need to talk this out. What you did last night to Ma was, well . . ."

"Totally whacked," Nat said.

"It made everyone extremely uncomfortable," Ash said.

"That dinner was a fuckin' soup sandwich," Duncan said.

"What the hell is a soup sandwich?"

Duncan forgot that his everyday expressions were a foreign language to anyone who hadn't served in the military, so he cleared it up for Clancy. "Think about it—what would it be like to try to eat a sandwich made of soup?"

"It would be fucked-up," Nat answered.

"Exactly. Cheers." Duncan clicked his ice tea to Nat's martini.

"All right. Let's sort this out." Clancy had summoned his official talk-the-guy-off-the-ledge tone of voice. "Da, what were you thinking?"

Frasier turned to look at his two sons. "I don't expect you to choose my side. None of you have ever chosen my side."

"There are no sides to this," Clancy said.

"Sure there are." Frasier spread his hands as far apart as they would go on the tabletop, nearly knocking over Nat's martini in the process. "This is your mother's side." He slammed his left hand down hard. "And this is mine." He did the same with his right hand. "It's been like that since I drove the fishery into the ground twenty-odd years ago."

Clancy shot a quick glance to Duncan before he spoke to his father. "It wasn't your fault the entire North Atlantic cod supply collapsed, Da. That was eighty percent of Flynn Fisheries' sales. You kept it going longer than other large fisheries up and down the Eastern Seaboard—that I know for sure."

"It wasn't just the overfishing, son." Frasier shook his head. "The company started going downhill as soon as your grandfather handed it over to me. I make a far better politician than businessman, and your mother always found a way to remind me of that. She was mad as a box of frogs when we had no choice but to turn the Safe Haven into a bed-and-breakfast."

"Shit happens," Clancy said with a shrug. "But here we are—we're all alive. The Safe Haven has been restored, thanks to Ash." Everyone raised their glasses. "And he and Rowan are operating it as an inn only in high season and only because they *want to*. Nobody's suffering."

Frasier nodded silently. "You boys don't understand. When a man loses his job or fails to keep a family business afloat, it affects the way his woman looks at him. Your mother and I were never the same after that. We had to rely on your mother's salary as principal of the school and barely had enough money to keep the Safe Haven from falling down. And then ..." Frasier looked up at the group with red-rimmed eyes. "Jesus, do we really have to rehash the whole development catastrophe?"

Though Duncan hadn't been around for most of it, he knew his parents had separated after they'd disagreed about what to do with the family land. Da wanted to sell the Flynns' three hundred prime oceanfront acres for a resort and casino, which would have made them multimillionaires, but Mona had refused.

Clancy shook his head. "You can't avoid the facts, Da. The longer the land battle went on, the more you and Ma couldn't stand the sight of each other. And then, to add insult to injury, you started seeing the woman who was the most vocal proponent of selling out—Sally! Sally the fairy! It was pretty clear to all of us that you and Ma used the development issue to duke it out."

Frasier shook his head and took a sip from his pint glass. "Yeah. That was a real ..." He raised his chin Duncan's way. "It was a real soup sandwich."

All of them laughed, which took a little bit of the edge off. Duncan knew it was time for him to step in.

"Da, look. We wanted to meet with you because we want you and Ma to begin negotiations. Both of you are miserable at the moment."

"I know *I* am." Frasier shook his head.

Clancy chimed in. "The question is—what do you really want? Do you want to stay married to Ma? Do you still love her? Because if you do love her and still want to be married to her, you've got to hustle it up. She's going to file for divorce unless you do something."

Frasier frowned, keeping his gaze focused on his Guinness.

Duncan spoke next. "Bringing Sally to a family dinner sent a clear message, and the message was that Ma was invisible to you, that she wasn't even on your radar as a person, that you had no respect for her whatsoever. Is that accurate?"

Frasier raised his head. His face was stricken with sadness. "No, son. I did it to shock her into paying attention to me."

Nat nodded. "Well, you shocked the shit out of me—that's for sure."

Clancy kept the ball in play. "If you love her, then you've got to suck it up, Da. You've got to put everything on the line and make sure she knows how you feel. Ma is so angry and hurt that she will never make the first move."

"It was that way with Rowan and me." Ash said the words so softly they could hardly hear them. He looked around the table, sheepish. "I misled her and she hated me—for good reason, as we all know—and I had no choice but to step it up."

A low chuckle went around the table, as everyone remembered how Ash had filleted his soul for Rowan in the most dramatic and public way possible—dressed up as a ship captain and taking center stage at the Mermaid Festival closing ceremonies, professing his love for her and begging for her forgiveness.

"That was epic," Nat said. "It's probably the best part of the documentary, to tell you the truth."

"I had to do the same with Evelyn." Clancy wrapped his hands around his ice water. "She didn't trust me, and the only way I could earn her trust was to put her and Christina first, ahead of my career in law enforcement, ahead of everything." He looked up and smiled. "Some things—some *people*—are worth doing that for."

"I wouldn't even know how to begin," Frasier said. "One bouquet of roses won't make up for all these years of arguing."

"No," Clancy said. "But a bouquet every week might help—but only if they are her favorite flowers, in her favorite color, and in her favorite kind of vase."

Duncan leaned toward his father. "In military terms, it would be like chipping away at an enemy combatant's weaknesses until you're close enough to execute. So with Ma, you just keep wearing down her defenses."

"He's right," Clancy said. "You knock on her door. You buy her a copy of her favorite book or a Blu-ray of her favorite movie."

Duncan laughed. "Hell, Da. You could even write her poems about sea spray and mermaids if you have to—just get in there and chip away at her resistance."

Frasier's eyes went big. "Poems?"

"Duncan has a point," Clancy said. "But don't do any of it unless it's really what you want. Above all, you have to be honest with her now. No more playing games and hiding behind your hurt."

"Exactly," Duncan said. "Because if you don't want Ma anymore, the only honorable move is to let her go, and do it now."

Frasier shook his head and sighed. "I do want her. I do still love her. I will always love her. But *dammit*, that woman is stubborn."

Clancy and Duncan gave each other a sideways glance, and then Duncan said, "Ma is not the only stubborn person in the Flynn family. Two bullheaded people have worked themselves into this impasse, and it's going to take guts to break out of it."

"It's in your hands, Da." Everyone raised their glasses to Clancy's pronouncement.

"Hooya!" Duncan said.

Chapter Five

Twenty-four years ago ...

Lena sat cross-legged on the end of the bed while Duncan played something called *Nemesis* on his Game Boy. It was a good thing she'd brought a book, because Duncan liked the game so much that he'd hardly noticed she was there. This was the third time now that she'd brought his lunch and sat with him for a while. She wasn't sure if he liked her to visit, but he never told her to leave.

"What's the game about?"

He didn't look up. "War." His thumbs moved so fast she could hardly see them. "There's a spaceship battle, and my orders are to kill the bad guys."

Lena gathered her knees to her chest. "What did they do?"

"Huh? Who?"

"The bad guys. What did they do that makes them so bad?"

Duncan paused the Game Boy and looked at her like she was crazy. "I don't know. Nothing, I guess. They're just enemy spaceships and they have to be destroyed.

Watch." Duncan turned sideways so she could see the action on the tiny screen, one ship sending out death rays and bombs and other ships blowing up. All of it happened with really bad beeping music that seemed to just go on and on and never change.

"Okay." Lena didn't see what was so great about it. She picked up the book Duncan's mother had given her to read. She told Lena that she used to read it to her kids when they were younger and that they still enjoyed it. The book was called *The Mermaid of Bayberry Island*. Lena could tell it was a kids' book because it had a lot of pretty color pictures of pirates and mermaids and sea captains. But some of the words were hard to read, even for Lena, and she'd been the best reader in all of second grade at her school in Rhode Island. She had a certificate that said so!

With the spaceship battle going on in the background, she flipped through the pages until she found a place she wanted to start reading.

Once the mermaid fountain was finished and shown to the people of Bayberry Island, rumors began that she had magical powers. People claimed the mermaid could find true love for anyone who wanted it.

Lena studied the colorful full-page drawing of the mermaid of Fountain Square. She decided the statue was the most beautiful thing she'd ever seen. She had long hair, nice eyes, and a friendly face. Her skin looked so soft. Lena decided that if the mermaid were real, she would be one of those ladies who always smelled good and wore lipstick. But the one thing she couldn't stop staring at was the mermaid's tail. Lena had so many questions. Where was her belly button? How could that happen? The statue's arms were like everyone else's, with hands and fingers and an elbow and everything else that was supposed to be there. So what happened to her legs? Everything from the hips down was covered in sparkly scales. Where her feet should be she had a wide fantail. Its shape reminded Lena of a real-life dolphin or whale tail, only a lot fancier.

Sure, she had seen drawings of mermaids before. Her mother used to tell her mermaid stories she'd learned as a little girl growing up in the Azores. But never had Lena seen anything as interesting and perfect as this drawing.

"Where's the fountain?"

"Huh?" Duncan frowned in concentration at his tiny black-and-white screen. His spaceship was still killing everything that got in its way.

"The mermaid. Where is this mermaid statue? How long does it take to walk to Fountain Square?"

Duncan paused his game and glared at Lena, who was holding up the book. "Are you kidding me? You want to talk about the mermaid?"

She held her chin high. "Yes, I do."

Duncan grabbed the book from her hands and began laughing. "Ma gave this to you, I bet."

"She did." Lena snatched it back.

Duncan smiled. It wasn't a sweet smile. He looked like he was up to no good. But it was the first smile Lena had seen from him at all, so she thought it was wonderful.

"You know, I can save you a lot of time. You don't have to read the book. I'll tell you the real story."

Lena sat up straighter. "Really? You will?"

"Sure." Duncan dropped his electronic game to the comforter and leaned back against the headboard. He crossed his arms over his belly.

"So there was this dude back in the eighteen hundreds, Rutherford Flynn. He was my great-great-grandfather. He came here from Ireland and started a fishing business. It's called Flynn Fisheries, and my dad is the president now. This house was built by Rutherford."

She felt her eyes bug out. "Really?"

"Yeah. So Rutherford gets super-rich and owns a lot of boats, and one day he's at sea when the weather turns. You know, back then they didn't have satellites or the Weather Channel, so they never really knew how bad storms would get or exactly when they'd show up."

Suddenly, Lena felt scared. "Did he *die*?"

Duncan tipped his head back and laughed. It was strange that such a big, loud noise could come from a puny and sick boy. The laugh soon turned into a cough, and the cough sounded so bad and lasted so long that Lena was about run down to get Duncan's mother. But like it was nothing, he held up his hand for her to wait. He finished coughing, then kept talking. "Remember I said he was my great-great-grandfather?"

She nodded.

"Then he couldn't have died, right? He went on to have a boy, who had a boy, who had my dad."

"Oh." Lena suddenly felt like a stupid little girl.

"It's okay. So you want to hear what happened?"

She nodded, excited again.

"All right. So this really bad nor'easter hits the fleet, and Rutherford tries his best, but pretty soon he realizes they're all going to die. Water is everywhere. The boats are being blown sideways. Almost every man on the island was out that day, so if they died, then every family on the island would have been destroyed."

Lena slapped a hand over her mouth.

"So my great-great-grandfather is about to give up and let the sea swallow them whole, when he looks down into the stormy water and sees . . ."

Lena waited while Duncan coughed a few times. She jumped up and sat on her haunches, ready to hear what happened next. He was teasing her. "What?" She smacked her hands onto the comforter. "What does he see?"

"A mermaid!"

She gasped.

"And she stares up at him from down in the water and guides all the boats safely to shore. Everybody is cheering and stuff, and as soon as my great-great-grandfather touches land, he tells his men he has to find her and jumps right back into the stormy sea, like a crazy person. They drag him out again and get him to a tavern, where the owner's daughter nurses him. You know, she gives him soup and dries him off and stuff."

Lena nodded. "Go on!"

"Well, he wakes up a couple days later, sees this really pretty girl taking care of him, and freaks out. He thinks she's the mermaid. He *swears* she is! And he goes down on his knees and begs her to marry him."

Lena tipped her head to the side, blinking in disbelief. "He married a mermaid?"

Duncan laughed, coughed, then laughed again. When he looked at her, his eyes had softened. He seemed a little nicer. "How old did you say you are?"

"Seven."

"I'm ten. That's a *lot* older. I am way more mature than you."

"So?" Lena crossed her legs once more and settled onto the comforter. "I had a friend who was only four and one who was nine. Can you finish the story now, please?"

"You got it." Duncan cleared his throat, and that's when Lena noticed how his shoulders poked up under his T-shirt. She tried hard to be quiet, but he was so skinny it scared her. For the first time, she wondered—how sick was he?

"Are you going to die?"

"What?" His face froze.

"I just . . . I wondered if you are so sick that you're going to die."

Duncan looked away. She saw that he was working hard to breathe, and she watched as he grabbed his inhaler and took his medicine. When he finally faced her again, his face looked blank.

"So. You wanna know what happened to the mermaid girl?"

"Yes!"

He chuckled. "Right. So Rutherford marries the tavern keeper's daughter, and later, after they have kids and get even richer and build this house and everything, he becomes mayor and decides to have a fountain made in honor of his wife. He gets some famous artist to do it, and they have this big party to reveal it. The cover gets pulled away and there she is—a mermaid! And nobody knows what to say."

"Why? Didn't they like it?"

A smile slowly spread on Duncan's face. "Now I'm going to tell you the *real* story, Adelena Silva, something you won't find in any book. Pay attention and never forget what I'm about to tell you." He paused.

"Go on!"

"If you say so. Here's the truth: my great-great-grandfather was a nutcase. You know, cuckoo for Cocoa Puffs."

Lena felt her mouth fall open.

"Of course his wife wasn't a mermaid! But he *thought* she was. And my ma thinks so, too, and she's in charge of a whole group of women who dress up like mermaids and have meetings in our dining room. So the real story is that everyone on this island is a little crazy, and so are you if you think that stupid story is real!"

Lena let her hands fall to her sides, overwhelmed with disappointment and numb with sadness. But Duncan kept smiling, like he was happy he'd just destroyed something. She didn't understand it.

Slowly, Lena got off the bed and lifted the book into her arms. She stood over Duncan, trying to figure out what she saw. Those eyes stared at her—burning blue and alive—like he was ready to fight her. Suddenly, she understood. He was mad because he was sick. He couldn't have any fun, so he didn't want anyone else to have fun either. He didn't think good things happened, so he didn't want anyone else to think so either. It made sense, she decided. If she were sick like that, she would be mad, too.

"Well? You got something to say?"

Lena shrugged. It was going to be hard to be friends with a boy like Duncan. He was mean on the outside and scared and lonely on the inside. How could you be a friend to someone who pretended he didn't want or need a friend?

"I guess I'll see you tomorrow," she said.

Lena wandered down the back staircase to the apartment she shared with her mother. It was right off the kitchen, very small, but her mother said they had everything they needed. Lena had her own bedroom. They had their own TV, bathroom, and something her mother called a kitchenette. Lena shut her bedroom door, plopped down on her bed, and rolled onto her stomach. She opened the book and began reading again. This time she would start at the very beginning, so she didn't miss anything.

Duncan was wrong about Rutherford and the mermaid, of course. He said those things only because he was angry and had never been to the Azores. Lena knew that someday, when he felt better, Duncan Flynn would be able to believe.

Maybe she would help him.

Chapter Six

Lena tossed her wallet into her canvas bag and exited the farmers' market near the public dock. Her mind was on the painting she'd been tinkering with all morning and her sudden desire to make grilled eggplant for dinner, an urge that, unfortunately, required a trip to town. She breathed in the cornucopia of smells to be found on a summer day during high-tourist season—the briny sea and ferryboat diesel fumes mixed with fried clams, boardwalk fries, pizza, and sunshine—and headed toward her car in the public parking lot. Out of nowhere, her body began to buzz with awareness. Lena looked up. And spotted him.

Duncan towered above most everyone else on Main Street. He walked at a steady pace, with a strong stride. He was about half a block from the water and headed right toward her.

Lena slipped under the awning of Frankie's Fish-n-Chips, pulled a bistro chair into the shade, and sat with her back against the restaurant's cedar-shingled wall. Her heart was beating like crazy! What was she—eleven years old? She took a deep breath and told herself to calm down and blend in with the dozen or so tourists dining al fresco. She slumped in the chair and covered the lower part of her face with her shopping bag.

A mother of two glared at Lena, moving her chair to act as a buffer between Lena and her offspring. Good grief! Since when did a woman with a tote full of eggplant look like a threat? Especially in a place where festival-week tourists dressed like zombie pirates just to go out for ice cream.

From the shadows, Lena watched Duncan approach the very doorway she'd just exited. It gave her chills to think that if she'd dawdled near the squash only two extra minutes, she would have run right into him!

She sighed, resting her chin on her tote, simply enjoying the sight of him. The first and most important thing she noticed was that he had come a long way in the month he'd been home. Her mother had told her that when Duncan first arrived, he'd had trouble walking. Today he seemed steady and sure of himself, even in a crowd. On closer inspection, Lena did detect a slight limp, but only because she was looking for it.

It wouldn't be much longer before he was ready to return to work, and the thought of that squeezed her heart.

It was embarrassing, but Lena wasn't just examining his gait. The truth was that she had never known, and would never know, a man as crazy sexy as Duncan Flynn. The only reason she wasn't gawking in shock was because she'd caught a glimpse of Duncan last year during festival week, when she had stopped by the Safe Haven to pick up her mother. Duncan had been coming out the kitchen door with Clancy, and the two of them had been laughing. Lena had carefully backed away from the bed-

and-breakfast so as not to draw attention to her car. She had noticed her hands were shaking.

"He looks like a movie star nowadays, doesn't he?" her mother had commented.

Lena hadn't answered.

Her mother had turned in the seat to look at her. "Don't you think he looks like a movie star, *menina*?"

Lena had kept her eyes on the road.

"Lena?"

"Who are you talking about, Mother?"

Mellie had laughed all the way to the house.

Duncan was thirty-four now, six foot two, hard and chiseled and maybe just slightly leaner than she recalled him being the year before. Despite his injuries, he remained a study in masculine lines and motion, sleek and in control. It was no wonder a group of women had just stopped in their tracks and stared as he walked by.

He was that kind of gorgeous.

When Duncan disappeared into the market, Lena felt her body relax. There was no denying it. She was a coward. The reason she hadn't run into Duncan in the month he'd been home was because she was afraid to. She had waited till the very end to stop by Frasier's dinner party, in the hopes that Duncan would have already called it a night.

And just now she'd run away from him.

Lena gathered her tote and wound her way through the bistro tables, once again headed toward the parking lot. She longed to spend time with him, to hear him laugh and see him smile, but the truth was, she was too afraid to risk getting her bubble popped.

What if he was nothing like she'd built him up to be all these years? What if he was not the man of her imagination? What if she'd been wrong so long ago and had continued to be wrong every year since?

What if Duncan was not her one and only?

Duncan sat at the desk in his room at the Safe Haven, the only light coming from his laptop, his whole body nothing but a ball of frustration. He couldn't keep putting this off. Duncan placed his fingers on the keys and forced himself to start writing.

> *July 28*

> *Dear Nestor and Beth,*
>
> *I think of you both every day, and I know I'll be visiting you in San Diego soon. I'm headed to Little Creek next week to meet with Capt. Sinclair, my first official step toward getting back to active duty. I still have a ways to go before I can even think of passing my physical screening and dive medical, but I'm running again, and hope to start swimming in the choppy Atlantic soon. (No pansy pools for me!) As Justin used to say— "It ain't a good swim unless you damn near drown."*

Duncan stopped typing. Would the Jaramillos want old jokes from their dead son? Would they hear Justin's voice in their heads and laugh with him, or would they think Duncan was being flippant about death? *Their only child's death.*

"Shit."

He could change it later. Right now he needed to keep typing. It had been two months since the Jaramillos had come to visit him on the rehab unit at Walter Reed, and he hadn't yet reached out to them. That was unacceptable.

As I continue to get stronger, my memories of the ambush become clearer. I believe it is my responsibility to share with you some of the details of that night, not because I want to cause you additional suffering, but because it is my duty, as Justin's best friend and teammate, to share everything I know. I realize the Navy has given you an official report, but I am the only man on earth who can tell you about the last seconds of your son's life. It was a promise we made to each other during Hell Week, when we both knew we would be among those going through. We said that if anything ever happened to one of us and the other survived, we would be the eyes and ears for our families. I am not a writer, but I will do my best to help bring you closure.

Duncan paused, his trembling fingers resting above the keyboard. He had to keep going. He owed them this.

Justin was on point for our eight-man insertion team that night. He never flinched, never hesitated. Your son was the most courageous man I've ever known, and he remained so all the way through the last seconds of his life. Even when he knew he was facing death, his concern was for his team.

We were dropped in a godforsaken stretch of rocky hills in the Middle of Nowhere, Kandahar Province. Our orders were to stake out a single-story shack that intel indicated was the hiding place of one of the region's high-value terrorist targets. We'd been stalking him for six months. So with night-vision binocs, we lay on our bellies in the rocks until we could verify that the structure was occupied and our target was on the premises. We got the order from base to execute the mission, which was to take the target alive and kill his bodyguards and lower-level soldiers.

All these months later, we know the target had been tipped off and escaped via an underground tunnel—but not before the structure was rigged to explode upon our entrance.

I will never forget how it unfolded. Justin signaled for me to cover the rest of the squad while he took the front door with Mike and Scotty. He sent Terrence to the back, Paul and Jax around to the sides, and Simon, who was running coms, remained stationary behind a boulder just thirty feet from the structure.

I can't tell you how many times I've wondered why Justin made that last-minute change to the mission profile and put me where he did. I should have been at his side, right there at the front door when they blew the lock and rammed it in.

But I was crouched behind an old burned-out Jeep parked about a hundred feet from the front door. I monitored the windows through my night-vision rifle sight, scanning back and forth, three windows in all. But I saw no movement. And just like that, a sick feeling flashed through me.

It was over in a split second. Everything happened at once—they popped the door; a tiny pin-prick of red light flashed three times in the darkness; Justin screamed, "Get down!" A rolling wall of pressure and heat smacked me and sent me flying. The force of the explosion lifted the vehicle up in the air and tossed it on top of me. I was trapped under the weight, flames everywhere, debris flying over my head. I could not move. I strained and pulled, but I was trapped. I realized my skin was on fire under my vest. The pain in my left leg was brutal. But I knew it was my duty to find anyone alive from my team and get them out.

But I didn't. I couldn't. I failed Justin and all of my brothers and I'm sorry.

Duncan stared at his hands on the keys. Why were they covered in blood?

I'm trapped. Trapped. Trapped. Stinging pain. The metal taste of blood in my mouth. Still hearing shit hitting the ground in the distance. And then the faint sound of my name being called . . . "Flynn . . . Jesus, Flynn." And then everything went silent . . . time passed . . . hours . . . Then there was the sound of the helo. Medics handling me. Shouting and screaming. A tourniquet on my leg and burn pads on my side. I kept asking, "Where are they? Where are they? Who survived?" And then nothing . . . not until I woke up in a recovery room in Germany.

Duncan pushed himself from the desk chair, sweat pooling in the hollow of his collarbones. He glanced outside—dark. How long had he been sitting there staring at the laptop screen, the words flowing in his head but not on the keyboard? It didn't matter. He needed to get out of that room and get some air.

He laced up his running shoes and headed down the back steps to the kitchen, hoping to hell he didn't run into any of the bed-and-breakfast's guests. The place was filled to capacity with couples and families and would remain that way until fall.

Duncan moved without making a sound, down three

flights of stairs, through the kitchen, out the side door, across the lawn, and down the beach access steps. His feet hit the sand. He jogged to the water's edge, finding that sweet spot of hardened sand, not wet enough to collapse beneath his weight but not so loose that he couldn't get traction. And he took off.

Within minutes, the rush of sea air into his lungs had cleared his mind. He told himself he was a world away from the blast, the blood, the pain, and the cries of his dying friend. That's whose voice he heard. There was no question—Justin called out to him just before he died.

And Duncan had failed him.

He ran, directing his awareness down, down into his body, feeling the miraculous ease of movement he had that night. He decided to shoot for three miles, halfway down the public beach and back, which would be his longest run to date. Finally, all the hard work was paying off.

Duncan listened to the rhythmic thump of his stride on the sand, his perfectly timed breath, and felt the salty seawater spray against his face.

"Hey, sexy."

A gaggle of junior high school girls lounged on beach towels, smoking cigarettes and looking for trouble. Duncan had a hard time understanding how parents could let girls that age go free range—it never ended well. He would never allow Serena or Christina to behave like that.

He ran right past them.

"Hey! We were talking to you, Gramps!" The girls burst out into a fit of giggles just before one of them said, "I don't care how old he is—he is hot!"

Duncan chuckled to himself, keeping his focus on his run, which was a challenge since the beach was a teenage wasteland that night. He smelled pot about every ten yards. There were dozens of illegal beach fires and as many parties, with kids making out on blankets and beer cans clattering in trash bags. Everything from Latin dance music to pop country to hard-core rap was broadcast from portable speakers, so loud it could be heard over the roar of the sea. Duncan almost tripped over a lip-locked couple rolling around in the surf like they were gunning for a remake of *From Here to Eternity*.

He kept on, in search of silence and privacy, but it was nowhere to be found on the public beach. He slowed his run as he neared a newly built chain-link fence. A large white metal sign read, NO TRESPASSING. PRIVATE BEACH. SECURITY CAMERAS. A quick scan of the surroundings revealed that no such cameras existed, so Duncan hopped the fence. While suspended in the air, an instant before his feet hit the sand, he realized where he was. This was old Harry Rosterveen's land, now Adelena Silva's property, and she'd given it the ridiculous name of Moondance Beach. Too bad *Sea Spray* was already taken.

Though his only near-contact with her had been the night of Da's ill-fated birthday dinner, she'd pop into his thoughts every now and then. How could she not? Her paintings were all over the Safe Haven. Once his mother discovered Duncan had removed that witchy-woman mermaid portrait from his room, she went and found him another one—even bigger and with even more naked flesh!—and slapped that sucker right up over the mantelpiece. "Maybe you'll like this one better," she said.

He didn't.

Since Lena made her living painting mermaids, it was a sure bet she was just as flaky as his ma, but that didn't mean she'd shoot Duncan for trespassing. Shy, artistic chicks weren't usually the type to carry rifles.

After about ten more minutes of running, the exhaustion caught up to him. He'd run as far as he'd planned but had to get all the way back. So he slowed to a walk, waited for his pulse to return to normal, then plopped down in the sand for a stretch and a rest.

As much as he disliked them, he couldn't really blame the tourists for coming here. Bayberry Island was a pretty place, and though he'd traveled most of Asia, Europe, and North and South America, he'd seen none prettier. Duncan lay back, tucked his arms behind his head, and indulged in a little stargazing. It was a perfect spot for it, with very little light pollution and a new moon. He could see the cloudy sweep of the Milky Way and a fiercely bright Jupiter taking center stage. The Big and Little Dippers hung suspended overhead. And suddenly, a meteor shower burst across the sky, shooting out from the constellation Aquarius and arcing overhead, flashing and diminishing as it dipped below the northwest horizon line.

And that's when he noticed something moving.

Duncan's gaze shot to the water, where he saw a great swish of a tail breaking the surface not twenty yards from shore. What was it—a dolphin? He blinked. Waited. Nothing. Wait. It hadn't been a tail at all—the head and shoulders of a person now appeared above the waterline. His instinct was to jump into the surf and carry out a rescue, but the swimmer was in no obvious distress. Something told him to be still. To wait and observe. So in stunned silence, Duncan watched a form rise slowly from the surf. He blinked again. Okay. He had to be hallucinating. It had happened to him once in the smothering heat of Afghanistan, so why not here and now? Maybe he had pushed himself too hard.

Without making a sound, Duncan flattened himself into the sand, disappearing, remaining perfectly still while he stared in disbelief. This was better than any hallucination. Hell, it was better than any wet dream he'd ever had.

Not twenty feet away, a woman had materialized. She was gloriously naked, her pale skin gleaming in the starlight, a stream of dark hair flipped over her left shoulder and cupping a breast. As she continued to rise from the water, the rest of her loveliness was revealed. Duncan saw a slim waist, flared hips, and a dark vee between a set of perfect thighs.

He stopped breathing. He willed himself to be invisible. And she walked right past him, so slowly it was like she was in a dream state. That was when he saw her face in profile — lovely, delicate, and somehow bold. That was a strong woman. But who *was* she?

No way.

Could this vision be Adelena Silva, Mellie's daughter? It was her beach, after all. But when had that timid little squirt become a mesmerizingly gorgeous woman? Duncan squeezed his eyes shut, telling himself he had to be confused. Sure, the babe who'd just come out of the water reminded him of someone — some*thing*, really. A moment, maybe. A fleeting sensation. And though he couldn't quite put his finger on why she seemed familiar, he was certain she wasn't Adelena.

Right?

Duncan opened his eyes. He watched her as she continued down the beach, his brain now on high alert. *Pay attention*, it said. Then he saw it — the feminine curve of her calf and the daintiness of her ankle. Put a frilly little sandal on it, and that was the leg he'd seen in the dining room of the Safe Haven.

Duncan waited until she was far enough up the beach that he could make his exit. Because he had been lying still for so long, tensed up and on alert, he had become quite stiff. He grunted as he pushed himself from the sand, somehow got himself over the fence, and headed down Safe Haven Beach. He jogged the three miles back to the bed-and-breakfast, his mind racing as fast as his heart.

"Gather 'round, ye maids." Mona paused, swallowing hard as she blinked back tears. Oh, of all the ridiculous things! Here it was, three weeks before the festival, and she suddenly doubted her ability to step into the role of president of the Bayberry Island Mermaid Society. She'd held the job for forty years, for goodness' sake, and she could conduct their rites in her sleep. Just because she'd found a suitable replacement and had finally retired last year didn't mean she'd lost her knowledge and experience. She needed to calm herself.

Mona took a steadying breath and joined the sacred circle along with her friends. "O, Great Mermaid. Hear this plea of pure heart."

The ladies gazed up at the face of the bronze goddess, who began to glow in the first hint of morning light. Eight female voices said in unison, "Hear this plea of pure heart."

Mona continued. "O, Great Mermaid! We are twenty-one days away from our celebration of your power and grace. Your followers are already arriving. Bless the pilgrims who come to pay their respects. Bless the travelers who return again and those who come for the first time. Hear the pleas of those who yearn for their heart-mate."

The women responded together, "Hear them."

"Help them remain open to the mystery of the sea."

"Open them."

"Ease their resistance to true love."

"Assist them."

"Allow . . ." Mona felt her eyes begin to sting. She sniffed. "Allow the water of love to flow through the hearts of all who come here."

"Guide them."

"Light their way to—" Mona had to stop. She felt as if she were about to burst into tears.

"You okay, Mona?" Polly Estherhausen twisted the tip of her flip-flop back and forth, extinguishing her cigarette butt on the brickwork of Fountain Square. "Would you like one of us to take over?"

As soon as the question escaped Polly's mouth, she realized how insulting it had sounded. She raised her shoulders and winced. "Oops."

No one was gazing at the mermaid now—they were all glaring at Polly.

"I'm sorry, okay?"

"I think we need to do some kind of sensitivity training. You know, as a group." Abigail Foster peered through the pale pink light into the faces of the eight members present. "Should we take a vote?"

"Sensitivity?" Izzy McCracken seemed puzzled. "I think we're all plenty sensitive as it is. I mean, I suffer from gluten sensitivity. And I know Barbara can't use those kitchen gloves because of that stuff . . . Oh, what's that called, again? You know, what condoms are made of?"

"Latex?" Barbara Butcher offered.

"Right."

"I have sensitive skin." Layla O'Brien seemed happy to join the conversation. "Every brand of sunscreen I've tried breaks me out."

"And that's not even counting emotional sensitivity," Izzy added. "I cry every time that Folgers commercial comes on. You know the one I'm talking about."

"Oh, for the love of all that's holy." Polly pushed her wig back into place and rested her fists on the waistband of her spandex mermaid tail. "Just say it, Abigail. You don't want to fix our *group*. You want to fix *me*! Last fall I needed anger management. Last festival week you wanted me to stop using the *F* word. Last winter you told me I needed to sit under a full-spectrum sunlamp because I become a raging bitch after every Thanksgiving, like clockwork."

Abigail crossed her arms under her coconuts. "Your mood swings are more accurate than the *TV Guide*, Polly."

"That's a symptom of menopause, you know," Izzy offered. "But that ended forever ago for you, didn't it, Polly?"

"I wish Darinda were still here." Mona couldn't believe she'd said that aloud! Tentatively, she raised her eyes to see each of her fellow mermaids cringing with guilt. She had not intended to take a passive-aggressive jab at them. It wasn't her preferred way of dealing with conflict, but she was clearly off-balance that morning. "I apologize," she told her friends.

"No." Barbara approached Mona and took her hands in hers. "We are the ones who are sorry. We let you down,

Mona. You *finally* got a break from serving as president, and then Darinda up and quits."

"It wasn't like she *wanted* her mother to break her hip." Izzy's cheeks flushed. "She had no choice but to move back to the mainland. It's what any of us would have done."

"Yes, but not a single one of us offered to serve out the rest of Darinda's term." Abigail pursed her lips. "We just assumed Mona would do it."

"And that wasn't right." Barbara squeezed Mona's hands tighter. "One of us should have stepped up. You've carried this organization for nearly half a century, and you should be allowed to retire."

"She's right!" Layla scanned the faces of the other mermaids for support. "She has her grandbabies now, and Duncan is home, and then there's the Frasier issue."

"He's not still dating Sally, is he?"

Polly shook her head at Abigail. "Open mouth, insert fin."

Everyone got quiet. The only sound to be heard was the tinkling of the fountain, the cries of seagulls, and the distant whisper of the ocean. Mona wandered over to a bench and sat down, suddenly more exhausted than she had a right to be. The other mermaids followed, unnaturally silent, finding places to sit or stand near Mona.

"Have you talked to him since his birthday?"

Mona chuckled at Abigail's question. "No."

"Is he still calling you?"

Mona shrugged. "Calls, flowers ... He even wrote me a ridiculous poem about sea spray and mermaids and shoved it under my front door."

Polly nearly choked. "A whaaaat?"

"My question is, why all of a sudden? I think it's because he embarrassed himself in front of the family with the whole Sally thing," Mona said.

"Ha! He should be embarrassed! What an ass!"

Mona continued. "Honestly, I think our marriage is beyond repair. I've been thinking I should call a lawyer later this week and file for divorce—three years is a long time to be stuck in limbo."

"I know what you mean!" Layla smacked her palms against her spandex-covered thighs. "I was stuck in Lubbock with my ex for three years and I nearly lost my mind!"

"We will be with you every step of the way, Mona."

Everyone agreed with Barbara.

"And Duncan? Is everything all right with him?"

Mona put on a brave smile. "He's great. I believe he's going to make it back to active duty. It's been remarkable to watch how focused and determined he is, and I'm happy for him." She paused, careful to put a lid on her disappointment. "Really—I am. I am happy whenever my children are happy. I just wish that he would have discovered something—someone—worth staying for."

"Oh, no!" Izzy slapped a hand over a coconut. "He can't go!"

Mona sighed. "We gave it our best shot."

"Lena's painting ...?" Barbara didn't have to finish her question.

Mona shook her head. "I replaced it with another one and he took that one down, too. Number three is in there now, covered with a beach towel. He says they give him headaches."

"Aha!" Abigail nodded knowingly. "He is not completely immune, then. Maybe there's still time."

"No." Mona placed a hand along the side of her cheek, rubbing her temple. "Neither of them are in the right place. Duncan is already gone to Afghanistan, if not in body then in spirit. Lena has gotten lost in her art—I'm not sure how much of that magical little girl still lives inside her—and she's shown no interest in him at all. It's just not working."

"But they are each other's heart-mate!" Izzy began crying, pulling a tissue from her shell to blow her nose. "Ever since they were children! It's the truest of true loves!" Izzy appeared panicked. "We've got to stop Duncan from leaving!"

Mona shook her head. "He is blind, and she will not make the first move. This has all been for nothing."

Layla gasped.

"I don't know what to believe anymore," Mona said, hearing the despair in her own voice. "Sometimes I look back on the last forty years and wonder if I was a fool to spend so much of my life in the service of love."

Polly struck a match on the park bench and lit another cigarette. She took a puff, blew the smoke over her shoulder, and lowered her chin. "I'm just going to spit this out—all right, girls? I'm gonna be blunt, and I might offend some of you."

Abigail feigned shock. "Say it isn't so!"

Polly ignored her. "The writing's on the wall, maids. We're old. We're cranky. We've got grandkids and wayward husbands and a whole range of illnesses—hell, even our bowels are irritable! We've hit a dead end." She took a drag on her cigarette. "We've tried for years to get somebody—anybody—under the age of forty to join our society, but our recruiting efforts have failed. Who wants to hang out with a bunch of whiny old hags in mermaid outfits? We're a throwback to another time and place. We're irrelevant."

"Absolutely not!" Abigail stomped her Easy Spirit walking shoe onto the bricks. "Who will coordinate the festival? Who will register Island Day vendors and hold auditions for the children's play? Who will decorate for the Mermaid Ball?"

Barbara shrugged. "This thing has become way bigger than us. The Chamber of Commerce and the festival board of directors run things nowadays. They don't need us anymore."

"But we *are* the festival!" Abigail seemed shocked that no one was taking her side. "If we disappear, who will testify to the power and mystery of the Great Mermaid? Without her—without the heart and soul of the legend—then what's it all for?"

Everyone lowered their heads.

"Let's face it," Polly said, her voice just above a whisper. "None of us was even willing to serve as temporary president when Darinda left. Rowan, Annie, and Evelyn have repeatedly refused to consider joining—hell, Rowan and Annie have made fun of us since they were kids! There isn't a soul on earth to lead the next generation of mermaids!"

No one had a comeback for Polly. Layla used the back of her wrist to wipe away tears. Izzy stared down at her Birkenstocks. Mona sat on the bench, watching the pale sunlight hit the faces of the Mermaid Society members the way it had for one hundred and twenty-seven years.

Was Polly right? Was this really the end?

The Great Mermaid stared out to sea, as stoic and unchanged as the day she was unveiled. She never grew old. She never doubted herself in the face of change. But she was made of bronze, of course—not flesh and blood—and though she might possess mystical knowledge of true love, she would never know the human heartache associated with losing it.

"Polly is right," Mona said. "Without some kind of miracle, the Bayberry Island Mermaid Society is dead in the water."

Chapter Seven

Duncan's eyes popped open with the sun. He lay still for a moment, aware that something had changed. First off, he was sore as shit. Six miles had been too much, and he would need to rest his hamstrings and calf muscles for a couple days. But the change went beyond physical. Something had shifted in his mood. He was excited to begin something. It was almost as if he had a new mission . . .

The water woman! There was no way she had been a dream.

Duncan rose from the bed and took a quick shower—well, quick*er*. In just over a month, he had managed to reduce the time required for grooming and dressing from forty minutes to twenty minutes. Not bad. He caught himself humming as he slipped his feet into his favorite old Docksiders and headed down the back stairs to the kitchen.

It was a typical summer morning, ovens filled with baked goods while trays of fresh fruit, bacon, and scrambled eggs were ferried out to a noisy dining room by the summer waitresses. It was controlled chaos, and the controller was Imelda Silva.

"*Não,* Svetlana! That's the cottage cheese. We need cream cheese for the bagels!" Mellie rolled her eyes and shooed her summer employee toward the walk-in refrigerator. When she turned back, she caught Duncan reaching for a miniloaf of banana bread right off the cooling rack. She smacked his hand.

"Good morning, dear Mellie."

"Get!"

"But I'm starving."

She pointed to a stool at the large butcher-block table in the middle of the room. "Then sit down like a person. Have coffee and juice and maybe some eggs."

Duncan couldn't help but smile at her showmanship. Mellie liked to pretend she was annoyed with everyone and everything, but Duncan had always been able to see the laughter in her dark almond-shaped eyes.

Wait.

Those eyes. They looked familiar. They were similar to the eyes of the witchy-woman mermaid painting.

He went still as a strange heat radiated from his chest, through his body, and out to his limbs. He knew he was staring at Mellie but couldn't seem to stop himself.

"What's this all about? You're acting strange today. Now, sit down." She poured him a cup of coffee and fetched the container of half-and-half, then threw together a breakfast plate. Duncan dug in, realizing that the word "starving" may not have captured just how hungry he was.

His plan was to eat and get out of there. Looking into Mellie's eyes was suddenly way too uncomfortable.

"You good?"

"Absolutely. Thank you for breakfast."

She frowned. "Where are you headed in such a hurry at nine in the morning?"

"I gotta go see Clancy at the station."

"Hmm." Mellie sat down across from him, folded her hands on the table, and looked him up and down. "Something is different with you today. What is it?"

Duncan shrugged, giving Mellie a quick, reassuring smile. "I'm feeling a lot stronger. I ran almost six miles last night, and I'm looking forward to my meeting with the captain next week."

"That's not it." Mellie shook her head and waved her hand at him. "It's not your running and it's not your captain."

Duncan laughed, wiping his mouth with a napkin and finishing his coffee in a single gulp. "I gotta go, Mellie. Thanks again for breakfast." He grabbed his dishes and placed them in the large sink, then kissed her cheek on his way to the side door.

He could feel her eyes on his back, and the sensation lingered long after he'd left the kitchen.

It was a twenty-minute walk to the Bayberry Island Police Department and Jail complex—if two old, weather-beaten clapboard buildings held together by a breeze-way could be called a complex. But Duncan enjoyed the sunshine and the cool morning air. He cut through a few alleys and parking lots once he got to the oldest part of town, knowing the shortcut to his destination. A bell jingled when he opened the front door and the assistant chief of police, Chip Bradford, looked up from his paperwork, his face breaking out into a big smile.

"Duncan! How you doing?" Chip stepped out from behind the desk and gave him a hug. "It's good to see you, man. You're looking wonderful!"

"Thanks, Chip. *Whoa!*"

Something made a sharp barking sound and leaped up to the level of Duncan's chest. He caught it in midair and came face-to-face with what reminded him way too much of an Ewok from the *Star Wars* movies. He stared at it for a moment, laughing. "Is this thing supposed to be a dog?"

Chip laughed. "Yeah, but that's all we know about her. She's a stray—no tags, no microchip, no collar. She was hanging around the back door last week, and we let her in when it started raining. She was soaked. We think a tourist dumped her."

"Classy." Duncan put the creature down on the old wood floor, shaking his head. "My brother is too soft. He should have called Animal Control."

"We did, but when Fred got here, Clancy told him never mind, that we were going to keep Ondine."

"Who?"

"Ondine. I named her that after the water sprite from mythology, you know, because she was nearly drowning in the rain."

"Of course." Duncan decided if he didn't divert Chip to some other topic, he could be there until nightfall. "Listen, is he around?"

Chip inclined his head toward the hallway. "In his office. He's finishing shift scheduling for festival week and told me not to bother him. Our moonlighters will be here soon."

The dog began sniffing and scratching at Duncan's shoe. He ignored her.

Chip went on. "Just between you and me, we got some new scheduling software, and it's a wicked piece of crap. Your brother's probably not in the greatest mood."

"Roger that." Duncan knew that every summer the Bayberry Police Department beefed up its force in order to deal with festival-week crowds. Most of the temporary guys were Clancy's buddies from his Boston PD days, more than happy to spend their vacations making triple overtime.

The scraggly little dog had just finished rolling around on her back, her tongue sticking out of her little mouth. Now she sat staring up at Duncan with big puppy eyes.

"It needs a bath," he told Chip.

"It's a she."

"*She* needs a bath." Duncan let himself through the gate that separated the public part of the station from the offices. He tapped on the chief's door, then pushed it open.

"Whoa!" He shut it and backed down the hallway. That wasn't meant for him to see—his brother pressing his wife down onto his desk, kissing the hell out of her, her legs wrapped around him. Duncan wandered farther down the hallway and leaned against the wall, deciding how best to apologize for the intrusion.

Thank God all they were doing was kissing.

Evelyn exited her husband's office first, her eyes averted. Clancy was right behind her, buttoning up his shirt, his eyebrows raised in annoyance at his brother.

"Very sorry about that." The worst part was Evelyn. Would she be angry at him? Embarrassed? Sure, he saw her often enough, but they weren't particularly close. Duncan wasn't even sure how it worked with a sister-in-law— he'd barely spoken to Clancy's first wife.

Right at that moment, he felt like a real tool.

"Evie, I didn't see anything. Really. And you have nothing to be ashamed about."

Evelyn kissed her husband good-bye, whispering, "See you tonight, Chief." As she passed Duncan, she winked at him. "Get your own girl," she said.

"See you at home, sweetheart." Clancy watched his wife exit the station, a shit-eating grin on his face. Honestly, Clancy looked just as dopey-in-love now as he had the summer he was fourteen, when a pretty, brown-haired festival-week tourist named Evie McGuinness stole his heart. As soon as the back door latched shut, Clancy's demeanor changed.

"What the hell, bro?"

"Sorry. Really. But I need to talk to you."

Just then the skanky little dog squeezed under the old swinging gate and came skittering down the hall, ears flying back, eyes focused on Duncan.

"Want a dog?" Clancy asked.

"Thanks, but no."

"She likes you."

"It's an unrequited thing."

Clancy laughed. "Well, come on in." He began tidying up a mess of papers scattered everywhere. They probably had been in order before the police chief rolled around with his wife on the desktop.

"Everything okay with Ma? Everybody at the Safe Haven good?"

"Yes. Sure." The dog was at his heels.

"So is this about Da? Have you talked with him lately?"

Duncan couldn't believe how annoying the dirty ball of fur was. She was bumping up against his right ankle.

"No, no. It's not about Da. I just have a few questions I need to ask you."

"This better be worth the interruption."

"Yeah. Again, I'm very sorry about that." Duncan sighed heavily and sat down in the chair across from his brother. The dog sat next to Duncan's foot. "Look. Do you know Adelena Silva very well?"

Clancy reared back. "*Lena*?"

"Yes. Lena. Mellie's daughter."

"Uh, no. Nobody knows Lena well. I don't even know if Mellie knows her well."

"You make her sound like the Unabomber or something."

Clancy must have thought that was funny, because he laughed pretty hard. "Nah. She's great. She's just, well, Lena is unusual. She does her own thing and doesn't seem to need other people for much." Clancy stopped talking and smiled. "Anyway, you're not exactly a social butterfly yourself. Does anyone know *you* well?"

Duncan attempted to answer his brother's question but stopped, unsure what to say. The truth was that Justin had known him well, and so had Mike and Scotty, Terrence, Paul, Jax, Simon, and the other members of his platoon. But he had a feeling that was not what his brother was asking.

Did anyone really know *him*? The whole man and not just the warrior? Duncan had never given it much thought, and now wasn't the time to start. The dog chose that moment to start licking his shoe. He shoved her away with his foot.

"Look. I need to run something by you. And it's going to sound really bizarre, but I want to tell you the whole thing and then you can tell me what you think."

Clancy leaned back in his office chair. "Sounds promising. Go for it."

Duncan leaned forward, his elbows on his knees. "I decided to go for a run last night. My plan was to do about three miles, but the beach was like *Animal House*—I was tripping over kids everywhere."

Clancy frowned. "I know. We rounded up sixteen kids last night—underage drinking and public intox mostly."

"My God. Were we that bad as teenagers?"

Clancy laughed. "Definitely."

"Anyway, so I ended up running a lot farther than I intended, just to get away from the hormone-a-palooza. And ended up on old Harry Rosterveen's land."

"Yep. Moondance Beach. It's Lena's now."

"Right. So I decided to chill for a few minutes and lie back in the sand to watch the stars. The sky was clear and the water was calm."

"You sound like one of the brochures in Safe Haven's lobby."

"Would you stop with the heckling and let me tell you what happened?"

"Sure." Clancy cleared his throat.

"So all of the sudden I think I see . . . No, I'm almost *positive* I see a tail flip out from the water."

"A tail."

"Yeah, a fantail. Like on a dolphin."

"How close?"

"I'm talking right up on the beach, maybe twenty feet from the sand."

"Well, that's not unheard of. Injured or sick dolphins and whales sometimes hang out in shallow water, where they feel safe. They've been known to beach themselves at night for that reason."

Duncan shook his head. "Thanks, Professor, but I know all that, and that's not what I'm describing to you. A fantail flipped out of the water with a splash, a playful kind of movement. But I didn't see it again. What I saw instead was ... I saw a woman."

"Say what?"

"So I'm pressing myself into the sand, making myself invisible, you know, total ninja shit, and I see a head and shoulders come out of the water. I see a woman walk toward the beach, right out of the water, and she's naked."

Clancy did that thing with his eyebrows again.

"She walks all the way out and, holy shit, she's the most gorgeous thing I've ever seen in my freakin' life. Pale skin, dark hair, an incredibly beautiful face. I'm talking *stunner*. Naked. A naked stunner of a woman, coming out of the water, right in front of me."

Clancy appeared slightly uncomfortable, crossing and uncrossing his legs several times. He might have been trying not to laugh.

"What? You don't believe me?"

"I didn't say anything! You told me to wait till you told me the whole story. This is what waiting looks like. Jeezus!"

The dog was back. She had decided to plop down for a nap, and she rested her little black nose on the top of Duncan's shoe. He ignored her and went back to the issue at hand. "Anyway, this woman is perfect and naked and she walks right past me, and I'm not even breathing. She looks so calm and peaceful, like she's in a trance or something. No shit. And then she heads up the beach and I get the fuck out of there."

Clancy's eyes were big. Duncan waited for a response. Nothing.

"Say something!"

"Oh, so now I'm allowed to speak?" Clancy spun around in his chair to face the credenza. He poured himself a cup of coffee, then found a Styrofoam cup in a drawer and poured one for Duncan.

He took a sip—and nearly spit it out. "This tastes like it just drained out of my combat boots."

"Good to the last drop." Clancy raised his mug in a toast. It was obvious to Duncan that his brother was stalling for time.

"Just say it, man."

Clancy nodded. "All right. Here's what I think. I think that you've been through a lot. Your injuries were severe, and that kind of trauma can affect your brain. I think you need to give yourself time to heal. Go easy on yourself. You might be pushing yourself too hard."

"So you think I'm nuts?"

"I didn't say that." Clancy took another swig of coffee, obviously weighing his words. "You want to be sure who you saw last night, correct?"

Duncan shrugged. "Sure. Just out of curiosity."

Clancy seemed puzzled. "Hold up. So you've never actually seen Lena? I mean, before last night you haven't run into her anywhere in the last, say, decade or so?"

"Of course not. I'm only here a few days out of the year, and I barely stay long enough to see my own family—why would I see her?"

"Point taken." Clancy sipped his coffee. "And you haven't looked her up on the Internet?"

Duncan shook his head. "No. It didn't even occur to me until right this second."

"Shall I do the honors?"

Just as Clancy turned to his computer, the dog jumped

in Duncan's lap and plopped down like she belonged there. He wrapped his hands around the little body, feeling how bony she was under all that matted fur, and put her back on the floor. She couldn't have weighed more than a sack of groceries.

He watched Clancy search the terms "Adelena Silva," "mermaid paintings," and "images." He got immediate results and turned the monitor toward Duncan so he could get a close look. The screen was filled with thumbnail shots of more mermaid paintings than should be allowed by law, plus pictures of Lena at art shows, parties, interviews, and fairs.

Clancy clicked on one image in particular, and it expanded to fit the entire screen. It was a photo of a striking woman with long, dark hair, laughing almond-shaped eyes, and a sexy half smile. In this photo she was wearing a burgundy velvet evening gown cut to her sternum, her slim throat draped with exotic-looking jewelry.

"*Holy shit.*"

"That her?"

"Oh, yeah."

"Hmm. So we have a confirmed sighting of our local celebrity skinny-dipping with the fishes. Want me to call *TMZ*?"

Duncan knew his brother was trying to lighten the mood, but his head was spinning. He didn't know how to process this information, especially in the context of everything else.

He really had seen a tail.

Then he'd seen a woman rise from the ocean.

The woman was someone he'd known as a kid.

She was the famous artist Lena Silva, known for her paintings of mermaids.

One of her paintings had caused him to have the most devastating sex dream of his life.

But now he realized that dream hadn't been about the painting. It had been about *her*.

"You all right?"

"Huh? Yeah." The dog would not give up and was now sitting by his shoe again, leaning her dirty fur against his calf.

"You sure you're okay?"

"Yes, except this lice-encrusted hair ball won't leave me alone, and I think your coffee just blasted a hole through my stomach lining."

Clancy smiled. "So what's the upshot here? Are you thinking of asking Lena out?"

"What?" Duncan jolted to attention. "Hell, no. I'm leaving as soon as the Navy clears me for active duty. Why would I want to start dating someone on Bayberry Island? Especially a chick who paints mermaid pictures?"

"It was just a question. No need to lash out." Clancy held out his open palms in the same gesture he'd used to calm down their father at the birthday dinner. It had to be a cop thing. "I think you should take Ondine home with you. Spending time with a dog lowers your blood pressure, relieves stress, and increases feelings of well-being."

"Not this dog. She just increases my need to take a shower."

"Do you want to hear what I know about Lena?"

He shrugged.

"Well, I know she's very good at what she does and she works hard at it. She always agrees to appear at Island Day to help us bring in the people, and they wait in line for hours to get her to sign a poster or take a picture with her. And I know she takes very good care of Mellie and is a big supporter of several charities here on the island, too."

"Sounds like a decent person."

"You two were friends when you were kids, right?"

Duncan nodded. "For a short time, I suppose we were friends."

"Well, I sure remember Lena crushing on you when you were in high school." Clancy grinned. "She followed you around like a lost puppy."

Duncan stared down at the lost puppy with the ridiculous name resting against his leg. A crush? Lena? He didn't remember.

"Something's bothering you," Clancy said. "Want to tell me what it is?"

Slowly, Duncan returned his attention to his brother. He heard himself laugh. "I am perfectly fine."

"Excellent news!" Clancy uncrossed his legs and leaned in toward Duncan. "I'm going to deputize you and make you serve your community during festival week."

"What?"

"Sure. Under Municipal Code Section 8, subsection 42-B, paragraph 2, as police chief of Bayberry Island, Massachusetts, I have the authority to appoint, at my discretion, temporary peace officers to ensure the safety of our many Mermaid Festival visitors."

"Nice try, man, but the United States Navy's not gonna look kindly on that. I'm on medical leave, but I'm still the property of Uncle Sam."

"Fine." Clancy sighed. "Then I'll ask you to help us out on the down-low, no police powers, just an extra set of eyes and ears—more of a volunteer tourist facilitator. You know, a facilitator-slash-bouncer."

Duncan squinted at his brother. "Now you're just making shit up."

Clancy couldn't suppress his laugh. "No, seriously. I would appreciate your help. You're here, right? In fact, you'll be here for the entire festival week, and I don't think that's happened since you were in high school. So why not pitch in? Or maybe you'd rather help Ma decorate for the clambake?"

Duncan pictured himself hanging Chinese lanterns around the dance floor and putting centerpieces on the tables.

"Exactly what would I be doing?"

"Just keep an eye out for shoplifters on Island Day and radio it in. Or maybe lend a hand with crowd control during the parade. Total civilian stuff."

Duncan grunted.

"Chip will find you a BIPD shirt and a pair of standard-issue shorts. I know we got some extras around here somewhere."

Duncan couldn't help but laugh. "Damn, man. A hallucinating, tourist facilitator in a pair of shorts. If that doesn't scream Bayberry Island, I don't know what does."

"Give yourself a break, Uncle Duncle," Clancy said, grinning. "You weren't hallucinating—you were just trespassing on private property and violating a citizen's right to skinny-dip in peace."

"Good." Duncan got up from the chair, the dog standing, too. "Then just do me a favor and throw my ass in the slammer until the Mermaid Festival is over. Please."

Chapter Eight

Sanders Garrett signed the freight receipt and told the driver to go ahead to the Bayberry Island Municipal Airfield, where he'd meet him within the hour.

He found Lena on her favorite perch, a Victorian chaise placed in front of the wall of windows facing the sea. The heavy piece of furniture was made of elaborately scrolled mahogany and covered with ripped and stained upholstery that might have once been velvet. Sanders knew Lena would never restore it. No matter that it was soaked with a hundred years of linseed oil—it had too much sentimental value in its lived-in state. It was her way of holding on to her late mentor and teacher in New York, Madame Broussard.

"Too early for wine?"

As she turned away from the window, Sanders could see she'd been lost in thought. Lena blinked at him as if she'd forgotten he was there.

She just kept getting more beautiful, he realized. He might have been biased—being her manager and dear friend—but each year seemed to add another layer of polish to Adelena Silva's beauty. Yes, there were remnants of the seventeen-year-old sprite he'd met at the Art Institute of Chicago all those years ago, but the girlish energy was no longer her dominant trait. Lena's personality had softened, her talent had deepened, and her beauty had blossomed all over the damn place.

"You're gorgeous. You know that, right?"

"Moi?" She batted her dark eyelashes and rested her fingertips against her paint-splattered oversized sweatshirt. "In this old thing?"

"C'mon." He pulled her up from the chaise. "Let's have a toast before I have to get back up on that rubberband-powered plane, shall we? This may be the last time you see me alive."

"Always so dramatic," she said, laughing.

That laugh never failed to take Sanders back in time, to the poorest—and happiest—years of his life. Art school was a time when nobody had a dime and too many of them shared an apartment that should have been condemned, in a neighborhood that should have been under martial law. And they didn't even notice.

Life then was delicious and juicy and their group lived off their passions—for painting, sculpture, graphic design, filmmaking, for the city of Chicago, and occasionally, for one another. They hadn't been trampled by reality quite yet, and they were free to be as unusual as they dared.

It amused Sanders that all these years later, the shyest and most humble of the bunch, Lena Silva, had become an international art rock star, while the most vocal counterculture rebel badass—himself—spent his days writing contracts, booking gallery showings, and managing the assets of those with real artistic ability.

Of his five clients, Lena had the biggest share of talent. She had the most of everything else, too—money, heart, kindness, and eccentricity. But as much as he loved her, Sanders couldn't relate to her lifestyle. Lena Silva was all mermaid, all the time, and she lived on an isolated little island known for its mermaid legend, for God's sake.

The only island Sanders could tolerate was Manhattan, and the only mermaids he believed in were the ones that flew off the gallery walls at well above catalog price.

As they exited the studio, Sanders's eye caught that old pencil drawing Lena refused to part with. It was a sketch of her face when she was about eleven, and though it had been done with a startling lack of skill, the artist had a good eye for detail—Lena's detail. The crude pencil strokes captured a young girl with a mixture of innocence and understanding beyond her years. It showed the face of a young girl in love.

It occurred to Sanders that Lena hadn't mentioned the artist in a few weeks. He would have to remember to ask her about him.

They grabbed a bottle of Malbec and two glasses, then squished together in the rope hammock on her side porch. The sun had dipped behind the house, and the combination of shade and breeze was delightful. Lena rested her head on his shoulder while he poured.

"Here's to another embarrassingly successful Paris show." Sanders clinked his glass to hers. It had taken three hours that morning to catalog and crate twenty canvases. All but one would travel from Bayberry to Boston, and then on to Galerie de la Mer in the city's Marais district—Sanders riding along as bodyguard. The last canvas was headed to Seattle.

"And a toast to one very happy dot-commer," Lena reminded him.

"Of course! Here's to *Rhonda on the Rocks*. May she enjoy sunning her double-Ds for the rest of her days. Cheers."

Lena took a sip and snuggled up to him, and for a few moments they didn't talk. Sanders began to notice the silence.

"You good, sweetie? You seem a little pensive today."

She shrugged. "You just emptied my studio of two years' worth of work. I'm not complaining, but it seems a little hollow in there right now, you know?"

Several weeks had passed since she'd mentioned her wounded warrior. Maybe the news wasn't good.

"Is he getting better?"

"Absolutely. He's doing great."

"Have you had a chance to talk to him?"

When Lena shook her head, her hair rustled back and forth on his neck. "You know my rule."

Sanders chuckled. Ah, yes. He knew all about her "Duncan Flynn rule."

As a gorgeous woman, Lena had never lacked for male attention. Men were drawn to her like moths to a bug zapper. But Sanders had watched every relationship she'd had since the age of seventeen implode. As far as he had been able to tell, the problem was Lena's no-frills honesty. When the time came to bring up the "L" word, she would calmly inform the man du jour that she would not be able to love him.

"I've loved the same man since childhood," she would say. "I don't think I'm capable of loving anyone else."

This revelation usually didn't go over well.

He respected Lena's devotion, but he didn't fully understand it. First off, the dude was a Navy SEAL, a precision-honed instrument of war, and Sanders couldn't imagine what he and a woman like Lena would have in common. And then there was the fact that Lena had never even *told* this SEAL person that she loved him. The man had left for the Naval Academy before Lena had even graduated from high school. So from then until now, she'd heard about him only through her mother. And that meant this soldier of hers had been out there fighting terrorists and getting himself blown up without ever knowing Lena Silva loved him.

Was it commendable of her to stay true to her heart? Sanders couldn't say—he didn't have much experience with such things in his own love life. Was her approach unusual? You bet. But was it stupid? That remained to be seen.

All he knew was that the night Lena had learned of Flynn's injuries, she'd fallen apart in a way he'd never seen before. Sanders had caught the next flight to Boston and risked life and limb in a flying Sprite can to get to her little island. He'd stayed for a week.

Lena sat up and looked Sanders in the eye.

"He has to come to *me*. That's the rule."

He smiled at her.

"He has to figure it out for himself. I've known him since I was seven years old. But Duncan has to put the pieces together and make the choice for his own reasons. Otherwise, it won't work."

"I know, Lena."

"He's stubborn and wickedly smart. He's a fighter, in every sense of the word, and he will need to fight to get me or it won't work. If he feels he's been reeled in some-how—like loving me is not one hundred percent his idea—then that's it."

"I hear you."

"But time's running out." Lena's dark eyes filled with tears. "He's doing so well that they're going to clear him to return to active duty, and he'll be gone. I can't help but think this is my one chance."

"Can I ask you something, sweetie?"

She shook her head. "I know what you're going to ask, and the answer is no—I'm not lonely. I haven't missed anything while I've waited for him. I have a suc-cessful career. I've had some wonderful lovers. And I've seen the world. But I am absolutely certain that if I am to share my life with anyone, it's supposed to be Duncan."

Sanders nodded. "Well, okay, but that's not what I was wondering."

"Oh." She pursed her lips.

"My question is, what if he's not everything you imag-ine him to be?"

Lena gave him a calm half smile. "He is."

"But—"

"If I'm wrong about him, then I'm wrong. Done and done. I can move on with my life. Is that the sane answer you were waiting for?"

Sanders laughed. He had never gotten anywhere with Lena when the topic of conversation was her mythical Duncan Flynn, but if he didn't try to bring her back to earth—at least temporarily—then who would?

"Just . . . one more question, okay?"

"Sure."

"Would you be able to handle it?"

A little crinkle popped up between her eyebrows. "What do you mean?"

"I mean, could you handle loving a man who's gone to God knows where, doing God knows what, for God knows how long? Could you deal with knowing he might not come home?"

Lena looked surprised. "Of course. I already am."

Duncan needed a little extra proof that he hadn't been seeing things that night on the beach. He spent a few days studying up on a variety of subjects, including Adelena Silva, of course, and the connection between posttraumatic stress and visual hallucination.

During his three months at Walter Reed, Duncan had been evaluated for PTSD and had participated in private and group counseling sessions. The docs wanted to know how the deaths of his teammates and his own injuries had affected his mental state, and they'd found that aside from his issues with guilt and grief, which they'd said were to be expected, he was perfectly normal—for a Navy SEAL. His own research seemed to back that up. He exhibited no other examples of psychosis.

When it came to Lena, there was no question in his mind that she was the woman on the beach. The Adelena Silva he watched in online interviews possessed the same serene expression he had seen that night. She had the same laugh he'd heard at the Safe Haven, and it turned out she was just as exquisite in clothes as she was out of them.

Lena didn't sound like a nut job when she was interviewed on camera and in print, which, he had to admit, surprised him. She never claimed mermaids were real. In fact, she never even mentioned the Bayberry Island

Great Mermaid legend—an attribute Duncan found outrageously sexy. If that wasn't enough, Lena Silva didn't dress like a mermaid or claim that she herself happened to be one.

All in all, she sounded sane.

"Reality is subjective," she told the host of a TV morning show. "If people want to believe there are mermaids in the sea, who am I to say they're wrong? But my paintings aren't field studies. They come from my imagination."

But in another interview, Lena did briefly wander off into la-la land. She was talking to a women's magazine about the symbolism in her paintings. "I have always been fascinated by what lies beneath the surface, in the ocean and in people," she said. "That's where the magic is. And yes, my underwater scenes are mysterious and exotic—and sometimes a little over-the-top—but then again, so am I."

Right.

Duncan would bet he'd spent a lot more time beneath the surface of the ocean than Ms. Silva had, yet he'd never seen a whole lot of magic down there. The deep was brutally cold, dark, and silent, and it wasn't a place humans would care to frolic. There was exotic beauty there, to be sure, but only those with adequate equipment and training could survive long enough to see it firsthand. In Lena's mind, the sea was a playground. For a Navy SEAL, it was a hellish training ground for mastering underwater demolition, combat diving, search and rescue, and your own fears. The ocean was nothing to fuck with.

So now that Duncan was sure *whom* he'd seen on the beach, he wanted to understand *what* he'd seen. Had it been a dolphin? A minke whale? For that he needed to see it again.

So for four nights in a row, Duncan made his way to Moondance Beach. He came at different times to cast a wide net, arriving between twenty-three thirty-two and zero two fifteen. The first two nights he rested his quads and hamstrings and walked the round-trip. The next night he ran. And the fourth night he decided he was ready to swim.

Duncan pulled on his wet suit and fins and waded into the ink black water off Haven Cove. It was an immediate rush to be back in the sea. He used a combination of freestyle and combat sidestroke, shooting up the shoreline at a good clip. His legs moved freely, with little pain or stiffness, and he felt himself smile. God, how he'd missed this.

He knew Haven Cove like the contours of his own face, exactly where the undertow was fierce, where it got rocky and shallow, and where the waves crashed the hardest or rose the highest. This stretch of ocean was where he had found his core. Once puberty had put the brakes on his asthma and bronchitis, this was where the ocean had taught him to trust himself. Distance swimming had taught him there were no limits. It was right here, at the age of twelve, that for the first time in his life Duncan had pushed beyond what anyone thought possible.

He hadn't stopped since.

But after four trips to Moondance Beach, he'd found nothing. No Lena. No fantail. Aside from spending time with slimy seaweed and dead jellyfish—and feeling sand crabs skitter across his face—he'd come away empty-handed. Duncan decided he would give it one more shot,

and if nothing happened, he'd let the whole strange episode go, just file it away with all the other weird shit he'd
witnessed in his thirty-four years. He was leaving for Virginia in two days, anyway.

On the night of his last recon, he decided to swim
again. It was the last thing he'd expected, but the swim
became a kind of meditation. As he cut through the water, each lungful of air propelled him against the current.
His body fell into a rhythm. His mind emptied. He felt
stillness even as his speed increased. And at some point,
about a half mile from Lena's private beach, his emotions exploded. Duncan sobbed as he swam, never losing
his momentum. For the first time since the ambush, he
cried for Justin and all his teammates. He cried because
of how unfair it was, what a fucking waste of life. Exceptional human beings were dead, and it shouldn't have
happened. But it had.

As he turned toward shore, Duncan was grateful that
he'd had his breakdown in solitude, in the dark, in the
waves, where no one could possibly hear him and where
his flood of tears spilled unnoticed into the Atlantic.

He hopped the private fence, took his place in the
sand, and waited. Nothing. No dolphins, no whales, and
no naked women. There was nothing but a gentle July
breeze and the in-and-out breath of the waves.

He woke with a start as the tide began tickling his
toes. The sun hummed lightly against his eyelids. *Some
Navy SEAL you are*, he thought, pushing himself to a
stand and stretching. He froze.

All around were fresh footprints—dainty female footprints in the sand.

Chapter Nine

Twenty-three years ago ...

"Why did Grandmother say you were a witch?"

Lena's mother dropped the string bean in midsnap. Her hands hovered over the large glass bowl as if she had forgotten how to move, her eyes staring out the window over the kitchen sink.

"*Mãe?*"

When her mother answered, her voice was strangely flat. "Adelena, I have explained that your grandmother was angry that your father left. She needed to blame someone, so she blamed me. Sometimes people try to make themselves feel better by hurting others."

"But why did she call you a *witch*?"

Her mother quickly dried her hands with a kitchen towel and lifted Lena off the stool. Her grip felt too tight against her ribs.

"Where are we going?"

"Let's go for a walk."

It was an unusual thing for her mother to do in the middle of a summer day. She was always busy at the Safe

Haven, but she had been working even harder lately. She said she was afraid she might lose her job because the fishing company had closed. Mother said the Flynns used to be very rich, back in the old days, but weren't anymore and might have to turn the mansion into a hotel.

Lena knew this already, because she sometimes heard Mona and Frasier in the first-floor parlor, talking in whispers that could be heard all over the first floor.

Lena's mother held her hand firmly and walked to the mudroom, where she grabbed their sun hats. Then they headed out the door and across the lawn. In the last year, Lena had grown used to living in the huge old house by the ocean, but every once in a while, like on summer days as perfect as this one, she would find herself blinking a lot, amazed that this was the place she got to call home.

She had discovered that if she stood in the right spot, the Safe Haven looked like a castle. It had five skinny, pointy towers. Her favorite was the one that looked in the opposite direction of town. She liked to climb up to the top floor, sit on the dusty wood floor of the empty, circular room, and stare out at the blue water and the wild fields that curved around the other edge of the island. It was a place where hardly anybody lived, which she thought was strange. People on Bayberry were always worried about weeds and uncut grass, because they thought the tourists wanted everything neat. But if Lena were a tourist, she'd rather visit a place that was wild and natural.

"Where are we going?"

"To the beach."

Lena's head snapped around, and she stared at the

side of her mother's face. In the last year, her mother had stood in the sand just once, and that was because she was in charge of the food for the festival clambake. As much as Lena wanted to ask her mother the reason for the sudden walk on the beach, she decided against it.

She had a feeling that today would be about listening.

"I think you are old enough now," her mother announced, once their feet were in the sand.

"I'm eight."

"I know, *menina*." Mother pulled her against her side. She could feel and hear her body let go with a heavy sigh.

"Do you remember the legend of my village? The one I told you about before we came here?"

"Yes."

"Tell me what you remember."

Lena concentrated. "There was a man who went out to fish one day and suddenly knew he had to go to one certain spot, a place he'd never fished before. He fished and fished and didn't catch anything. Then, just when he was about to go home, he pulled in a net and there was a beautiful, red-haired mermaid."

"Hmm. And what did she tell him?"

"That she had been waiting for him."

They walked together along the beach, dodging Frisbees and Nerf balls and letting the water wash over the tops of their feet. "And what else did she tell him?"

"She said that if he was brave enough to cut out her gills, she would grow legs and become his wife."

"Mmm-hmm. That's right."

Lena waited. She thought her mother was getting ready to tell her something, but it seemed like forever before she spoke again.

"In our village, people thought the women in my family were descended from that mermaid. For more than two hundred years, my female ancestors were accused of having special powers."

"Like what?"

Her mother shrugged. "Well, back then, if a woman was very wise in a certain way—like with using plants for medicine or healing sick people—the people in charge of the church and the town would get uncomfortable."

"Why?"

"Because women weren't supposed to be in charge of anything back then."

"Well, that's silly."

Her mother laughed and hugged her tighter. "Very silly, indeed, Lena. But sometimes it came to a sad end for these women. Some were accused of being seductresses and witches and were hanged."

Lena stopped walking. Almost immediately she began to cry.

"Oh, *menina*, I know it is terrible, but those sort of things don't happen anymore. People are smarter now and know more about science and how the world works. But ..."

Lena waited, sniffling. "What, Mama?"

"The women in my family still had to deal with that old story. It followed us around over the years. I was the only girl in my family, and my parents decided when I was twenty that it would be best if I went to America. I did. And four years later, I married your father and moved into his mother's home. I never would have talked about it with your grandmother, but I did tell your father and he shared it with his family."

Suddenly, everything made sense. Lena broke out into a smile. "So it was that old story? That's what Grandmother was talking about?"

"Yes. But that is all behind us. You will never have to worry about that because you are not in my village. You are American. And you carry your father's name. The connection has been broken."

Lena stayed quiet for many moments, letting everything sink in. In one way, it was exciting to think there were witches in her family—that she might be a witch, too!—even if they were only pretend witches. But in another way the story made her feel sad for her mother. She had to run away because of the wrong things people thought of her. First she ran to Rhode Island, and then she ran to Bayberry Island.

Lena felt her eyes widen. "Did you come here because of the mermaid legend?" Lena was half expecting her mother to laugh and tell her what a silly thing that was to say. But how she answered surprised Lena.

"I think in some ways, yes. I have nothing against stories of mermaids. I think they are beautiful stories. I just don't want people talking about me being one of them. Trying to convince people you're not a witch or a seductress gets tiring."

"How did you know to come here?"

For the first time during the walk, Lena's mother looked down at her daughter and smiled a big, beautiful smile. "I saw a news story about the festival and I thought, now, that looks like a pretty place. Those people seem very full of joy. They have a sense of humor. And I thought that a place with beauty, legends, joy, and a sense of humor sounded perfect for us."

"Oh." They walked for a little longer. Her mother started humming one of her Portuguese songs. And Lena remembered there was one other question she had.

"Mama? What is a seductress?"

"Oh my goodness!" Her mother glanced at her watch. "We'd better be heading back to the house. We have green beans to snap!"

Chapter Ten

Rowan was beyond exhausted. It never failed to amaze her how one eighteen-pound, nine-month-old human could rule the lives of everyone around her. All Rowan wanted to do was sleep—plop her face into the exquisite softness of her pillow, curl up next to her husband, and close her eyes.

Serena had other plans. After sleeping for six hours, she began talking to herself in her crib, which segued into screaming at the top of her lungs so loudly she would wake Ash and the guests. So Rowan left the family's second-floor apartment near the guest rooms. She came down to the B and B kitchen and closed the doors for sound control. There she would find the tried-and-true antidote to Serena's unhappiness: the pots and pans. So that was what Rowan was doing at nearly three in the morning on the Wednesday before festival week—pacing back and forth across the big kitchen, with every light blazing, so that Serena could point at, coo, and converse with the sparkling stainless-steel cookware suspended from the pot rack.

"Aren't you just the most brilliant baby ever?" Rowan

nibbled kisses along her neck and cheek until she squeaked with happiness. Serena began jumping up and down in Rowan's arms, reaching out so she could touch a sauté pan. She turned to Rowan with shockingly alert blue eyes, pleading, excited, and curious.

"You win, little girlie. Let's rock 'n' roll."

Rowan retrieved the pan, along with a stack of plastic storage containers and three wooden spoons, and sat Serena on the kitchen rug to play. As the happy banging began, Rowan shuffled over to the coffeepot, surrendering to the beginning of yet another ungodly early day.

The pediatrician had assured Rowan and Ash that it was normal for a nine-month-old to wake up and demand stimulation of some kind, and in fact, it was a sign she was reaching a developmental milestone. Rowan filled the coffee filter and hit the power switch, thinking how she, too, was reaching a milestone. Nine months as a mother, and she no longer remembered a time when Serena wasn't in her life. Or Ash. It was as if she had never been anywhere but with her husband and daughter.

Rowan's life had changed so fast. This time two years ago, Ash had showed up at the Safe Haven in a rainstorm, needing a place to stay. The Rowan Flynn he'd met at the front desk of the Safe Haven had been bitter and hating life and certainly not expecting anything wonderful to be just around the corner. But in a matter of days, rocky though they were, she was swimming in a sea of contentment and hope. And then came Serena, the most miraculous change of all.

The lesson Rowan had learned: no one ever knows what is right around the corner.

She tipped her head. She had just heard something.

She peered toward Mellie's apartment, knowing it was too early for her to be up. Maybe she was just using the bathroom. Rowan was about to pour herself an emergency cup of coffee when the door leading to the back stairway creaked open and a set of pretty dark eyes peered into the kitchen.

"Lena?"

Oh, crap. Rowan's voice had been laced with disbelief and judgment, something she'd not intended. She might as well have said, *What the hell are you doing here in the middle of the night?*

And Rowan already knew the answer to that question. Thanks to Serena's sleep issues, she was well aware that something was going on between Lena and Duncan. This was not the first time she'd seen Lena sneak in or out of the Safe Haven in the wee hours, and lately, Duncan had started coming and going in the middle of the night himself. This was the first time Rowan and Lena had come face-to-face, however.

Lena lowered her gaze to the floor. And after a pause and big breath, she pushed the door all the way open and entered the kitchen. When she finally looked at Rowan, there was defiance in her expression.

"Would you like some coffee? I just made a fresh pot."

Lena glanced around the room, checking to see if anyone else was around. Just then the baby began pounding on the sauté pan with her favorite spoon, and Lena's gaze flashed to the percussionist sitting on the rug. She broke out into a huge smile and laughed.

"My God, she is so beautiful, Rowan. What a wonderful gift she is."

Rowan felt her chest flood with pride. "Thank you. We kind of like her."

Lena laughed again, but suddenly she seemed to remember she was standing in the middle of the Safe Haven kitchen in the wee hours of the morning. Embarrassment clouded her face. "I should go."

Rowan wondered how she could possibly convince Lena that there was no reason to feel awkward. If she and Duncan were having a good time, then hey, more power to them. Rowan knew all about following your bliss—it's what she had done with Ash.

"Please don't go. I would love some company."

Lena didn't exactly jump at the invitation. It was understandable. Though they had grown up together in the same house and were about the same age, they had never meshed. There had been several reasons for that.

First off, Rowan had always been a rowdy tomboy—sailing, waterskiing, beach volleyball, swimming, ice hockey, cross-country skiing—while Lena was quiet and reserved. She liked to wander the island by herself, read, or draw. For that reason, their passions didn't often overlap.

Then there was the Annie issue, of course. Starting in preschool, Rowan and Annabeth Parker had become inseparable. They still were. And though Rowan and Annie never intentionally pushed Lena away when they were kids, she preferred to keep her distance. It was if she knew there was no room for a third best friend.

Lastly, Rowan always suspected that Lena drew a line between herself and the Flynn kids because she was the housekeeper's daughter, which was something Rowan had never understood. Mellie never made that distinction as far as Rowan knew, and her parents loved Lena like one of their own. Whatever division Lena felt was of her own making.

And now, all these years later, Rowan had come back to Bayberry Island to live and raise a family. Lena was back, too, living and working from a private estate on the island's North Shore. And yet that old, senseless distance had continued.

Until Duncan came home.

Rowan had seen Lena more in the last two months than she had in the last decade, and if that wasn't enough to indicate something was going on, Lena had agreed to don a mermaid costume and represent the Safe Haven from the parade float. She had never participated in festival week before, and even Mellie seemed surprised that she'd agreed to cover for Rowan this year. So, as Lena stood there wondering whether to accept Rowan's offer, there was more at stake than a cup of coffee—she was in the process of coming out of her shell.

"So you know?"

Rowan wanted to tread lightly. "About . . . ?"

"The gifts," Lena said. "You know that I've been the one bringing gifts to Duncan."

Rowan did her best to hide her surprise. Of course she had always suspected as much when they were kids, but she was sure all the current nighttime coming and going was not just about a few shells and cattails.

"Uh, yeah. I figured it was you back when we were kids. You and Duncan were very close for a while, and I saw how kind you were to him."

"Who else knows?"

Suddenly, Serena cried out. Rowan hadn't seen what happened, but the baby now had a red welt forming on her cheek. Her guess was that she had just accidentally whacked herself with the spoon.

"Oh, sweetie. I'm here. Mama's here." Rowan bent

down and retrieved the baby, holding her close and stroking her back. She murmured through the sobbing, "It's okay, darlin'. It'll feel better in just a minute."

Lena stood in the doorway, her face twisted in concern for Serena.

"Would you mind holding her for a sec while I get a cool washcloth to put on this boo-boo?"

Lena's eyes widened. Serena's howling escalated into great air-sucking sobs.

"It will just take a sec."

"Of course." Lena stepped into the center of the room and stretched out her arms. The instant Rowan placed Serena in her care, the baby stopped crying. Serena didn't even wind down to it; she just stopped. Now the silence rang in Rowan's ears.

"Well, check that out," she whispered. "Do you babysit?"

Lena chuckled, beginning to gently sway with Serena as the baby stared at her in awe. "Shhh, little one. See? Mama was right. Everything's going to be just fine."

Impressed—and just a little puzzled by how easily Serena had taken to someone she didn't know well—Rowan ran a linen dish towel under cold water, then wrung it out.

When Rowan turned around, she saw Lena gliding through the kitchen, singing softly. The melody was somewhat melancholy and Rowan didn't understand the words, which were Portuguese, but Serena's face was lit up with wonderment. She began giggling.

When Lena realized Rowan was watching, she went still and stopped singing. "Oh. Here you go." She tried to peel Serena from her embrace, and the baby started to cry again.

"Do you mind sitting with her for a bit? She's clearly

very happy in your arms. Here—just hold this against her cheek if you don't mind."

Lena took a seat at the kitchen table with Serena, smiling like she'd just won the lottery. The baby relaxed against her and laid her head on Lena's chest. She didn't even fuss about the cool towel that Lena pressed against her skin.

Rowan turned toward the coffeepot and smiled to herself—that pair was the cutest thing ever. "Cream? Sugar?"

"Both, please."

By the time she brought two mugs to the table and sat across from Lena, Serena's eyelids were growing heavy.

Lena looked up at Rowan with a pleading expression and whispered, "Who else knows about the gifts?"

"Nobody that I'm aware of."

"No one?"

Rowan knew the "no one" in question was Duncan. "If he knows it's you, he hasn't said anything. And I've never mentioned my suspicions to Clancy or even Annie. But my mother—"

"Oh, *great*."

Rowan snickered. "I told her my suspicions when I was little, and she told me she'd figured it out a long time before I did. Then she told me not to tell anyone, and I haven't."

Lena nodded seriously.

"How could she not know? Ma watched over Duncan like a hawk back then. But I don't think she would ever make a big deal of it or do anything to embarrass you, Lena. And she clearly has never told him." Rowan waited for a reaction from Lena but didn't get one. "Does *your* mother know?"

She nodded. "Of course. She watched me like a hawk back then, too. But she doesn't know that I know that she knows. And she doesn't know that I know that you and Mona know."

The women laughed softly, careful not to disturb the very peaceful baby in Lena's arms.

"People can be so ridiculous sometimes," Rowan said. Lena smiled. "This is true."

"So." Rowan fiddled with her coffee cup. "Are you ever going to tell Duncan that it's been you all along?"

Lena's pretty face flushed bright red. "I . . . No. I want him to figure it out. He needs to put two and two together."

Rowan tipped her head to the side, deciding how to phrase her next question, since not only was it a delicate topic, but it really wasn't any of her business.

"Lena, are you hoping this leads to something long-term? I only ask you this because . . . well, I don't want you to be hurt, and sometimes Duncan can be such a . . ." Rowan searched for an alternate word for "dickhead."

"He's a very intense guy. He's focused on only one thing."

"I know."

Rowan took a sip from her cup. "I didn't realize you two have been keeping in touch over the years."

"We haven't."

Okay, now she was totally lost. "So you've only recently reconnected?"

Lena's mouth turned up in a mysterious smile and her eyes sparkled. Rowan had always thought Lena was a pretty woman, but in that instant, she saw a spectacularly beautiful woman—a woman in love. *With Duncan Flynn.* Rowan swigged some more coffee, just to keep her mouth occupied.

"Not yet."

"Not . . . *what*?"

Lena tucked her chin to her chest and checked on Serena, now asleep. "I know it sounds strange," she said, looking at Rowan again. "But Duncan doesn't know how I feel about him—how I've always felt. And I . . ." She shook her head. "If he doesn't figure it out soon, then I don't think he ever will."

Rowan couldn't help it—her mouth fell open in shock. She tried to piece the story together in her head, but it was a strange one, indeed. Lena was sneaking gifts into Duncan's room the way she had as a kid, but he was as clueless as ever that it was her. Lena had real feelings for him. But the two of them hadn't reconnected.

"Um, have you spoken to him since he's been back?"

"No."

"But you want to, right? You want to get to know him again?"

Lena laughed, causing Serena to stir. "Sorry," she whispered.

"It's okay. So *do* you?"

"Of course." She smiled shyly. "But I'm not the kind of woman who follows a man around town and pretends to run into him at the squash stand at the farmers' market or something ridiculous like that."

"I hear you."

"If it's going to happen, it will happen because he suddenly wakes up, sees that I'm standing right in front of him, and is intrigued enough to do something about it."

Rowan froze, her eyes jumping to the back of the kitchen. Duncan stood framed in the staircase doorway, his face stoic, unreadable. In his hand he held a colorfully painted shell, no doubt Lena's latest present. He advanced silently toward the table.

Rowan said, "Uh, Lena—"

"What I really don't want is your family inviting us both to dinner one night as a setup and then saying to me, 'Oops! We forgot to mention that Duncan would be here!'"

"Lena—"

"I don't think Duncan would appreciate that, either."

"You're right—I hate being played."

Rowan moved faster than she ever had in her life, sliding from her chair, sweeping around the end of the table, and taking the baby from Lena before she dropped her. Rowan took Serena and retreated toward the dining room door, giving the two lovebirds room to . . . rumble?

This was going to be interesting. Rowan hadn't seen her brother interact with a woman since back in high school, when girls threw themselves at him. Back then, he used them and swatted them away when he was done. Rowan had no idea if his attitude about women had changed over the years. In fact, she'd never even heard her brother mention a woman's name. The truth was, Duncan was a complete mystery to her.

Rowan knew she shouldn't stick around. Whatever was about to happen here was a private matter between two adults. But then she thought, *Well, maybe for just one minute.*

Duncan's entire life had been about proving to himself—and others—that he could endure any hardship and rebound from any setback. He could swim miles in rough seas, walk days through burning deserts, climb seventeen-thousand-foot mountain peaks, and trudge through swamps. Duncan could fly a plane, sail a forty-two-foot sloop by himself, rappel out of a Black Hawk helicopter, and in a pinch, drive a tank. He spoke five languages. He could do a hundred push-ups in ninety-eight seconds and tie a bowline twenty-five feet underwater. Yet nothing in his tool kit prepared him for the instant Adelena Silva turned toward him in that kitchen chair and looked up into his eyes.

He was flooded with everything at once—a rush of memory and emotion that pistol-whipped rational thought. There she was. She was the girl from his childhood, the seductress from his dreams, and the woman from the beach. His reaction made no sense whatsoever, but he felt something inside him uncoil and go perfectly still. It was her, his woman of the waves.

Lena stood to greet him. As she moved, her scent slammed into Duncan's brain. It was the same elixir he smelled in the dream—delicate but earthy, like a garden after it rained.

A sly smile curled up the corners of her mouth, and at that moment Duncan truly believed that not touching Lena Silva would be the one thing he could never endure, a loss he could never recover from.

And yet, at the same time, anger welled up from somewhere deep inside him, and as much as he wanted to devour her, he wanted to send her packing for messing with him the way she had. She'd invaded his privacy, for fuck's sake! Just walked through his door in the middle of the night. Over and over again.

"You look great, Duncan."

Good God, she was a foot shorter than him and her waist was as big around as his thigh.

"If it isn't the famous Lena Silva, painter of mermaids." Duncan displayed what he held in his right hand. "And decorator of clamshells, I presume?"

Her gaze flashed to the shell and then back to Duncan's face. "Busted," she said.

Oh, shit, this was all wrong. He needed to get in the shower, shave, dress, and be on the seven a.m. ferry to the mainland. His flight to Richmond left Logan Airport at noon. His appointment with Captain Sinclair was at zero eight hundred tomorrow. This was one hell of a time to get distracted. It was one hell of a time to suddenly decide he wanted a woman—*this* woman.

The sound of someone clearing her throat came from the dining room. Both Duncan and Lena turned to see Rowan swaying with the baby in her arms. Duncan had forgotten she was there.

"I guess I'll say good night, then."

" 'Night, Row," he said.

"Thank you for the coffee, Rowan."

They listened to his sister's footfalls on the main staircase, and the sound reminded Duncan of a ticking clock.

"Look, Lena. I don't know what to say. Thank you for thinking of me, I guess. For the stuff when I was a kid and for now. But—"

"You're welcome."

Just then he remembered all those interviews he'd watched online. Lena could hold her own, and she was doing it again with him. "You really had me going. I was convinced it was my mother."

Lena allowed her smile to spread. She looked sweet, but even before she said a word, Duncan knew she was about to put an end to their chat. "Sometimes we don't see the whole picture," she said, touching his forearm with the barest brush of her fingertips. "It was good to see you again. I wish you the best."

She turned to go.

And he did it. Dammit, he knew it was a boneheaded move. He wanted a clean break from Bayberry when he went back to active duty, no messy apologies or explanations or promises to make—or break. Not to anyone in his family. And certainly not to a woman he hadn't seen since high school.

Yet none of that mattered.

Duncan set the shell on the table, placed his hand on her shoulder, gently turned her around to face him, and Jesus, he did it. He cupped her face in both palms and slowly, slowly, lowered his mouth to hers. He didn't have the words for the feelings that hit him. He had no frame of reference. Except for one—the dream. It was the same sweet mouth and the same loving response. It was the same swell of emotion inside of him. It was the same damn woman.

Duncan had planned for the kiss to be what the Navy might call a small-scale contingency—using the least amount of pressure required to stabilize a situation. In other words, he wasn't planning something overtly sexual, but he didn't want a dry peck, either. He wanted to give her a respectable kiss.

As it turned out, the universe didn't give a damn what he had planned. The instant his lips touched hers, Lena moaned, melted under his touch, and molded her body to his. Before he knew it, Duncan had gathered her up, set her on the edge of the kitchen table, and proceeded to make a meal of her.

This wasn't even remotely his style. He never let himself go with women. His three-pronged approach was always the same: remain detached, stay in control, and keep the exit strategy in mind at all times.

So what the hell was this? What was happening to him? How had a female half his size managed to hijack his body and soul with a single kiss?

It wasn't a normal kiss; that much was obvious. It was as if a dam had busted inside of him, and there was no stopping the unleashed energy, as if there was no limit to what he wanted from her, what he had to have, and the lengths he would go to get it.

When she arched up beneath him, he could feel every curve and sweep of her body, where her firm flesh pressed against him, where it became soft and yielding, and how much this warm and sensual creature wanted him, too.

Suddenly, she pulled away, pressing her palms against his chest to create distance between them.

"Wait. Stop." Her plea was whispered into his ear. "This is not the way."

And just like that, the spell was broken. Duncan quickly separated from her, looking down on the sexy, panting, disheveled mess Lena had become. He recognized those lips, the heavy-lidded eyes, the wild fan of dark hair. And on the table near her shoulder, right where Duncan had placed it, was the intricately designed clamshell, with those trademark swirls of light and color. He had been an idiot not to see that it had been Lena all along.

She was absolutely correct—what just happened between them was not right. In fact, Duncan didn't know what the fuck he had been thinking.

He offered his hand, and Lena placed her impossibly

soft and small one in his. He gently pulled her from the table.

"I don't know what that outburst was all about, and I apologize." Duncan realized he sounded like a robot, but maybe that was a good way to balance out the insanity of the situation. He'd just lost his fucking mind. He'd just acted on pure instinct and animal lust. "My behavior was unacceptable. I hope you can forgive me."

Lena shook her head and smoothed down her hair. By the time she looked up at him, her eyes had filled with tears. "I'm sorry, too." He watched her straighten her shirt and he nearly laughed at his own ridiculousness. He'd had the presence of mind to throw her down and devour her, but he hadn't even noticed how adorable she looked in those clothes—a Red Sox T-shirt and a pair of white jeans, her feet bare.

Suddenly, an image flashed in his head—the way Clancy was lost in Evie, the way he had kissed his wife that day at the police station. What had just happened with Lena wasn't that different. There were similarities, weren't there? But then Duncan decided such a comparison was absurd.

He couldn't get off this island fast enough.

"I heard you're headed to Little Creek," she said, still standing right in front of him. Her voice wobbled, but she pressed on. "I wish you the best getting back to active duty. I know that's what you want. Please take good care of yourself, Duncan."

With that, she rose up on her tiptoes and delivered a quick kiss to his cheek. Without another word or glance his way, she left out the back door.

Duncan touched the spot where she had just kissed

him, puzzled by how foreign his own cheek felt. He examined his lips and had the same bizarre reaction.

Enough already. He'd had enough of pretty shells and heart-shaped rocks and decorated feathers and Lena Silva . . . *and this whole crazy damn island*. Duncan wished he were already on the plane to Richmond, one step closer to getting out of here and back where he belonged.

Chapter Eleven

Twenty-two years ago ...

L ena loved the sensation of skipping over the water. Duncan controlled the rudder of his little Sunfish sailboat, carefully aligning the sail so that it drew tight with the wind. She took a quick look at him—she didn't want to stare—but these days Duncan looked like a different person.

He was healthy. He was better. He hadn't used an inhaler for four months and hadn't had an episode of bronchitis for six. He had just turned twelve, and Duncan's skin was golden from the sun and he smiled and laughed all the time.

The doctors said it was because of puberty. Lena knew what that was, but she didn't want to think about it.

Duncan anchored off Haven Cove so that they could go swimming, and then they ate cheese sandwiches on the boat. Later that afternoon, they went on a hike through the nature preserve and Lena showed him the fallen osprey nest she'd found.

They both bent down to get a closer look.

"Don't touch it," she said.

"Do I look like I'm touching it?" Duncan asked. "You're such a bossy know-it-all, Lena."

"Oh, yeah? Then why did you just spend the whole day with me?"

Duncan chased her all the way out to Shoreline Road.

As they walked back to the Safe Haven, Lena looked over at him. She noticed how one black curl from his head had curved perfectly around his ear. It was beautiful.

He turned his head. "What?"

"You'll still be my friend, right?"

"Huh?"

"I mean, now that you're all better, you'll still be my friend?"

Duncan picked up a rock and threw it down the road. "Sure. We're still friends. Don't make such a big deal about stuff, Lena."

Chapter Twelve

The Joint Expeditionary Base at Little Creek–Fort Story, Virginia, was home to the largest naval amphibious training facility in the world. Duncan had first placed his boots on its red clay soil nine years before, and he remembered that day in detail. It was the day he discovered why he was put on this earth.

More than a year had passed since he'd been on base, and his return had a surreal quality to it. The man who had shipped out for another six-month tour in Afghanistan was not the man who made his way down the sidewalks of the base today. Duncan carried a hollow sensation in his gut—Justin and the rest of his insertion team would never walk here again. He figured he was experiencing firsthand something he'd heard other injured comrades talk about: one day you discover that what seemed like the end of the world to you had no discernible effect on a command, a base, or a nation. You might be privately doing battle with pain and surgeries and rehab, but life in the U.S. Navy had been going on, and would continue to go on, without you.

It was a standard-issue August day in the Virginia

swamplands, which meant that the humidity was thick and the air was hot and heavy. It was much cooler on Bayberry Island, no doubt, thanks to a steady ocean breeze. Duncan almost stopped walking.

How had such a random thought breeched the wall of his mind? Why was he thinking about Bayberry Island when his entire career was on the line today? And worse yet, it bugged the hell out of him that he couldn't get Lena out of his head. . . the way she tasted, her scent, the sound of her husky laugh. This kind of pointless distraction was the absolute last thing Duncan needed, and he told himself there would be no more of it. Besides, he'd already wasted enough time thinking of that kiss while on the ferry and on the plane.

The question was, why? Why was he allowing some silly woman who brought him rocks and feathers—and who basically *stalked him,* for God's sake—into his thought process? She didn't belong there. She would never belong there.

He kept walking. Duncan was wearing his service khaki uniform for the meeting, but found that it felt foreign to him. Recently, his wardrobe had consisted of hospital gowns and rehab shorts, and before that it was a combat suit, pants, and brain bucket with all the Navy SEAL trimmings: night-vision goggles, bolt cutters, breaching charges, his HK M4 assault rifle, a grenade launcher and a grenade or two, and his favorite fixed-blade knife and Gerber pliers and everything else. Justin had once remarked that he looked and felt like a walking hardware store, and that was how he got his nickname: Ace.

Duncan was saluted by two masters-at-arms on duty in the lobby of Training Command Building, passed through security, and headed down the long hallway to the office of his commanding officer. Every breath he had taken since the ambush, every time he'd stared down the pain and won, every push-up, every run and every swim and every time he did more than what was required of him—it was all for this meeting. Duncan was certain that once he opened this door, his life would find its true north once more, and he could once again serve his country.

He would do it in honor of Justin, Jax, Terry, Paul, Mike, Simon, and Scotty.

"You're not hearing what I'm telling you. This is not an exaggeration. It was a complete disaster." Lena heard Sanders sigh into the phone. He was about to say something, but she cut him off. "It could not have gone any worse."

"Do you want me to cut my Paris stay short? All the paintings will be cataloged and stored by tomorrow, and anyway, this show will basically put itself together, the way it always does. I can fly out of de Gaulle tomorrow night."

"No." Lena paced back and forth in her studio. She hadn't been able to paint for the last two days. She hadn't been able to sleep or eat or concentrate. All she had done was walk the beach, swim, and beat herself up with abandon. "I just need you to listen. There's no one else who will understand."

She suddenly heard the sound of a siren, car horns, and traffic noise. "Where are you?"

"Well, I'm about to get a taxi to meet someone for dinner."

Lena stopped pacing. "Oh. I'm sorry, Sanders. Really. Just go."

"It's all right. Hold on a sec, love." Lena heard him give directions in French to the driver. She knew the place he was going and bet the "someone" he was meeting was someone special. "Okay. I'm all ears. Now tell me what happened."

Suddenly, Lena felt ridiculous. It hit her—how absurd had it been for her to profess she loved a man she didn't even know? How delusional? How flat-out nuts? And here she had been whining and mooning over Duncan to poor Sanders for as long as she had known him. Like a broken record.

"I'm crazy-pants, aren't I?"

"What?" Sanders laughed. "Why do you say that?"

"No. I'm serious—I'm whacked. Running around my entire adult life claiming to be in love with a stranger. If I had a friend like me, I would take her to the nearest hospital and make sure they strapped her down. Why haven't you ever done that?"

Sanders groaned. "Lena, you are not crazy. Are you one in a million? Absolutely. You embrace the world with passion and you believe in magic, and that's what makes you such a great painter. Now, back up and tell me what happened."

She did, and when she got to part where Duncan picked her up and lay her on the kitchen table, Sanders told her to stop.

"I've got to roll down the window for some fresh air."

"Sandy!"

"All right, but am I missing something? I thought you were going to tell me he was a complete asshole to you or didn't remember you or told you he was going to have you arrested for breaking and entering."

Lena gasped. "Oh, my God. You did? No, no . . . I never even imagined something like that could happen."

"Clearly." Sanders mumbled something to the driver Lena couldn't hear, then came back to the conversation. "But instead he kisses the hell out of you and you get so turned on you nearly pass out. This is bad, how?"

Her mouth fell open, then snapped shut in indignation. "Well, because it was a little scary. You know, unexpected. I felt . . . I don't know . . . I felt like I was having a sexual meltdown, like I was out of control, and if I didn't put an end to it, there wouldn't be an end. And that's not how I pictured it happening."

"Okay. And how did you picture it?"

"You know, the two of us slowly getting to know each other again. Having deep conversations and opening up to each other . . . and maybe then we could segue into a really good kiss or two."

She heard Sanders chuckling. "Lena, if there's one thing I've learned about relationships, it's that you have to work with what you've got. So if what you've got is that your childhood crush has grown into a sexy hunk of burning love who can't keep his hands off you when he sees you for the first time in a couple decades, then don't knock it."

Lena collapsed on the old chaise. "But I want him to know me. I want Duncan Flynn to open his eyes and see me, not just *do* me."

"Honey, I get it. Your first encounter didn't go the way you'd fantasized about it all these years. But you've finally had that real first encounter. It actually happened. There was chemistry to spare. The next time you see him, maybe calmer heads will prevail."

She sighed. "He's back on the mainland right now, interviewing with his commanding officer. He's going to leave again soon."

"Lena, just be yourself and do your thing, and if he comes around again, don't try to control the outcome. Leave room to be surprised. Who knows? Maybe he's been out there his whole life being in love with you, too."

She hissed. "Yeah. Right."

"Are you going to be okay?"

"Of course." She sighed. "Festival week is starting and I'm doing the parade thing I told you about, and then the annual Island Day arts-and-crafts-show appearance."

"Sorry I'm not there this year."

"It's fine, Sandy. They always have a nice tent set up for me, and the police department keeps an eye on the crowd. I'll be fine."

"I'm glad. Well, I'm here. I better go."

"Have a good time. Don't do anything I wouldn't do."

Once Sanders had finished laughing and said goodbye, Lena remained there on the chaise, stretched out, enjoying the feel of the afternoon light spilling down on her. She closed her eyes, felt the heat on her face, and for the hundredth time in two days, she replayed in her mind the delicious moment she'd turned around and was face-to-face with him again.

Though she'd caught a glimpse of him at the market, it hadn't prepared her for being in the swirling vortex of his personal space. Duncan Flynn was tall and scruffy, broad in the shoulder and more muscled than any man she'd ever seen in person. Those eyes were the ones that had lived in that scrawny little boy so long ago—burning blue and alive—and still looking for a fight. Eyes that intense on an asthmatic kid were one thing, but on a

Navy SEAL they nearly knocked her over. Maybe that's why she could offer no resistance when he'd lifted her up and laid her on her back.

"Holy crap!" Lena rubbed her hands all over her face, as if she could erase the images stuck in her head.

The truth was, Duncan was the polar opposite of every male she'd ever had in her life. Her lovers had been artists like herself, men whom some would classify as hipsters and metrosexuals, sexy in their own right, but certainly not a force of male nature. Of course she knew Duncan had become a Navy SEAL, but she had no idea that his physical presence would be so powerful it could suck the air out of a room—and her lungs. Masculine strength and sexuality rolled off him in waves.

Damn straight he was a hunk of burning love.

Lena grabbed the sketchpad and charcoal she'd left on the floor near the chaise. She began to draw. As the image revealed itself, she had to laugh.

Every muscle, bone, and tendon came to life from strokes of the charcoal. His black hair was cut close, the bridge of his nose high and strong. His eyes smoldered, and his wide mouth stood out from the rough beard, its edges curled in teasing sensuality. As Lena continued to work, it became clear that this would be a nude study, and her usually dependable fingers trembled as they released the details . . . the hard line of his hip, the swell of his quadriceps, the muscled calf and elegant ankle and foot. Her breath caught as she executed the perfectly sculpted upper arm and powerful forearm. And what was it that dangled from his large fingers? It was a single osprey feather, sleek with black and white stripes.

She felt her breath hitch as she finished the sketch, shading the muscles of his abdomen, his ribs, adding the dusting of dark hair on his chest and the distinct line that led to . . .

Lena stopped. She blew across the sketchpad, and a cloud of charcoal dust rose, hovered in the sunshine for an instant, then trailed away.

She decided that some of Duncan Flynn should remain in her fantasies, at least for now. Like Sanders said, she should leave enough room to be surprised.

Duncan had never felt so ridiculous in his life. As threatened, Assistant Chief Chip Bradford had found him a pair of Bayberry Island Police Department navy blue cotton shorts, along with an official baseball cap and a white polo shirt embroidered with the department logo. The problem was, the shirt was too small. Chip apologized, explaining that Deon Ware, one of Clancy's annual moonlighters, had already claimed the largest size they had.

Chip looked him over. "It's not that bad. Really."

Duncan looked down at how the cotton blend hugged his abs like a wet T-shirt. "If you're a male stripper maybe," he replied.

So looking like he was the main attraction at a bachelorette party, Duncan set out to do what he hadn't done since high school—help out his family during the Mermaid Festival.

"Mandatory fun"—that was what they called this sort of quasi-recreation in the U.S. Navy.

"I appreciate your help, man. Seriously." Clancy had acknowledged Duncan as he rushed from the station's back door. "Remember—one p.m. at the parade staging area in the museum's west parking lot. I've got my cell if you need me, or use your radio to call dispatch."

"Hooya, Chief."

As Duncan watched his brother drive off in his department-issued Jeep, he realized that an unexpected benefit of being home had been getting to know Clancy. He was a good man, and good at his job. Everyone on the island genuinely liked him, and the tourists respected him. Like Da, Clancy had an easygoing way with people, and he made friends wherever he went.

Duncan had missed out on that genetic trait. He'd had only a handful of friends outside of the Navy, and within the ranks of his SEAL team, he'd had only one true confidant. Duncan had no idea what it would be like to go through life as laid-back and content as Clancy was. He couldn't be that mellow if his life depended on it.

Clancy was similar to Duncan in one respect—he'd escaped Bayberry Island after high school and had graduated from college on the mainland. His life had led him to serve four years as a Boston cop, and then, when old Chief Pollard was getting ready to retire, he'd asked Clancy if he would consider coming back and taking over the Bayberry Police Department. Duncan had warned him it was a bad move, that he could get stuck here forever with the falling-down bed-and-breakfast, the elderly parents, and the burden of being a Flynn. Clancy did it anyway.

Duncan had seen a big change in his brother now that Evelyn and Christina were in the picture. Clancy had that blissed-out look of a man with his life on lock—he had a job he loved and that challenged him, while having a peaceful home life with a wife and a kid who adored him almost as much as he adored them.

Rarely had Duncan pictured that kind of happiness for himself. He'd seen the sacrifices Navy SEAL wives had to make, and Duncan had decided he couldn't put someone through that. So his relationships with women tended toward hot, tumultuous, and short-lived, usually because the women soon decided they liked the idea of dating a SEAL more than the actual SEAL. Some women had been determined to "fix" him, smooth him out, make him more loving and patient and carefree. In other words, turn him into Clancy.

Not ever gonna happen.

"Any questions?" Chip leaned against the reception desk in the police department lobby.

"I got it."

"You're our eyes and ears out there."

"Damn straight."

Just then Duncan heard a skittering sound from around the corner, and he saw that little dog come barreling toward him. "Incoming," he mumbled, as the thing jumped up into his arms just like the last time he was there.

Chip seemed happy to see the dog. "Ondine really likes you. She doesn't run to anyone else like that."

"I'm honored." Suddenly, Duncan got a noseful of fruity sweetness and saw that the dog had been washed, fluffed, trimmed—and accessorized. She had a small pink bow stuck to her head to match the small pink tongue that lolled out the side of her mouth.

"We got her groomed."

"Lookin' good." He put her down on the floor, and she began running in circles in front of Duncan's feet. "Energetic little bugger."

"You sure you don't want her? We can't find anyone to take her, and she obviously loves you. That's why we got her groomed—you know, to make her more adoptable."

Duncan laughed. "I'm a U.S. Navy SEAL, Chip. The only dogs we have are trained to sniff explosives and find enemy hideouts. Can Ondine do that?"

While they looked down to see the creature licking herself, Chip said, "No problem. I just thought, you know, if it turned out you weren't going back to active duty, then maybe you could take her."

Duncan's entire body went deadly still. His mind emptied out. "Who said I wasn't going back?"

Chip looked startled. "Nobody! I just thought—"

"Hey, no problem." Duncan patted him on the arm. "I'll report in later today. Have a good one."

As Duncan headed for the door, he heard Chip snatch the dog as she tried to follow him.

What the hell? Why would Chip even think that?

Duncan made his way through the narrow, cobblestone streets of Bayberry's oldest section, nicknamed Cod Hill. It was built in the 1880s, back when the island was booming and housing couldn't be erected fast enough to meet the needs of the fishermen and their families. The very street Duncan now walked along was often featured in tourist brochures along with words like "quaint" and "picturesque." Right now "suffocating" was more like it. He couldn't shake off the claustrophobia Chip's comment had brought on. Had someone implied that Duncan wouldn't or couldn't go back to his full duties? Had someone said they wished he wouldn't?

He tugged at the neckline of the too-small polo shirt, suddenly feeling like he couldn't get enough air. He didn't want anyone—even his mother—talking about what he should or should not do. He wanted his family and anyone else who was interested in the direction of his career to just back the hell off.

As it was, sooner or later he would have to tell his family what happened at Little Creek. All he'd shared was that the meeting with his commanding officer went well and that he would return in September for physical screening and medical testing. All that was true. What he hadn't mentioned was that he was to be awarded the Purple Heart for injuries sustained in the field of battle, and the ceremony would take place in the fall.

He knew why he hadn't told them. He didn't feel worthy. He didn't want a medal. All he wanted was to go back in time to the night of the ambush and save Justin and the rest of his insertion team.

Duncan shook off his melancholy and focused on the view below him—Bayberry's historic wharf under a bright blue summer sky. The rear of the museum was straight ahead. Like most of the redbrick buildings and warehouses along the wharf, the museum was once part of his family's business. Even decades of disuse, wind, and sea spray couldn't erase the huge white letters soaked up by the porous brick: FLYNN FISHERIES, EST. 1879.

As he continued down the hill, Duncan had a bird's-eye view of the parade floats, which were bunched together in a disorganized lump resembling an interstate accident scene. It made him laugh—somehow, some way, the islanders always managed to pull this week off. The Mermaid Festival was held year after year without fail, with only a four-year pause during World War II. For the first time since Duncan was in high school, he would be around to see it unfold from start to finish. Ever since he'd left for college sixteen years before, the only event he made a point of returning for was the Flynn family cookout on the Wednesday of festival week. It was a promise he had managed to keep to his mother. Everything else was hit or miss, depending on his orders and his leave.

He stepped around a line of porta-potties and entered the mayhem of tuba players, papier-mâché-encrusted floats, Shriners, politicians, clowns, shiny fire trucks, and garden-variety crazy people. If anyone ever wanted a visual for why the Bayberry Island Mermaid Festival was called the Mardi Gras of New England, this would do it.

Duncan had reentered the world he'd tried to avoid since the day he was born, a world where it was de rigueur for grown men to be dressed as pirates, sea captains, sharks, mermen, and even versions of Neptune himself. Where women of every conceivable shape, size, and height swam in a teeming sea of mermaids. (Always a safe bet: each float would feature at least one mermaid sitting on some sort of throne.)

Within minutes Duncan had homed in on the person in charge. It was his personal favorite among his mother's mermaids, the unsinkable Polly Estherhausen. She looked particularly fetching in a multicolored sequined mermaid skirt and a bikini top made of coconuts topped off with a red-and-white-checked flannel shirt. She was also missing her long mermaid wig, so short gray spikes stuck up all around her multiple ear piercings.

Her eyes flashed his way, and she raised her clipboard in praise. "Oh, thank God! The cavalry's here!" She hugged Duncan and thanked him for offering to help with the parade. She planted a menthol-scented kiss on his cheek, adding, "Though I suspect you didn't exactly volunteer."

For the next hour or so, he and Polly divided and conquered. They walked through the bedlam and managed to get each float, musical act, random costumed person, baton twirler, and VIP in the proper order. Duncan finished up with the Falmouth High School color guard and went to meet up with Polly.

That's when he saw her.

Adelena Silva was attempting to climb up on the Safe Haven Bed and Breakfast float, but she was having trouble. It seemed her skintight blue-green mermaid skirt didn't allow for the leg movement needed to hoist oneself onto an elaborately decorated flatbed truck. Instinctively, Duncan rushed to help her but then froze as he came up behind her.

Taking a breath, he said, "Can I help?"

Lena froze, too. Slowly, she turned her head and looked up over her shoulder into his eyes. Duncan swallowed hard. That maddening painting had come to life, and the well-sexed siren he'd last seen lounging on the sea floor just placed her hand in his. "Thank you," she said.

And that left Duncan with a question of simple physics. Since she was unable to bend her knees enough to reach the running board, there were only two choices: Lena would have to remove her skirt or Duncan would have to pick her up and carry her on board. She seemed to understand the dilemma before he could spell it out for her.

"Uh-oh," she said.

"Yeah. Do you have a pair of shorts on under that thing?" As soon as Duncan said those words he knew it was a ridiculous question. That mermaid skirt was so tight it hugged every slight variance in her shape, all the way down to the ankles, where the fantail flared open to reveal a pair of delicate seashell sandals.

Lena glanced down at herself and laughed. "There's barely room for me under this getup. I'm afraid someone's going to have to carry me." Just then a frown crinkled between her eyebrows. "I can find someone else if you'd rather not do this."

That stung. Clearly, Lena would prefer he not put his hands on her, and he didn't blame her. "I promise I can do it without losing my sense of propriety."

She smiled at him. Oh, damn, but she was pretty— otherworldly pretty. Her face, chest, and arms had been dusted with some kind of iridescent powder, which highlighted her already spectacular seashell-covered breasts. Her lips were a deep rose, sparkly and soft. Her hair was shiny and straight and tossed over her shoulder. Her eyes had been made-up with a thick swoosh of eyeliner, mascara, and an even more sparkly eye shadow. Yet somehow, despite all this, she managed not to look like a caricature. Lena looked like a beautiful, perfect . . . mermaid.

"I won't aggravate your injury?"

"No."

"Then let's do it." She turned around to face him and reached up to rest her hands on his shoulders. Duncan reached underneath her thighs and behind her back and tossed her up into his arms. She weighed next to nothing. Lena wrapped her arms around his neck. "I'm ready if you are," she said.

Duncan wished he had two hundred steps to take instead of two, so he took his time getting onto the truck. He could feel the firmness of her thighs and the swell of her ass. His hand was wrapped around the bare skin of her back and side—hot and soft. So that he could prolong the inevitable, Duncan carried her over to the sequin-covered half shell that was positioned in the center of the float. It was obviously the mermaid's throne.

He carefully placed her in position and let her body

slip from his arms. While he was already bent, he gave her a bow. "Madam," he said.

She laughed, reaching for the rhinestone crown propped against the base of the shell. She placed it on top of her head. "Am I straight?"

"Hooya," he said, which made her laugh again.

Just then two young women working as seasonal help at the B and B clambered onto the float in their mermaid costumes, laughing and talking and clearly having no trouble hopping on board. Duncan and Lena both stared at the construction of their mermaid skirts.

Both costumes were unzipped all the way from the fantail to the upper thigh, leaving room to kickbox if they wanted to. The girls quickly zipped the skirts closed before they took their positions on the two smaller shells, then waved at Lena. She waved back.

Lena said, "Well, that answers that."

"I guess real mermaids don't need zippers," Duncan said, smiling. "Enjoy the parade."

Duncan continued smiling the rest of the day, even when every member of the New Bedford show choir complained about the sound check for their wireless mikes and threatened to pull their act from the parade.

"We're sure gonna miss that Lady Gaga medley," he said as he left to meet up with Polly.

"Is it any wonder I drink?" she asked Duncan.

"Hell, no."

"So did Lena get situated all right?"

Duncan's head snapped around. Sure, he liked Polly, but the truth was, she was first and foremost a member of the Mermaid Society. And Duncan knew that group of women was always up to no good. "Her mermaid skirt didn't have a zipper."

Polly shrugged. "That's a custom skirt for ya."

"Why is she wearing a custom skirt?"

"Mona gave it to her."

The situation didn't smell right. If Duncan allowed himself to go there, he could see a connection between Rowan being there in the kitchen that night, Ma giving Lena a zipperless skirt, Clancy asking him to help out at the parade and sending him out in public in a too-tight shirt, and Lena needing someone to help her onto the parade float just as he walked by.

To most people, that kind of conspiracy theory would seem beyond all possibility since it required a ridiculous amount of collaboration and a bit of omniscience on his mother's part.

But most people didn't know his mother. Or her fellow mermaids.

"Polly, you know I'm leaving, right? You know I'm going back to full duty."

She draped a red and white flannel arm over his shoulder. "Of course you are, and you make all of us proud."

"I'm off-limits for your mermaid bullshit. You know that, right?"

Polly sighed. "You're being outrageously paranoid, Lieutenant Flynn. By the way, nice shirt."

Chapter Thirteen

The most family-friendly day of festival week was Island Day, the Sunday when Main Street shut down and the street and public dock became an open-air market, a tent city of commerce, refreshment, and entertainment.

By ten a.m., Bayberry was busting at the seams, and Clancy looked as if he were about to do the same. Though the event had just opened, Duncan had already watched his brother deal with an entire day's worth of crises. There was a boat collision with injuries near the public dock, and both operators faced DUI charges. About six thousand dollars' worth of hammered silver bracelets and necklaces had been stolen from a vendor's car trunk. One of the chili cook-off judges had gone into labor and was on a helicopter bound for Martha's Vineyard Hospital. And Ondine, the dog, had bolted from the police station and was last seen eating out of a garbage Dumpster behind Frankie's Fish-n-Chips.

Duncan had been taking orders since before the sun came up. Clancy sent him to direct last-minute vendor traffic arriving by the car ferry. Next up was helping a freaked-out teenager who'd locked his boss's keys in a van full of iced cupcakes. Next Duncan was dispatched to repair the diesel generator used to keep the street fair's favorite ice cream stand up and running.

"At least the weather's clear for the time being." Clancy yanked off his ball cap and rubbed his hand through his hair. "There's a possible cyclone making its way north. It has the potential to wash out the closing ceremony. Good God, it's always something." He shoved his cap back on his head.

"You look pretty washed-out right now, yourself," Duncan said.

His little brother shook his head and then checked his vibrating pager. "Nope. I can't be. I got six more days of this shit, so if you see me in a corner somewhere, curled up in the fetal position, just kick me till I snap out of it."

Duncan chuckled, but Clancy's comment made him think. When they were kids, Duncan wasn't the nicest big brother in the world and had, on occasion, kicked his little brother when he was down.

"I think I've given you enough beat-downs for one lifetime," Duncan said.

A slow smile spread across Clancy's face. "Yeah. But after this week, we'll be even."

The two brothers grinned at each other, and something passed between them that didn't require words. Though he didn't have much experience with this sort of thing, Duncan was pretty sure he'd just apologized to Clancy for all the crap he'd put him through, and Clancy had accepted his apology. It felt pretty awesome.

"So anything in particular you want me to do next, Chief?"

Clancy patted him on the back. "Just walk the rows if you don't mind. Keep your eyes peeled. If any of the vendors need anything, do what you can to keep them happy. Radio in if something goes down."

"You got it."

"Oh, and if you see that damn Ondine, grab her, will you? I think we've found a nice tourist family to take her."

"Roger that."

So about an hour later Duncan found himself finishing his first lap through the jam-packed pedestrian thoroughfares between tents. The air was heavy with the scent of fried seafood, sausage, funnel cakes, popcorn, and barbecue, all doing battle with the chili cook-off downwind. Two music acts duked it out from opposite ends of the event, creating a mishmash of country and calypso. Tourists were attempting to dodge foot traffic while carrying their loot of wood carvings, shell crafts, blown glass, sand paintings, and mermaid paraphernalia ranging from clothing, jewelry, coffee mugs, and press-on tattoos to dream catchers, wind chimes, posters, flags, beer cozies, and garden sculptures. Along the way he reunited a crying toddler with his crying mother and unsuccessfully tried to catch two stray dogs, neither of which were the lovely and fragrant Ondine.

As Duncan approached the end of the arts-and-crafts row, he heard a ruckus nearby. It seemed to be coming from a tent set off by itself, nearly twice the size of the standard vendor stall. By the time he got to the scene, two women in their thirties were well on their way to tearing each other's hair out.

"All right, ladies. Come on, now. There's no need for this." Duncan pressed his body between them and got slapped on the ass for his trouble. For an instant he was speechless.

"I'm sorry!" The woman in a mermaid T-shirt covered her mouth in horror. "I didn't mean to touch your butt! I was trying to hit her!" She pointed around Duncan toward her sparring partner.

"She started it!" the woman in full-metal-jacket mermaid attire screamed in Duncan's ear. "She cut in line! I was here first, and I've been waiting more than an hour!"

Duncan used his body to keep the women apart while he radioed for backup. This whole attempting to serve and protect without any authority or firepower was a new experience for him. When the dispatcher asked for his location, he wasn't sure how to pinpoint it, so he craned his neck to find out where the crowd had assembled.

And there she was.

"Looks like I'm at Adelena Silva's vendor tent," he told the dispatcher, shouting over the women's continued arguing. "And it's a zoo."

Lena sat behind a large table draped in fabric that featured her trademark iridescent swirls of light and color. Directly behind her, a huge screen displayed a video loop of her work. Each image appeared for a few seconds, then dissolved into the next. He watched a view of the hypnotic scenes float by until, suddenly, he sucked in air. The painting from his room! There it was for the whole world to see, his very own personal dream vixen. The image faded, to be replaced by another, and Duncan snapped himself out of it.

What was he doing, again?

"Ladies, please." He spread his arms and held them apart while he returned his attention to Lena. She was attempting to autograph posters and coffee table books while the mob pressed in on her. From what Duncan could see, the line of her fans snaked past the row of food vendors and ended half a block away at the chili cook-off stage.

"Back off, bouncer!" One of the women stood on her tiptoes and got up in Duncan's face. "I don't see a badge or a gun, so what you gonna do about it?"

The other woman tried to kick her opponent while she was distracted, but instead kicked Duncan in the calf. *Oh, hell no.* After everything he'd been through, he did not plan on getting reinjured breaking up a girl fight.

"Do you want an autograph from Miss Silva, or do you want to spend the night in jail?" he asked.

The head-to-toe mermaid laughed and looked him up and down. "What are you, some kind of rent-a-cop?"

"Yes, ma'am. That's exactly what I am."

"You're superhot," the T-shirt woman said. "But this is none of your damn business."

Just then Chip jogged up to the tent and cut through the line to reach Duncan.

"Here you go," Duncan said. "I hereby turn these two lovely art aficionados over to your care. I'm going to lend Miss Silva a hand."

As he made his way toward the front of the line, Duncan continued to observe Lena. She was dressed in a filmy, soft green top that floated around her arms when she moved and fell loosely from one shoulder. The color and shape seemed to accentuate how pale and creamy her skin was, as well as the darkness of her eyes and eyelashes. She wore large, sea-green earrings that brushed against the side of that exquisite neck. And her hair . . . He'd never seen anything like it on another woman. It fascinated him, falling straight and glossy down the center of her back.

Lena took time with each person who came to the table and seemed genuinely interested in every visitor. When Duncan realized she was inquiring about names and hometowns and thanking each individual for enjoying her artwork, he knew he had to do something. At this pace, one of two things would happen—either Lena would still be sitting there during the Mermaid Festival closing ceremonies, or there would be a riot.

He cut to the side opening of the tent and pushed his way inside. Lena turned suddenly, her marker poised in mid-autograph. "You can't—" She stopped speaking. Her lips parted as her eyes opened wide. "What—"

"Why in the world would you try to do this by yourself?" Duncan asked as he entered the tent.

"I usually don't, but my manager is in Paris putting together a gallery show for me. I was told Island Day organizers would provide a volunteer."

"Well, here I am," was all he said. Then he got to work.

For the first twenty minutes or so, Lena felt awkward having Duncan in the tent with her. Not only did he take up a lot of room, but he seemed to be everywhere at once as he performed the duties of assistant, bodyguard, and event coordinator.

"Next five people step forward, please!"

No, her public appearances weren't usually organized like a SEAL team operation, but she had to admit that this particular Island Day appearance was shaping up to be one of the most enjoyable she'd ever had—and not just because it was well organized.

Lena felt electrically charged being this close to Duncan, like her nerve endings were going haywire. And though he was the perfect gentleman—for the second day in a row—she was uneasy. Would he ever kiss her again? Would he even dare to? Or had she enjoyed the first and only adult kiss she would ever receive from Duncan Flynn?

Occasionally, while restocking the poster supply or bringing her a fresh bottle of water, he would brush his fingers across her arm or bump her shoulder. She enjoyed it even though it was accidental. Or at least she assumed it was.

The first item on Duncan's agenda had been setting up two folding chairs about ten feet back from the table and instructing people to remain behind the chairs until they were called. She had to admit it was far less claustrophobic, and it allowed the two of them to develop a rhythm. Duncan politely but firmly moved the crowd along, giving each person about fifteen seconds to chat and get their autograph. For those who wanted photos, Duncan let them through to stand next to Lena for a single shot, then immediately ushered them out.

Clearly, he was not used to the quirkiness of Lena's fans and seemed surprised when a woman asked Lena to autograph her wedding album. She and her husband had been married in an Adelena Silva–themed ceremony, she explained, and she had dressed as a mermaid bride.

"Absolutely beautiful," Lena said, quickly looking at the photos. "I wish you many years of happiness."

"Next five people step up, please!"

She saw how Duncan bristled when a man stood in front of Lena, yanked up his shirt, and revealed an entire torso tattooed with one of her most famous paintings. When the man asked her to autograph his flesh below his belly button, Duncan stiff-armed him. "Keep your pants on," he told him, and then he leaned down to whisper in Lena's ear, "Are you kidding me?"

She giggled and whispered back, "I don't mind. I've had weirder requests."

"I don't think I want to know." When he pulled away, he was smiling. At *her*.

Lena was unable to move. That smile. How was it possible that a man could be so over-the-top macho and yet so beautiful at the same time? His eyes were the focal point of his face, bright with intensity, the color of the night sky under a full moon. His smile was straight and symmetrical, white teeth framed in pink lips, the upper being slightly thinner than the lower. But all that prettiness was set against a rugged backdrop. The smiling eyes were surrounded by crow's-feet and edged with thick, dark brows. His nose was of the no-nonsense variety, straight and strong. But somewhere beneath the dark stubble sprinkled on his chin, upper lip, and cheeks was the same boyish face she'd loved.

"What?" he asked.

Just like that, the charcoal drawing appeared in her mind, though it had morphed into a fully realized portrait in oils. There, in perfect composition, was the sloping musculature of his shoulders, the dusky purple of his eyes.

"You're right," she said. "You don't want to know."

By four p.m., Duncan had cleared the queue and informed latecomers that Lena would see them next year. He closed the tent flaps and began to dismantle her laptop, take down the video screen, and pack up what was left of coffee table books and posters.

She stretched, stiff from sitting for hours on end in the same position and in awe of how wonderful Duncan had been.

"I can't thank you enough. You were a lifesaver."

He glanced up at her from where he crouched over a box and smiled. "My pleasure," he said.

Duncan loaded up her SUV. What would have taken Lena hours of solo effort was accomplished in fifteen minutes. He held the door open for her as she climbed in and then waited for her to start the engine and buckle up.

Duncan leaned his forearms on the open window of her car. Lena smiled at him while trying not to stare at how the white polo shirt strained at his muscles. She pressed her knees together and summoned enough level-headedness to get through this last exchange.

The man made her dizzy.

"Who's helping you unload at your place?"

She did her best to sound nonchalant. "I've got it from here. Really. I'm fine."

A wrinkle appeared between his eyes. "I would be happy to do that for you."

Lena felt her heart start to bang inside her ribs. Was she ready for this? Was she ready for him to step into her world, her life? But this was what she'd always wanted, right? This was the imagined tale she had shared with Sanders a hundred times—that one day she would meet Duncan again, and it would be magical.

Her mouth had gone so dry she could barely speak. "Um, yes. That would be nice—but only if Clancy can spare you."

Duncan smiled, then straightened up and tapped his hands on the driver's side window ledge. "I was given direct orders by the chief of police to do whatever was necessary to assist our Island Day vendors."

"Oh." Lena blinked.

"In fact, his exact words were 'do what you can to

keep them happy.'" Duncan gestured to the empty passenger seat. "May I?"

"Of course. Yes. Sure." Lena thought she would pass out.

She drove the five or so miles to the island's North Shore, U.S. Navy Lieutenant Duncan Flynn riding shotgun. They talked about everything and nothing, and despite the traffic as the day's events wound down, the time flew by. But all the while Lena kept thinking, *I'm taking him home with me . . . I'm taking him home with me.*

Duncan had seen Lena's compound only at night, from down on the beach. So when the remote-controlled gates opened and he got a good broad-daylight look at it, the scope and style of the place shocked him.

The two-story structure sat on one of the highest points on the island and was a clean combination of cedar shingle, stone, glass, and more glass. He was no architect, but he noticed how it combined ultramodern lines with the traditional New England coastal style. Two giant stone chimneys bookended the house, and all the windows were trimmed with blue-green and white, which stood in bright contrast to the white cedar shakes. He could see a large greenhouse topped with at least six weather vanes of varying height, color, and design. The yard wasn't a yard at all—it was wild island land. It took a couple minutes to get all the way down the crushed-shell drive.

"Not too shabby, Silva," he said.

She laughed, and when he glanced over at her, he had to laugh along with her. Since Duncan wasn't an artsy kind of guy, he couldn't find the words to describe why he felt this way, but immediately he knew Lena belonged here. This was her place, and it suited her perfectly.

Beautiful. Unusual. Interesting.

She pulled into the attached garage and showed him a storage room off the back where she kept items for art shows.

As he unloaded the trunk, he asked her, "How many of these things do you do a year?"

"A year?" Lena paused, throwing a bag over her shoulder. Only then did Duncan have the time to appreciate the full effect of what she wore—figure-hugging black leggings and a pair of complicated-looking black sandals with a heel. Her floaty blouse was cinched in by a black leather belt that hung low on her hips, and her wrists were stacked with black and green bangles.

Holy shit, that girl is sexy.

"I travel about a week out of every month for media appearances and gallery events. I'm asked to do more, but I need to leave three unbroken weeks of each month to paint. Otherwise, what would I have to show?"

"Makes sense," Duncan said. "Do you like being out there, having people swarm around you like they did today?"

She laughed, almost as if she were embarrassed. "I do. I love meeting people who like my work, but just between you and me, a little bit goes a long way." She looked around. "I'm always so happy to come back home."

Duncan nodded. He found it interesting that her favorite thing was coming home, which was the one thing he had always avoided. He stacked the last box. "So when is that show in Paris you mentioned?"

"October."

Duncan closed the door to the storage area, feeling her eyes trained on his every move. "I guess you'll be in

Europe when I'm ... who knows where. Europe? Central Asia? But neither of us will be here."

Lena smiled stiffly, breaking eye contact for a second. "Do you know when you ship out?"

"I don't."

"Oh." Lena shifted her weight from one fantastic leg to the other. "So, um, should I drive you back? Would you like something cool to drink first?"

Duncan smiled politely. "Since I'm here, I'd like to see some of your incredible home, if that's not too pushy of me. And I'd kill for a cold beer."

"Ah, sorry." Lena shrugged. "No beer, but I'd love to show you around. I could whip up a margarita if you're interested. I need one after today."

"You got yourself a deal."

Lena went upstairs to change and told Duncan to make himself at home, which gave him a chance to look around without Lena seeing his jaw hit the floor. As funky as the place looked from the drive, the oceanfront side of the house was where the party really got started. The home was perfectly situated for maximum light, and since it was nearly wall-to-wall glass, the view of the Atlantic was spectacular. From where he stood in the huge and open kitchen, he could see most of the first floor. A great room spread out on the west side, dominated by a giant stone fireplace and a killer media setup. On the east side Duncan saw a dining room and sitting room, with a wide hallway leading off to what were probably bedrooms. He didn't think it would be polite to wander around by himself, so he took a seat at one of the counter stools pulled up to a vast kitchen island. He spread his hands out on the cool, ice-smooth quartz surface and wondered what the hell one petite woman needed with all this space.

Lena returned, now wearing a pair of Hawaiian floral surf shorts and a camisole top. Her hair was pulled up in a ponytail and her bare feet slapped against the wood floor when she walked. The earrings and bracelets were gone, but Duncan saw that her toenails were painted a bright pink. This girl was too cute.

"Can we get right to the margaritas? I'm in a tequila state of mind," Lena said with a smile.

Right then Duncan decided that Adelena Silva had her own version of a sense of humor. Sure, she was subdued and a little eccentric, but occasionally she'd come up with something sharp and funny, like the tequila comment, and it intrigued him. In all honesty, Duncan's only memory of her was as a mousy, shy girl who'd hung out with him because she didn't have anything better to do. She had been sweet to him even when he wasn't sweet in return.

But he certainly didn't remember her as being funny, or sharp, or gorgeous.

Duncan couldn't just sit there while she waited on him, so he squeezed the lime and tossed an extra handful of ice into the blender. Lena let the countertop Ninja do its magic. She pointed to where he could find the margarita glasses, and Duncan chuckled as he carried them over.

"Just an FYI—these are bigger than my head."

Lena laughed. "I've never heard anyone say the words, 'This margarita is too big.' Have you?"

"Can't say that I have." Duncan sprinkled sea salt onto a plate and gave the glass rims a good coating. He offered to pour. When Lena handed him the heavy glass pitcher, his hand skimmed across hers. A jolt of alarm surged through him. He managed not to visibly react, but he was astonished by how intense his response was. And strange. Lena was perfectly lovely and her touch was lovely, yet the contact made him want to bolt out of there and never look back.

Lena suggested they look around the downstairs first, and she showed him what she called the "guest wing," which had three bedrooms and three baths, a sitting room, and the main dining room. The great room had enough seating for twenty people and a huge flat-screen TV that doubled as a mirror when the power was off.

Duncan couldn't help himself—he'd never seen a place more suited to a Super Bowl party in his life. Or for watching Bruins games. Or the Celtics and Red Sox seasons. She almost had to drag him out of there. What one artistic chick needed with a tricked-out man cave he had no idea.

They went outside next, and she walked him out onto a deck that seemed to go on forever. Then she showed him a greenhouse filled with plants, beautiful pottery, and odd-looking metal sculptures. She told him everything was the work of friends from art school.

He pointed up through the greenhouse roof. "Did the sculptor do the weather vanes, too?"

Lena looked surprised that he'd noticed. "No, that's another friend."

"Sounds like you've got a lot of artist friends."

She smiled. "I bet you have a lot of soldier friends."

Duncan chuckled. "Most are Marines and SEALs, but yes—I do. You and I live in very different worlds, don't we?"

Lena nodded. "Indeed."

Next she took him around to the opposite side of the house, to a side porch. Duncan was surprised to find it was far more traditional than what he'd seen in the rest of the house. The outdoor living space was at least forty feet long and half as wide, screened in, covered by a knotty pine roof, and filled with plants, wicker furniture, and comfortable-looking pillows. There was a long rustic dining table and chairs and a huge overhead fan that looked like it could move some serious air when put to use. But his eyes were drawn to a two-person rope hammock strung diagonally from beam to beam, facing directly toward the beach.

"Whoa," he said. "One day, before the end of the summer, I'd like to rent out that hammock for a couple hours." He glanced down and smiled at Lena. "The next time I'm stuck in the desert, I can picture myself here."

"Of course," she said. "But in appreciation for your service, I'll waive the hourly rate."

"Much appreciated."

"Why do you do it, Duncan?" Lena's gaze was open and curious. "I mean, what drives you to keep going back?"

He shook his head, wondering how the hell he'd managed to end up at this particular intersection.

"I don't mean to pry."

"There's no easy answer to that."

"Maybe we could sit down for a minute?" Lena gestured to the hammock. "I think it's calling your name."

One, two, three seconds passed and Duncan could not move. A voice in his head whispered that he knew better than to accept that invitation. A minute could lead to another, which could lead to something more, and something more wasn't an option for him.

"I won't bite, Duncan."

But I might. "All right. For a minute."

Lena sat in one of the wicker chairs and Duncan

eased into the hammock with a sigh of relief. He leaned his head back and began to gently rock back and forth, feeling the soft breeze move over his face. He closed his eyes for a moment, feeling his whole body melt.

Eventually he said, "I should come clean about something, Lena." He kept his eyes closed. "I don't remember very much about you from when we were kids, and now that I know it was you leaving those gifts back then—and now—I feel . . . I feel ridiculous. It never once occurred to me that it was you. You weren't even on my radar screen."

"I didn't intend for you to feel ridiculous."

He opened one eye and studied her. "What *was* your intent?"

Lena curled her legs under her and took a sip from her margarita. "Well, back when we were kids, I figured you needed cheering up. When you came home after your injury, I figured you needed cheering up again."

"I see a pattern developing."

Lena laughed. "Look, I overstepped my bounds these last couple months. I invaded your privacy by putting things in your room, and I apologize for that. I wasn't thinking straight."

"How the hell did you get in without me hearing you? Did you put a spell on me or something?"

She shrugged. "I grew up in that house, too, Duncan. I know where every squeaky floorboard is and how to jiggle the door open without making a sound—I had a lot of practice. And though Rowan and Ash may have renovated that place from top to bottom, the floors are still the same. The door latches are the same." She tipped her head to the side. "Did you wake up the night I brought you the clamshell?"

"Nope. I had set my alarm for four a.m. so I could catch the first ferry. Finding you in the kitchen was a complete surprise."

She nodded.

"I really liked the feather."

"You did? I'm so glad!" Lena broke out into a smile that commandeered her whole face. "I found it right out there"—she pointed to a patch of wildflowers—"when I was headed out for my morning swim."

Duncan sat up a bit. "Do you swim a lot?"

"Every morning and every night when the weather cooperates."

Duncan drained the rest of his drink, feeling the tequila and triple sec flow right through his empty stomach and into his veins. "You're not worried about swimming alone?"

"Oh, no." She looked puzzled. "I feel perfectly comfortable. I don't go very far out, especially at night, and I've been swimming on this coastline since I was little. You know how that is."

Duncan nodded. Of course he wanted to ask her about her late-night skinny-dip, but there wasn't quite enough tequila in his bloodstream for that conversation.

"You are a kind person, Lena. I have a feeling I wasn't always kind to you in return when we were kids."

"You were sick a lot. You were angry at the world."

Duncan sat up in the hammock and rested his elbows on his knees. "Being sick isn't an excuse to be cruel. I'm starting to remember that I might have been an ass sometimes."

Lena looked down at her hands where they cupped the margarita glass. "The good news is, you're less of an ass nowadays."

Duncan put his head back and laughed. Hard. It took him a moment to stop laughing. "That was the nicest backhanded compliment anyone has paid me in a very long time."

She shrugged. "I only said it because it's true."

"I like you, Lena."

She sat upright, placed her glass on a side table, and put her cute bare feet back on the porch floor. She blinked at him. "I like you, too, Duncan."

"You're an intriguing woman."

"You're a complicated man."

That little voice in his head was now a screaming banshee. Over and over it yelled for his attention. Like a warning, like a mantra . . . *Don't do it. Don't say it. Don't go there.* Duncan ignored the warning and told the banshee that he had the situation on lock.

"Would you like to go to the clambake with me tomorrow night, Lena?"

She stared at him, her face blank.

"Unless you have a date."

"No!" Lena shook her head, then started over. "What I meant was, no, I don't have a date. I wasn't really planning on going."

"Neither was I."

"So . . . we're going to plan not to go, but go anyway? Together?"

"My thoughts exactly."

Had he lost his mind? Duncan knew there was no other explanation for what had just gone down. He had asked a woman on a date. He had asked Lena Silva, a resident of Bayberry Island, Massachusetts, to go to the clambake with him, where his entire family would be. *What the fuck am I doing?*

"I'll pick you up at six." The air stuck in his windpipe, making his words barely audible.

"I'll be ready," Lena said, not meeting his eyes. "Now, let's go see the rest of the house."

Duncan could tell Lena was nervous as she took him upstairs. Her breath was quick, and she drummed her fingers on the banister of the staircase as they ascended. It made sense. It had to be nerve-racking to give a man a tour of the upstairs of a house when, at some point, the tour would surely arrive at the woman's bedroom door. And then what?

Also, Lena might feel a bit nervous knowing that Duncan was inches away from her backside as she climbed the stairs, and that would be a legitimate concern—he couldn't take his eyes off of her. It wasn't like she was dressed in Daisy Dukes. Her shorts were just a few inches above the knee. But Lena had a set of slim and strong thighs, alluring hips, and a nice rounded ass. How was a man supposed to not notice?

Duncan had always believed that women were at their sexiest when they weren't trying to be, and he had no doubt that Lena's bare feet, surf shorts, and sleeveless T-shirt were part of her natural habitat. In the last week, he'd seen her in a wide range of clothes—jeans, dressy, casual, a skintight mermaid skirt, and nothing at all. He had to say that aside from the totally naked look, this was his favorite.

When they reached the top of the stairs, Duncan discovered how Lena would handle the bedroom dilemma. "There are only two areas up here," she said, gesturing to her right. "On that side is my bedroom suite." Then she gestured to the left. "And on this side is my studio space."

Duncan's interest had gone elsewhere—straight up. He leaned his head back and took in the most astounding skylight he'd ever seen. It jutted up and spiraled outward in the shape of a mollusk shell. When he glanced down at Lena, she was smiling.

"I'd bet at night you can reach up and touch the stars."

"If you like that, then you should see my studio."

Duncan was looking forward to whatever surprise awaited him next. "I'm ready when you are."

He was wrong about that. Duncan was not prepared for what he saw when Lena led him halfway down a long hallway and threw open a huge set of double doors.

"Holy shit." He took a tentative step inside, aware that his mouth had fallen open. "This place is unreal, Lena."

He moved into the center of the room, and his reflex was to stretch his arms out wide so he could gather it in. He hardly knew what to look at first. The room was at least a couple thousand square feet. The ocean-side wall was nothing but a series of huge windows, and the ceiling, featuring three skylights, rose twenty-five feet high. The room was alive with warm light, gleaming wood floors, and touches of painted brick. The view was jaw-dropping. With a quick glance, Duncan could see the turreted Safe Haven and the newly constructed Oceanaire Marine Institute growing up nearby. The only other way he knew to get a view like that was on board a private plane or helicopter.

Taking up the center of the room was a giant butcher-block worktable stained with splotches of paint and littered with small easels, canvases, knives, and other tools of her trade. Next to it was a paint-splattered metal stool and a huge contraption that looked like it could adjust for a whole range of canvas sizes. Duncan bet it had cost a fortune.

He scanned the length of the room, noticing an office area with a desk, computer, sound system, and a mini-fridge. But his gaze landed on a far wall that held a patchwork of shelving and storage spaces.

"That's where I stretch and store my canvases," Lena said. "I paint in a variety of sizes, and sometimes I even get commissions for murals. So I make what I need and stock whatever I'm not using right away."

Duncan gave her a sideways glance. "It sounds like hard work."

"It can be. But by this point I can do it in my sleep."

Lena showed him what she called the "brush room." The walls were fitted with racks of old pottery jugs used to hold paintbrushes of all sizes. Dozens more brushes were secured on metal strips along the wall and hanging upside down. The room had three sinks and a separate bathroom with a steam shower. The sinks were lined with soaps, rags, and containers of mineral spirits and linseed oil. Just then Duncan noticed there was very little solvent odor. He examined the walls until he located several huge ventilation fans.

"It's good you've got these," he said.

"I have to. I get terrible headaches if I don't."

Duncan wandered toward the center of the studio and once again took in the huge skylight. It was three times as big as the one in the hallway yet far less decorative. "Why do you need a skylight when there are so many windows?"

"Dispersed light from overhead doesn't cause glare like light coming from one direction through a window. And I can dim or block the light completely by remote."

He scratched his chin. "This is quite a setup you've got here. It's a much bigger operation than I imagined."

"Really?"

"Yeah. I guess I pictured you perched on a little chair with a brush and a beret."

That made Lena laugh. "Not hardly."

"I never envisioned something this ... *lavish*."

Lena held up her hands in a Clancy-esque gesture. "Wait a minute. I haven't always painted in a place like this, Duncan. I spent the beginning of my career in decrepit apartments and a garage or two. This is a dream come true for me."

"So you designed the studio?"

When she crossed her arms under her breasts, Duncan couldn't help but notice how it improved the view of her cleavage. It was wrong of him, of course. But he couldn't stop looking.

"I designed the whole house and hired an architect and a general contractor who could turn my ideas into reality."

Duncan stood still, letting that statement sink in. This pretty little painter of mermaids had a core of steel. She had the guts to live bigger than anyone else he knew and to do things other people thought were impossible. It just might be that the two of them had more in common than he'd first thought.

"Bravo Zulu, Miss Silva."

A small wrinkle appeared between her brows.

"That means 'way to go.'"

"Thanks." She grinned.

"You go for it, don't you, Lena?"

Her cheeks reddened. "I ... yes. I guess I do. You look surprised."

Duncan shook his head. "Impressed, mostly."

Suddenly, it occurred to him that he saw no actual paintings in this huge space. "Aren't you working on anything now?"

She shrugged. "I am. I've got a few things I'm fiddling with, but my manager just took two years' worth of work to Paris for my show."

"Gotcha." Duncan's eye was drawn to the only real piece of furniture in the studio, an antique upholstered lounge chair made of what looked like mahogany. The fabric was so worn in spots that the springs were visible. He was about to give it a closer look when Lena slipped in front of him, blocked his progress, and grabbed a sketchbook that had been on the floor nearby.

"Excuse me," she said, closing the sketchbook's cover and pressing it against her thigh. Her chest had broken out in red blotches and she was breathing hard.

"I didn't mean to invade your privacy."

Lena shook her head. "It's fine. It's nothing."

"So you don't like people seeing your work in progress?"

"Uh, it depends on the work."

For a moment the two of them stood quietly. Lena looked at the floor and Duncan looked at her, the sweet curve of her neck, her soft shoulder, how cute she looked with her hair pulled up like that.

Suddenly, her gaze snapped up. "Well, I've taken up a big chunk of your time today. I'll get my keys and drive you back to town."

"Are you okay, Lena?" Duncan reached out and touched her upper arm. Her skin was hot and silky, but that annoying banshee was back in his head—*don't do it; don't say it; don't go there*—but he did. "Thank you for sharing this with me."

She nodded. "You're quite welcome."

His body made the next move without waiting for the approval of his mind. He dipped his head and left a soft kiss on her lips. It wasn't the shock-and-awe kind of kiss from the kitchen, but it was the right kind of kiss for the moment. Besides, he wanted to show her he had another side to him.

"Okay," she said, way too brightly.

Duncan was not imagining it — Lena was trying to get him out of there. Since he wasn't one to force his company on anyone, he just smiled and said, "So I'll see you tomorrow?"

Lena nodded, her ponytail bobbing up and down. "I look forward to it. Just let me get some shoes on so I can drive you — "

"I think I'll walk."

And that's when he saw it.

A small pencil drawing hung on the wall right near the doorway. It was amateurish and definitely not the work of a real artist, but Duncan began to boil with confusion. Why did it look familiar? Had he seen it before? He moved closer, and even as the blood began to pound in his ears, he heard Lena just behind him, mumbling to herself under her breath. No wonder she was hurrying him out.

He came to stand right in front of the drawing. The frayed and wrinkled piece of paper had been carefully matted and framed, as if it were a treasured piece of fine art. As if it had immense value.

At the bottom right corner was the scrawled signature of the artist — Duncan Flynn, circa eighth grade. This was *his* drawing!

Duncan spun around.

Lena kept her dark eyes trained on his but didn't say anything.

"Why the hell would you keep a drawing I made of you when we were kids?"

"You don't remember?"

"Remember what?"

Lena tossed the sketchbook to her worktable and crossed her arms over her chest. "Are you truly curious about my reason for keeping it, or do you just want to tell me how pissed off you are that I did?"

Duncan tipped his head and laughed with disbelief. His stupid sketch was hanging on her studio wall, which meant she'd carried it around for twenty years! *Twenty years!* Why was she so attached to such a silly memory? Why was she so attached to *him*? Why had she continued to leave him little gifts?

Duncan's stomach twisted in knots—it was too much. Her devotion made him deeply uncomfortable; it suffocated him. The situation had gone from promising to a complete cluster-fuck in a matter of seconds.

"You kept it for twenty years."

"I did."

"I was fourteen."

"Yes, and I was eleven." Duncan saw that Lena was doing everything she could to stop herself from crying. The blotches on her chest had darkened. Her jaw was clamped tight. Her eyes were welling over. And he had no idea why. Why was the sketch such a big deal to her?

"You don't remember that day, do you?"

Duncan shrugged. "What day?"

"That day." Lena pointed to the drawing, her finger shaking.

"Not really."

She nodded, then swiped the back of her hand over her eyes. "If you don't remember the day, you won't remember my reason for keeping it."

Duncan raised his hands in surrender. Seriously, this whole exchange baffled him. "Well, I don't get it. Sorry. I guess you have your reasons." He let himself out the door. "Talk to you later, Lena."

He heard her small voice say, "Thanks again for everything today."

He didn't reply.

Chapter Fourteen

Twenty years ago ...

On a Sunday afternoon in early October, Duncan didn't have anything better to do, so he started looking around the house for Clancy. He found him slouched on the couch, watching the National League playoffs.

"Who's winning?"

"The Dodgers, but they're going down."

"How do you know? Are you some kind of psychic?" Duncan plopped down next to his brother.

"No." Clancy mocked him. "Are you some kind of asshole? Wait—I can answer that. Yes! You're an asshole!"

Duncan knuckle punched him in the upper arm. "So you want to ride bikes?"

"No."

"Want to go see if we can get on Da's computer?"

"No."

"Want to arm wrestle?"

Clancy let his jaw fall open. "Oh, my God. No, I don't want to arm wrestle. I am watching the game, butthead."

Duncan got up. "You're just afraid to lose."

"I am not."

"Sure you are." Duncan wandered out to the lobby and through the dining room. There were only four guests there that weekend, and compared to the crazy summer they'd just survived, it was too quiet. Even the cute Russian girls who were there to help out during the tourist season were gone.

He pushed open the kitchen door and headed for the refrigerator. He stuck his head inside and looked around.

"Get out of there," Mellie said. "Dinner is in two hours."

"But I'm starving."

"Good, then you'll have a nice appetite at the table. I'm making turkey tetrazzini."

"That sounds like a disease." He grabbed a banana off the counter, too fast for Mellie to swat his hand, and headed out the back door.

Out of the corner of his eye he saw Lena. As usual, she was curled up on a wicker chair on the side porch, her colored pencils and sketchpad in her lap and her Walkman headphones over her ears. She was wearing one of those stupid scrunchies at the top of her head. All the girls seemed to like them, but Duncan thought they looked like balled-up sweat socks. Who wanted to stick a sweat sock in their hair?

Duncan finished his banana and tossed the peel in a nearby trash can. He threw open the screen door and jumped from the grass to the porch in one leap. Lena gasped and looked up. He must have scared her.

"Sorry about that."

She couldn't get the headphones off fast enough. "Hey, Duncan!" She smiled at him the way she always did.

"Hey." He eased himself into the next chair over and propped his feet on the wicker table. "What did you think of the track meet yesterday?"

"You were awesome. Totally awesome."

"Thanks." Duncan leaned back and put his arms behind his head. "So you saw me compete?"

"Oh, sure! We all did—except, you know, during the cross-country race when you disappeared because everyone ran into the woods, but we clapped when you crossed the finish line."

"Yeah. That's cool."

Lena went back to drawing, but she kept her headphones looped around her neck.

"Did you stay for the long jump event?"

"Yeah. Congratulations on winning that, too."

"Thanks."

They sat there like that for a few minutes. Lena wasn't the easiest person to talk to, because she was so quiet sometimes. But he thought it was cool that she went to his track meets. And swim meets. And soccer games. She went to more of them than anyone in his own family.

"What are you drawing?" Duncan leaned forward in the chair and craned his neck over her sketchpad. "Let me see that." He snatched it from her lap.

"Hey! I'm in the middle of drawing!"

"Man, no kidding. One of these mermaids doesn't even have a head."

She clicked her tongue against her teeth and rolled her eyes. "Give it back."

"Maybe."

She snatched it from him before he could react, which made him laugh. Lena was all right, even though she was from a younger generation and everything.

"Is that all you do? Draw and paint and stuff?"

She put the pencils on the table and stared at him. "Of course not. You know I do other things, because you used to do some of them with me—you know, walk through the nature preserve, read, play backgammon, listen to music, watch movies . . . talk."

He shrugged. "Yeah, but most of that was from when I was sick, so I don't do those things anymore."

Lena smiled at him, but it wasn't a "funny ha-ha" kind of smile. She almost looked a little sad. "I'm very glad you got better, but I do miss hanging out like we used to."

She picked up the pencils once more and was about to replace her headphones when Duncan said, "Remember when you used to draw me?"

Lena's head snapped up. She blinked at him. "Sure. Why?"

"Oh, I don't know. I was just thinking that I should draw you sometime. You know, just to see if I can do it. I'm really into challenging myself these days, you know. I want to see how good I am at everything."

Lena's eyes got big. "You want to draw me?"

"Sure. Why not? There's nothing better to do."

So Lena turned the sketchpad over to a fresh page and asked him what he wanted to use as a medium.

"A medium what?"

She giggled. "You know, do you want to use charcoal, pastel chalk, pencil, ink, colored pencils—"

"God, I don't want any of that art stuff. Just give me a pencil."

"How do you want me to pose?"

Duncan was at a loss. "Man, I don't know. Do what you normally do, I guess."

"I've never posed for anyone before."

"Why not?"

She laughed. "Because I'm always the one drawing, silly."

"Oh." Duncan propped the sketchpad on his knee and signed his name in big, dark letters at the bottom right of the page. For some reason, Lena thought that was funny.

"What's the problem?"

"You sign it after you've finished, Duncan," she said, smiling. "Signing a sketch is bragging to the world, 'Hey, look, everybody! I did this!' So right now you're basically bragging that you haven't done anything yet."

Duncan thought about that for a minute. "Well, I am going to do something, Lena. I'm going to be famous one day, like compete in the Olympics, or play professional hockey, or maybe even be president of the United States. But I'm definitely going to become a Navy SEAL, so this autograph could be worth a lot of money someday."

She squished her lips together, then said, "If you say so."

After a few antsy minutes, Lena settled on a pose. She tucked her legs underneath herself and leaned an elbow on the wicker chair arm. He started to draw—but mostly erase, until he discovered that the less he worried about what was coming out onto the paper the better it looked. At one point he asked if she had a sharpener, and she did, of course, because she always carried around a big case for her art supplies. After about a half hour, she demanded to see it.

"Did you make me look like an opossum or something?" She laughed as she grabbed at the sketchpad. She stopped laughing. After a moment she looked up at him, confused. "I thought you didn't know how to draw."

He shrugged. "I don't."

"But . . ." She looked down again. "This kind of looks like me. You got the hair right, and the shape of my face, and the nose and mouth, which are the hardest to do."

"You're just messing with me."

"No! Really. It's kind of good!"

He knew that compared to how good Lena was, his drawing looked like it had been done by a kindergartner. Duncan reached over, yanked the page out of the sketchbook, balled it up, and tossed it over his shoulder.

Lena yelped like she'd been hurt. "What did you do that for?"

"Because it sucked."

Lena jumped from her chair and snatched the wadded-up paper. She sat down and used the sketchpad to try to press it flat. "You're too hard on yourself, Duncan Flynn."

"What's that supposed to mean?"

She glanced up at him, frowning. "You think you have to be perfect now that you're not sick anymore, like you have all this stuff you have to prove to the world."

"That's stupid. I don't have anything to prove to anybody."

"You're not going to win every single race or every single jump, because you're not perfect. You know that, right?" Lena's eyes widened. "Nobody's perfect, Duncan. No drawing is perfect."

"Whatever."

"But . . ." Lena smoothed the paper. "This drawing is good. See?"

Duncan rose from the chair, stood next to her, and

bent down to check out what she was talking about. Lena used her delicate-looking finger to point out the things he'd done the same way she would have. "See how you added shadow here over the eye to give it depth? And how you suggested a lot of dark hair without having to draw it all in?"

"I guess. Sure."

"But more than anything, you saw me. What I mean is, you drew me, a little bit of my personality, not just some random person. And that's why it's good."

Something snapped in him. He didn't know what his problem was, but all of a sudden Lena wasn't just Lena Silva, the little kid who'd been nice to him when he was sick. He suddenly smelled her, and she smelled like rain on summer grass. He felt how close she was to him. And all of a sudden Lena looked different, too. She was pretty, with those nice dark eyes and all that hair and that open smile of hers. She would probably grow up to be a very good-looking girl someday.

Duncan felt a rush of heat all over his body. He didn't know what was happening to him.

Lena continued to talk about the drawing, and he leaned in closer. Without warning, she turned her head and their faces were almost touching.

Well, what was he supposed to do? Back away and make a big deal about the fact that their lips almost met? Because that would make her feel bad about herself, like she had rabies or something. And he didn't want her moping around and crying.

So he kissed her. And oh, boy. Lena definitely kissed him back.

Everything went still. His brain began to hum and his legs felt weak. She placed her hand on his chest, and he almost cried like a baby. He rubbed her back and she arched into it like a cat. And the two of them seemed to hang in the middle of space, just kissing.

Duncan closed his eyes, and as he began to breathe with her, strange and wonderful feelings washed over him. For a second, it really felt like they were the same person, together, discovering stuff that no other two people in the history of the world had ever discovered before.

He pulled away and looked down at her face. Lena was shocked. Her mouth fell open and all she could do was stare.

Now, that was way weird. "Are you okay?"

She nodded, her mouth still open.

"I . . ." Duncan just realized something, and it made him feel like an idiot. "That wasn't your first kiss, was it?"

She nodded again.

"Oh, man." Well, that was a buzzkill. How could he have forgotten that she was three years younger than him? What he had done was probably illegal in the Commonwealth of Massachusetts. His da would haul him over the coals if he found out. Chief Pollard might even throw him in jail.

The only thing Duncan knew to do was pretend the kiss wasn't great and it wasn't special to him. Even though that was by far the best kiss of the seven he'd experienced, he had to convince Lena it was no big deal.

But how do you undo a kiss when it's already been done?

Obviously, Lena wasn't going to have any suggestions, since she still sat there and stared up at him like a space cadet.

"We should probably forget this ever happened, okay?"

That seemed to wake her up. "What?"

"This." Duncan motioned back and forth between the two of them. "I never sat here and drew a terrible picture of you, and we never kissed, okay?"

Oh, man. That made her cry. So after all that, she was still going to mope around and cry anyway. Duncan wondered how long it would be until he understood girls.

He squeezed his head between his hands. "I didn't mean to hurt your feelings. It's just that, you know, I'm older than you. A lot more mature. I'm in eighth grade. And besides, you're really kind of like my little sister."

She didn't say anything, just blinked, making tears roll down her face.

"Don't be mad."

She sniffed.

"I like you, Lena. A lot. It's just that . . ." He couldn't stand the way she was looking at him. At that point he realized that it didn't matter what he said. He wasn't going to make it any better.

"Okay!" Duncan smiled at her like it was just another day. "I guess I'll catch you on the flip side, Lena."

He cleared the porch steps in one leap and never looked back.

Chapter Fifteen

Lena got back from her swim about two a.m., too exhausted to rinse off the seawater and sand. She grabbed a glass of wine, locked the back doors, and headed upstairs, not even bothering with the lights. She made her way into the studio. Her plan was to sit in the dark, stare out at the moonlight on the water, and reach deep down inside herself to try to remember ...

Why? Why had she been so sure all these years? Had she been a fool to believe? Had the time come for her to let it go? Let *him* go?

The sadness had been unshakable. She'd gone numb when Duncan said he didn't remember the afternoon he made the pencil drawing. He didn't remember! That afternoon had been the turning point of Lena's life. It foretold her art, her passion, her career. And he didn't even remember. Apparently, the moment they shared all those years ago wasn't interesting enough for Duncan to file away even as a curiosity.

Lena let her head fall back on the chaise. She thought of the night she told her mentor, Jacqueline Broussard, everything about Duncan, the drawing, and the kiss.

Their conversation had taken place just two weeks before Jacqueline died and, as always, her teacher had listened with care, speaking only when Lena welcomed her
opinion.

"I received a message along with his kiss," Lena had
told her mentor. "It was clear and calm and very matter-
of-fact, not the hormonal emotions of a girl. The message
was from outside of both of us. It wasn't the voice of
anyone I knew, but I sensed she was a very wise woman—
maybe even a goddess. Isn't that bizarre?"

Jacqueline smiled. "You are an artist, my dear. You
swim in a veritable sea of the bizarre. And there is nothing more bizarre than the human heart."

Lena laughed at that.

"You feel deeply, Adelena, and your spirit travels beyond what most people are equipped to embrace. Now,
please go on. Tell me about the message."

Lena had looked down at her hands, embarrassed to
go on. She had never told anyone the details, not even
Sanders. And since she'd never told the story aloud before, she had no idea how absurd it would sound.

"It's all right. I am not here to judge, Adelena."

She looked Jacqueline in the eye. "When his lips
touched mine, I understood something that had always
baffled me—why my mother chose to come to Bayberry
Island, of all the places in the world."

"Interesting."

"I got an answer even though I hadn't asked."

Jacqueline laughed. "Ah, yes. Isn't that the way it usually happens? So what answer did you receive?"

Lena took a deep breath, aware she was about to step
into seriously strange territory. "I suddenly knew, without a doubt, that my mother came to Bayberry so that

Duncan and I could find each other. I don't think she realizes this. I'm telling you, Jacqueline, the understanding was overwhelming, and even as a kid I realized I had been given a glimpse into something very old and very powerful, and it just blew me away."

"Were you frightened?"

Lena shook her head. "I didn't have time to be scared. The kiss was beautiful and intense, and all the while I kept picturing words in my mind: 'It will take time. He must come to you. Do not give up.'" She looked at her teacher, wanting help. "So I've carried that message with me all this time, and I haven't given up on Duncan Flynn."

Jacqueline reached over and took Lena's hands in hers. "Who do you think was speaking to you? You must have an idea."

Lena stiffened at the question.

"You don't have to say, my dear. I already know. And as far as this man goes, if he is in fact your destiny, then you can do nothing to hurry things along. Do you understand?"

Lena nodded.

"My only advice to you is this—live your own life and find joy in it. If Duncan is your true love, he will be drawn to your light, but only when you both are ready."

Lena sighed, so wishing Jacqueline could be with her tonight. She placed her wineglass on the floor and covered her face in her hands.

What a stupid move! She had been so excited about sharing her life and work with Duncan that she'd forgotten all about the drawing. For her it was a familiar part of every studio she'd ever worked in. She'd had it professionally framed with most of the money she'd earned from her first professional sale, and she'd taken it with her all over the world. And yesterday she'd been so focused on Duncan not seeing her charcoal sketch of him that she'd forgotten all about the old drawing. She hadn't been able to get him out of the studio before he saw it.

There was anger in Duncan's eyes when he'd turned to face her. He resented that she'd kept a piece of him. He bristled at the proof that they had a history. Good God! How awful would it have been if he'd seen her charcoal study of him—nude? She closed her eyes tight.

You can do nothing to hurry things along . . .

As the moon danced upon the water, tears slipped down her cheeks.

The Safe Haven kitchen was buzzing today. Though the clambake had started forty years before as a simple tourism-appreciation event put on by the Flynns, those days were long gone. The mermaids had taken over the planning when the fishery went under and the family could no longer afford to host the affair. That had led to a committee, ticket sales, professional caterers, disc jockeys, and banquet tables. Clambake tickets were now the hottest thing going during festival week. Clancy just informed everyone gathered in the kitchen that he'd arrested scalpers on the public dock that morning, trying to sell passes for twice their original value.

"Man, if I had known that, I would have hawked mine online," Nat said.

"Who'da thunk?" Rowan said, grabbing another baking sheet from the cabinet. For reasons Duncan didn't fully understand, the Flynns (and by that he meant his sister) insisted on providing some of the desserts for the clambake. She said it was a way to keep the family involved.

Duncan hadn't helped the family with clambake preparations since high school, and right then he was kicking himself for getting hijacked on his way back from a run.

"Come help me with the mascarpone mixture," Rowan had called out to him.

"I'd love to, but I'm a sweaty mess," he said, gesturing to the T-shirt stuck to his torso.

Rowan curled her upper lip. "You sure are. Grab a shower and come right back down."

And now, not only had Duncan helped assemble a lifetime's worth of tiramisu, but he had been elected chief pacifier rinser and conscripted to play the role of an evil pirate captain in Christina's latest melodrama. The story was about a mermaid bent on saving the world from a one-eyed pirate named "Stinky Joe."

"I'm not stinky. I've got two eyes. And my name is not Joe."

Christina marched over to where Duncan sat with Serena and explained the what-what to him. "Uncle Duncle, this is my play. I am the star. See? I am wearing a tiara, for gracious' sake!" Christina grabbed the crown as it began to slip from her head. "So if I say you are Stinky Joe the evil pirate, then you are." She exhaled deeply, as if she couldn't believe what a diva Duncan was being. "Now it's time for you to attack, so make it scary."

"I'm scared—of her," Ash whispered from the sink.

"We sleep with the lights on," Clancy mumbled.

So from his seat at the table, he waved around a plastic sword as Christina jumped and twirled and carried on. Duncan checked on Serena. She sat in his lap, staring at him with her piercing gaze, chawing away on her binky like there was no tomorrow. The fact that she still reminded him of a cigar-chomping Marine Corps master sergeant he once knew made him slightly uncomfortable.

"If you're going tonight, we could really use some help with cleanup."

Duncan pretended his sister's announcement had been directed elsewhere.

"Come on, Duncan." Clearly, Rowan wasn't fooled by his silence. "Everybody's doing something, and you're here, right? So you might as well pitch in."

Duncan cleared his throat. "I've already made desserts. I've been an evil pirate. And anyway, I'm helping you tonight, aren't I, Clancy?"

His brother popped a carrot in his mouth and shrugged. "I don't know. You put in a lot of hours at Island Day yesterday. I heard you provided some excellent crowd control."

"Yeah." Duncan stood up. "Christina, I need to take a quick break. I'll be right back, okay, sweetie?"

"What?"

"I promise." He leaned down and kissed her forehead.

Duncan looked for someone he could hand the baby to, but everyone was busy. Ash was up to his elbows in carrot-cake batter. Nat was washing dishes. Annie and Rowan were taking stuff out of the oven. And Evie was running the mixer. Mellie was barking orders and keeping everyone in line.

The only other person with a free hand was Clancy. Duncan looked at him and tipped his head toward the back door. "Can I talk to you for a minute?"

"Sure." Clancy smiled at Evie and checked on Christina, who had already returned to her performance blissfully unaware that her dad was taking his leave. "Let's go while the going is good," Clancy said.

"Do you want the baby carrier?" Rowan called out. "It's hanging on a hook in the mudroom. Grab her sun hat as well!"

On the way out, Clancy snatched the pale yellow contraption and a white bonnet with a string. "Ever used one of these?"

"A baby hat?"

Clancy roared with laughter. "No, man. A baby carrier."

Duncan shook his head. Looking at it, he had a hard time believing something designed for his little sister would fit him.

"Ah, c'mon. Let's give it a try. Yellow is so your color."

Clancy pulled a strap up over Duncan's left arm and loosened it to its maximum length. He did the same with the opposite arm, then pulled on the seat to make sure it was secure. "Hand her to me. I'll buckle her back here while you snap up in front."

When all was said and done, Duncan was trussed up like a roasting chicken, but baby Serena seemed happy, her little legs kicking at him as they walked.

Duncan turned to Clancy, alarmed. "Where's the hat?"

"I already put it on her."

Duncan rolled his eyes in relief. "Thank God, because I don't even want to think what would happen to my ass if Serena got sunburned."

"Yeah. That's best left as an unknown."

They ended up wandering along the side yard, heading out toward the carriage house and into the cedars beyond. Which was fine by Duncan, since the beach was crowded and the B and B's front lawn had become the setting for a cutthroat croquet tournament. He needed some privacy.

"I got a problem," Duncan said. He figured he should cut to it, since he knew Clancy was on break and had to get back to work.

"Let me guess. Your problem is about five foot two, with dark hair and dark eyes, her naked flesh dripping water as she comes out of the surf—"

"This is serious."

Clancy's eyebrow arched high. "Okay. No problem. So what's going on?"

Duncan sighed. He really had no one else to confide in but his brother. These last couple months had reminded him that Clancy was an honorable cop and a first-rate family man, and he hadn't given Duncan a single reason to doubt him. But the truth was, Duncan had never relied on Clancy to be the protector of his secrets. He'd never bounced real troubles off of him.

"Hey, man, whatever it is, I'll keep it to myself. It won't go any further. Is it something that happened at Little Creek?"

Duncan glanced over at his younger brother. What people said was true. They really did look alike. They had the same face shape, the same dark hair and blue eyes, though Clancy's were lighter in color—and in temperament.

"Please don't tell anyone, but I'm getting a Purple Heart. The ceremony is in mid-October, probably soon after I get cleared from medical."

Clancy's eyes went huge. "Oh, wow. Man, that's awesome. Really. What an honor."

Duncan shook his head. "I'm not sure I want anybody

to go. I don't want kudos for being the only man from my insertion team who's still alive."

Clancy's eyes popped wide. "I can't imagine how hard it is to carry around that much guilt, but you're getting the medal for a reason, man. Don't dismiss it. What you did to try to save your friends was exceptional. It was an act of bravery."

They walked quietly for several minutes, the wind rustling through the cedars. Serena was happily kicking and patting Duncan's neck with her sticky hands.

"And," Duncan added, "you're right—I also have a problem with Lena."

Clancy tilted his head. "Really, now."

"Yeah. Look, she's a very interesting woman—hard worker, smart, funny, beautiful—and I know she was always nice to me when we were kids. But I'm learning that . . . well . . ."

"She's the one giving you all those gifts?"

Duncan laughed. "Rowan told you?"

"Yep."

"Yes, there's that, but I got over the weirdness of that once I spent some time with her. She really means well. The problem is, well, there's an old spark or something between us, and yesterday I asked her to go to the clambake with me."

Clancy stopped walking, nearly tripping on an exposed pine tree root. "Okay. Sure. Whoa."

"She showed me around her house. You ever seen that place?"

Clancy shook his head. "Just from the outside. It's pretty wicked, huh?"

Duncan blew out air. "She's got this art studio that's . . . I don't even know how to do it justice. It feels as big as an aircraft carrier. It's her world, you know? And she showed it to me."

"Something happened?"

Duncan laughed. "Maybe I'm making too much of this. That's why I wanted to ask you what you thought. But we're in there for a while and having a great conversation. Then out of the blue, she gets nervous on me and tries to shoo me out. Just as I'm heading to the door, I see a drawing on the wall and I . . . Jesus. This is just so weird."

"What? C'mon! You're killing me, man."

"It's a drawing of Lena that I did when I was fourteen. You know, a couple years after I'd grown out of all the bronchitis and asthma and I really thought I was *the shit*."

"I vaguely remember a time like that." Clancy laughed. "But I didn't know you liked to draw."

"I don't. I didn't. But that one afternoon, Lena and I were hanging out on the side porch and I drew a picture of her. I crumpled it up because I thought it sucked, but she grabbed it and started telling me it was good. And then something happened between us. Honestly, I had forgotten all about it until I saw that drawing in her studio."

Clancy frowned. "Go on."

"I kissed her that day. I was fourteen and she was eleven and, looking back, the kiss was way too intense for kids that age. Don't get me wrong. We didn't take it any further, but the kiss itself was kind of, I don't know, powerful, I guess. So it turns out that after all these years, Lena's still got the drawing I did just before I kissed her."

"Hmm."

"It's professionally framed, very nicely matted and everything like it's a freakin' Picasso or something, and there's my signature, big as day. It's right there hanging in her studio, twenty years later."

"Did you ask her about it?"

"Yeah." Duncan pinched the bridge of his nose. "She got mad because I didn't remember that day. And I was ... Man, there was something about the whole situation that didn't sit right with me. It made me feel trapped."

"Oh."

"She told me if I didn't remember the day, then I wouldn't understand why she kept it. And I left."

Clancy looked confused. "But now you do remember?"

Duncan remained quiet for a moment. "I walked home from the North Shore, thinking. I realize now that I intentionally pushed that memory aside. I didn't *want* to remember Lena or that kiss. It was more than I could deal with when I was fourteen."

Serena had started to fuss. Duncan asked, "Did her pacifier fall out?"

Clancy peeked over the edge of the backpack. "Yeah. Hold up. It's stuck between the strap and your shirt. Okay—we're locked and loaded again."

Duncan didn't know what else to say. It bothered him—the whole thing bothered him. That he'd shoved the memory away. That he'd had some kind of connection with Lena that he'd forgotten all about. That such a powerful kiss happened when they were kids, and it was followed twenty years later by that kiss in the Safe Haven kitchen. It made his head spin.

"Look, Duncan. Two people can have the same experience and remember it in completely different ways—it's normal. That's why eyewitness testimony is so unpredictable in criminal cases. What I'm saying is, that day obviously meant a lot to Lena, and she wanted to remember it."

Duncan nodded in agreement.

"I think the real question is—why does that bother you? Are you worried she's a little obsessed with you? Is that what you're asking me?"

Duncan shrugged. "I don't know what I'm asking. All I know is I have absolutely no business blowing on whatever spark is still there between us. I'm outa here, Clancy. I'm not staying. And though Lena is great, she's not *my* great—you know what I mean? I don't have room for something like that in my life."

Clancy gave him a sideways glance.

"What?"

He shrugged. "I don't know, man."

"Just say it."

Clancy shoved his hands in the pockets of his police shorts. "You've always had it figured out. At twelve you set a course and you've never looked back. I've watched it happen—you wouldn't let anybody or anything get in your way, and you sure as hell didn't have time for any scenic detours."

Duncan jolted. "Scenic detours? I've had plenty of nice-looking women in my life, if that's what you mean."

"I'm not talking about *women*. I'm talking about *a woman* or your own damn family. The only reason we've had a chance to even . . ." Clancy caught himself. He shook his head. "Never mind."

Duncan couldn't believe it, but his brother actually looked like he could cry. "Go on."

"All right." Clancy focused on Duncan. "The only reason you got to meet Serena here"—he pulled on the baby's foot—"or play 'Stinky Joe' with my little girl is because you got seriously hurt. If you hadn't been hurt, we wouldn't have had this time with you. And ... that would have been a damn shame." Clancy clamped his jaw tight. "I never fucking thought I'd say this to you, Duncan, but I've missed your ass."

Duncan felt his body freeze up. This was so unexpected. It was downright surreal. "I'm going back to active duty." He heard the flatness in his own voice.

Clancy laughed. "Oh, we know. It's what you were meant to do. We get it."

Duncan shook his head and tried to find the words. "I owe it to my friends, man. I owe it to my best friend, Justin. They're all dead, and the only way I can make any sense of it is to serve in honor of them."

"You sure about that? Haven't you already done your part? The Purple Heart might indicate the Navy thinks you have."

Duncan tipped his head. "Say what?"

"Listen, all I'm asking is this: who exactly do you go out there and risk your life for, Duncan?"

That was obvious, but Duncan humored his brother. "My fallen friends. My fellow SEALs. My country. The way of life I hold dear. The people I love."

Clancy gave him a crooked smile. "Who exactly do you hold dear, brother? Who do you love? Because to be honest, I've never seen you do much holding and loving. What I've seen is a lifetime of pushing away."

He was a little early, but Duncan figured he and Lena needed to iron out a few things before they spent an entire evening together. Lena had surely been thinking this thing to death as much as Duncan had. His plan was to ask her just one question: can we figure this out together? And if she said yes, they'd go from there.

Duncan clutched the flowers and rang the doorbell. Nothing.

He rang it again.

Nothing.

Duncan went around to the garage and jumped high enough to see through the windows. Her SUV was parked inside.

This is bullshit, he thought. It wasn't right to pretend not to be home. She hadn't answered his calls or texts, either.

He rang the bell again and thought he heard music. Maybe she wasn't hiding—maybe she just hadn't heard him at the door.

He turned the doorknob and the door opened wide with barely a touch. Instantly, he got hit with a full-frontal blast of rock 'n' roll surging down the stairs. He recognized the tune.

"Lena?"

First he looked toward the kitchen and great room. Then he craned his neck to look down the guest wing. Maybe the size of the house was the problem—the girl needed an intercom system or at least a set of walkies.

"Lena? Hey, Lena; it's Duncan!" He waited. "Hello?"

Since he'd already entered her home without an invitation, how much worse would it be if he headed upstairs? He repeated her name three times on his way up, and still no answer. At this point, he was starting to worry that something might be wrong.

He got the lay of the land as soon as he reached the

second floor. He smelled the oil paint. The music thumped out of her studio. Exhaust fans whirred and light spilled out into the hallway. She was painting.

"Hey, Lena?"

Duncan turned toward her studio and froze. He might have even stopped breathing. What he saw baffled him, fascinated him, and turned him on—immediately. He knew he had no right to watch this. He should turn right around and leave. He was invading her privacy more than she had ever invaded his. He'd been asleep when she brought him gifts. Duncan had just walked in on Lena while she was in the middle of deeply personal creative work.

Yet he couldn't walk away.

Lena sang along to the lyrics, her movements like a sad and slow dance. There she was, barefoot and damn near naked, pouring her heart out as she sang, swayed, and painted.

Duncan blinked a few times, just to ensure that this wasn't another dream. He was watching a wild creature lost in a raw artistic process—a private process. Lena reached and swayed and sang while slashing paint at the dark canvas. Everything in the room was in movement—her body, her brush, her voice, her hair, even the painting itself, with its moody swirls and strange shapes.

She wore nothing but a thong and a skintight camisole top that she'd knotted under her breasts. There were great swaths of black, red, and blue paint all over her forearms and striped around the back of her perfect hips. Duncan sensed the flowers slip from his fingers and hit the floor. He couldn't stop staring, but he was aware that he couldn't remain there like a Peeping Tom, either.

Duncan leaned down to retrieve the flowers and

slipped into the studio. He reached into the office area and killed the volume.

Lena spun around with a cry, moving so fast and wildly that she nearly lost her balance. Her eyes were startled but fierce, ready to fight whoever had just invaded her sacred space.

"I'm sorry." Duncan took a step toward her.

"What the *hell*?" Lena breathed so hard her paint-smeared belly pushed in and out. It was completely wrong of him, but Duncan's eyes swept down to the thong.

There wasn't a whole lot more in the front than there was in the back.

"What the hell are you *doing* here?" That's when Duncan noticed her eyes were red, as if she'd been crying. "You have no right to just walk in on someone like that!"

"I called your name. You didn't hear me—"

"You're damn right I didn't hear you! I was *working*!"

"I'm here to pick you up for the clambake, Lena."

She frowned and shook her head. "What?"

"We have a date."

Lena tossed her paintbrush and palette to the worktable and put her paint-covered hands on her hips. "A date? Funny, but you left me with the distinct impression that our date was off."

Duncan heard himself moan. This was so not in his wheelhouse. "Did you check your voice mail today? Your texts?"

Lena spun around, scanning the studio for her phone. She hissed. "No. I don't even know where my phone is."

Duncan decided it was now safe to approach the irate artist. "You need a security system or a Rottweiler or *something*."

She squeezed her eyes shut. "I have a state-of-the-art system, thank you very much."

"Well, it's not worth a damn if you don't turn it on."

Suddenly self-conscious, Lena tugged her camisole down over her belly, squeezed her legs together, and crossed them in front of her—as if she could hide how ungodly hot she was. "What do you want, Duncan?"

"I want to take a beautiful woman to a clambake on a beautiful summer evening."

Lena raised her hands in exasperation and let them slap her thighs. "I don't get it. You ran out of here yesterday like you'd seen a freakin' ghost!"

Duncan chuckled a little uncomfortably. "I did." He took a step even closer. "Look, Lena, I'm sorry about how I handled things yesterday. On the walk home the pieces started to fall into place, but by that time it was too late. I'd already come across as an insensitive bastard and I'd pissed you off."

She crossed her arms under her breasts and stuck out a hip in defiance. Clearly, she wanted him to grovel a bit more.

"I remember now—that day was our first kiss."

Her body language relaxed a little, but there was nothing close to a smile on her face.

"I'm not the world's most sentimental guy. It's one of my primary failings."

That got a small twitch at one corner of her mouth. The tension released from around her eyes. "Why?"

Duncan realized this was a trick question. "Why what?

"Why do you want to take me to the clambake?"

Duncan had thought it was going to be much trickier than that. He smiled. "Because I made a commitment. I told you I would pick you up at six, and here I am, a little early, I admit. But I honor my commitments."

Lena let go with a bitter laugh. "You sure know how to make a girl feel special, Lieutenant. Do you think I should go like this?" Lena twirled around and pretended to hold an invisible skirt. "Or am I underdressed?"

Duncan had always found sarcasm a complete waste of time. On the other hand, he wasn't used to putting it all out there with women. But as he looked at Lena standing in front of him, hurt and confusion on her lovely face, he figured he could at least try to give her what she needed.

"Honoring my commitment is not the only reason I'm here." His eyes shot over to the pencil drawing across the room. "Seeing that picture hit me wrong yesterday. My brain doesn't work that way—I don't keep mementos and souvenirs, and I don't treasure memories of things that happened a long time ago. Seriously, the only trinkets I own are the ones you've given me since I've been home."

She tilted her head, listening.

"I think I forgot that day on purpose. I didn't want any loose ends when I left Bayberry for the Academy. I told myself you were just a nerdy kid who used to visit me when I was sick."

"I see."

"But I'm seeing more of the picture now. I remember how good you were to me when I was angry at the world. And I definitely remember that kiss. There was something *unearthly* about it."

"Unearthly." Lena's eyes widened.

"The kiss, not you."

"I'd have to agree with that assessment."

Duncan took yet another step toward her, easing her sticky hand into his. "I like you, Lena. I liked you then and I like you now. I can't say I understand everything between us or what that kiss was all about. But I do know there's no reason for us to make each other miserable just because we happen to be on Bayberry at the same time."

Lena lowered her chin. Her dark eyes softened, and she gave him one of those half smiles. "I need fifteen minutes to clean up." As she walked past him, she kissed his cheek.

It was only then, once Lena had left the room, that Duncan got a good look at the painting she'd been working on.

He took an instinctive step back, his heart suddenly thudding. It was an underwater scene, but this one wasn't a sparkly fantasyland where mermaids frolicked and sunbeams filtered down from above. This shit was dark.

The world she'd created was black and ugly. Sharks swarmed. The water was streaked with blood. Any plant life looked burned or skeletal—and eight lifeless bodies floated off into the gloom. Though it was a huge leap to make, Duncan was sure this painting was about the ambush. The setting may not have been Afghanistan, but the essence of the image captured it perfectly.

If artists channeled emotions into their work, then there was only one way to interpret this painting. Lena was feeling the pain and horror of war—on Duncan's behalf. She was grieving with him.

"I'll be damned," he mumbled to himself.

Chapter Sixteen

"Give me that before you hurt yourself." Rowan removed a large catering dish full of coleslaw from her mother's grasp and slipped it into its designated spot on the buffet line. "The caterers are here to do that, Ma. All we have to do is smile and look pretty and throw it on plates as people walk by."

"Well, they're running behind schedule." Mona frowned. "Everything was supposed to be ready by now. People have started to show up."

"Ma." Rowan rested her hands on her mother's shoulders. "People started showing up at two in the afternoon. And they'll be straggling in until ten. But the food will be served from seven to nine and that's that. Don't worry so much."

Mona shook her head and sighed in frustration. "You know how I get."

"I know." Rowan pulled her mother close for a quick hug. It seemed that in the last year she'd aged more than in the previous five put together. Her arthritis flare-ups were more frequent and the unresolved mess with Rowan's father had drained her. At least her mother had finally hired a lawyer. It wasn't what Rowan had hoped for, but at least it was forward movement of some kind.

Her dream was for her parents to be at peace with each other. How exactly they arrived at that peace—still married or finally divorced—was no longer the biggest concern.

Annie and Evelyn had been enlisted to work the buffet line this year and were already at work with Mellie and the caterers. The mermaids began arriving. Polly gave Rowan a big squeeze as soon as she saw her. "You know you'd look even more beautiful in a nice fantail skirt, honey."

The woman never stopped her campaign to convince Rowan to join the Mermaid Society. She patted Polly's cheek. "Let it go. I beg you."

Polly answered with a typical bawdy laugh but hung on to one of Rowan's hands. "Fine. But it is a sight for my old eyes to see you so happy these days. You have a beautiful family, Rowan Flynn-Wallace. You are blessed."

Rowan pulled back to get a better look at one of her mother's truest friends. Unless she was seeing things, Polly was near tears.

"What's all this?"

Polly sniffed. "Ignore me. I get emotional for no reason nowadays. I wake up some mornings, feel my creaky bones, and just look at myself like *What the fuck?* I'm telling you, getting old is not for pansies."

Rowan was relieved to hear Polly sounding more like herself. "Scared me there for a minute, Poll."

Izzy McCracken arrived, along with Abigail Foster, Layla O'Brien, and Barbara Butcher, and all were decked out in their mermaid finery. Rowan had been observing the Bayberry Island Mermaid Society since she

was a toddler and was well acquainted with their cos-
tuming hierarchy. The merms had everyday-meeting
wear, ritual wear, and festival-week wear. It was during
festival week that they pulled out all the stops—longer
and glossier wigs, fancier coconuts tied on with sequined
ribbon, lots of sea glass and shell jewelry, and elaborately
decorated mermaid skirts.

"Does everyone have a food service hat?" Abigail
waved a clear plastic elasticized cap over their heads.
"We don't want a repeat of last year, people! No long
polyester hair in the pasta salad!"

The ladies continued on with the jobs at hand. Ma had
been right—guests were swarming in. Rowan looked out
on a sea of round banquet tables arranged on the beach
to see that there were few seats left. At least there was
very little wind coming off the ocean this year. Nothing
was more aggravating than trying to keep sand out of the
crab cakes and clams casino.

Suddenly, Rowan heard her mother gasp. Her first
thought was that she'd fallen and she immediately went
to find her. But no. Ma was upright, staring at the line of
guests coming down the beach stairs, her mouth wide-
open.

Polly wandered up to stand behind Mona. "Holy hop-
scotching Jesus," she whispered.

A loud crashing sound caused Rowan to turn around—
Mellie had just lost hold of a stainless-steel tub of condi-
ments. It had clattered to the table and sent packets of
ketchup, tartar sauce, and cocktail sauce shooting to the
four corners of the food tent. She held her hand to her
heart. *"Oh, meu Dues!"*

Rowan spun around, looking for the source of all this
shock and awe. She found it. Duncan looked positively

studly in a crisp white button-down shirt and a pair of dark jeans. On his arm was Lena, relaxed, smiling, and draped in a pale yellow sundress.

Rowan waved frantically for Annie and Evelyn to stand next to her.

Evelyn grabbed Rowan's arm. "Am I hallucinating?"

"O to the MG." Annie got out her smartphone and began taking pictures.

Rowan was horrified. "What are you doing?"

"Nat won't believe me unless I have proof."

By that time, the rest of the merms had abandoned their volunteer stations to cluster near Mona. There was a great deal of whispering and shushing going on.

Duncan gently cradled Lena's arm in the crook of his elbow. Lena's loose hair fell over her shoulders and brushed against Duncan's shirt. The fact that Duncan didn't immediately adjust for more personal space shocked Rowan.

"He's so freakin' handsome," Annie said.

Everyone watched, their heads turning in silent admiration as Lena and Duncan headed out toward the tables. Duncan found two seats together and pulled out Lena's chair, then tucked her in once seated.

Rowan began smacking Annie's forearm. "Look at him! He's a perfect gentleman! Did you just see that?"

The women watched Duncan lean down and whisper in Lena's ear. It seemed as if he was asking her what she'd like to drink.

"Holy shit—he's going to the bar! He's getting her a cocktail!" Annie kept snapping away.

Rowan turned her attention to her mother. Right there, not ten feet away in the sand, she saw something she'd never seen in her life. Mona Flynn and Imelda

Silva stood with their arms around each other, their heads inclined and touching. It wasn't that they didn't like each other, because they had loved each other for a long time. But Mellie and Mona had never behaved like BFFs.

Though it was possible she would be intruding, Rowan came to stand with the two women.

"What do you make of that, Rowan?"

"I'm not sure, Ma."

Mellie shook her head and mumbled to herself in Portuguese.

"C'mon, now, Mellie. You can't keep your thoughts to yourself." Mona wasn't letting the moment slip by.

"I said . . ." she shook her head. "I never thought I would see my Lena . . . Her men friends have always just been stories to me, when she spoke of them at all. She certainly never brought anyone home to meet me."

"Same for Duncan." Mona chuckled. "Maybe they have always preferred the ones already *at* home."

The women watched Duncan bring a glass of wine to Lena and sit down next to her. The pair talked and laughed. Duncan leaned forward and whispered something to her and Lena nodded. For the first time ever, Rowan saw her brother as just a guy—a normal guy.

She thought back to a conversation the three siblings had once had. It was at Clancy's wedding to his bat-shit-crazy first wife. Rowan and her brothers were hanging out on the patio of the reception location, and Clancy must have been feeling lucky, because he decided to give Duncan a hard time.

"Do you think you'll ever get married, bro?"

Duncan scanned the summertime surroundings with a stoic, manly expression, modeling his Navy dress whites. Rowan figured he was doing his best impression of *An Officer and a Gentleman*. "The topic doesn't even interest me," he replied.

Duncan and Rowan laughed.

"I guess you're just too type A for marriage," Rowan suggested.

"Yeah," Clancy said. "If 'A' is for asshole."

As Rowan watched Duncan now, smiling and laughing with his body and face relaxed, she knew they had been hard on him. Clancy's wedding day wasn't long after Duncan had returned from his first tour in Afghanistan. They'd had no idea what was going on in his head or his heart, and Duncan clearly hadn't been able to share it. They had been jerks to him.

"Well, lookie here. Our last success story." Polly slipped in next to Rowan. She sighed with deep satisfaction. "We should pat ourselves on the back for a job well done on this one, girls."

"Polly!" Mona dropped from Mellie's embrace and turned, her face bright pink with anger. "Shut up," she hissed.

When was the last time anyone had ever heard Mona Flynn say those two words? Never.

Izzy stepped forward. "I don't see the harm at this point, Mona. It's not like we're going to get any more opportunities to see the results of our work."

"What are you talking about?" Mellie asked. She put her hands on her hips. "Did you mess with Adelena?"

"Oh, for God's sake, everyone." Polly shook her head. "We'll be defunct by October anyway, so what does it matter?"

"Maybe this really is our last happy ending," Layla said,

her lips trembling. "We've certainly had a good run—Annie and Nat, Rowan and Ash, Clancy and Evie ..."

Mona hissed, *"Shut. Up."*

Rowan rubbed her forehead. Her brain hurt. What was going on here? Were the merms taking credit for her marriage? That of Annie and Nat? And her brother and Evie? Now? After they'd spent years vigorously denying any meddling? Rowan had to laugh—these women were ridiculous.

One of the caterers waved her arms to get Rowan's attention. She began tapping at her wristwatch.

"Defunct?" Rowan scanned the faces of the mermaids. "What do you mean by *defunct*?"

Mona shook her head. Polly turned away.

"We've decided to shut down the Mermaid Society after all the loose ends are tied up from this festival week. We're going to close the books, cancel our non-profit status, and just put an end to it."

A low humming went through Rowan's body. The news shocked her.

"Say what?" Annie asked.

Polly shrugged. "You know, we're going to pull the plug. Why should we hang around and die a little more every day?"

Rowan's gaze flashed to her mother. "What is she talking about?"

Mona's mouth was tight, and she had crossed her arms over her coconuts. She was angry, angry, angry.

Abigail spoke up. "Mona, don't be mad at Polly for telling the truth."

"Ma?"

"Fine!" Mona took a deep breath and addressed

Rowan. "By unanimous vote, we have decided we're an anachronism—a throwback to another time—and we are no longer relevant in today's society. We've decided it's time for us to let it go."

Annie, Evelyn, and Rowan shared a glance. Annie said, "But there's been a Mermaid Society as long as there's been a mermaid."

"That is incorrect," Izzy said. "The fountain was unveiled in 1885, and the Mermaid Society was not born until three years later."

"Well, it still seems kind of drastic to end it now," Evelyn said. "Don't you all enjoy getting together? I always thought it was a kind of girls club."

"Not quite," Mona said.

"We're getting old, Annie." Abigail addressed the younger women. "And, Rowan, your mother deserves to relax at this point in her life. The truth is, now that Darinda went back to the mainland, we have no choice."

"Nobody wants to be president," Barbara said.

Layla concurred. "We are worn the hell *out*. By now every one of us has some kind of sensitivity."

Rowan cupped her mother's elbow in her palm. "I didn't know you were planning to do this. It's so ... permanent."

Mona's eyes flashed with grief. "There is not a living soul to hand the society over to, let alone a woman who understands its history and respects its role in the culture of our island."

Suddenly, it all made sense to Rowan. She looked over to see Annie gazing skyward and Evelyn shaking her head.

"I see. So this is a guilt trip. You're trying to make the

three of us feel guilty because we've always said weren't interested in joining."

"No, my dear daughter." Mona shook her head. "It's not a guilt trip. It's the truth. I'm sixty-nine. Polly will be turning sixty—"

"Hey, hey. Watch it."

Mona continued. "And anyway, it's not just that you haven't shown interest, Rowan. You have repeatedly ridiculed our sacred mission and called us crazy for believing in the powers of the Goddess of the Sea."

Rowan felt Annie move closer.

"You and Annie have considered yourselves above becoming members of the Mermaid Society. So, even if you suddenly decided you wanted to join us, we could not, in good conscience, leave the mystery of the mermaid in your hands."

Izzy pursed her lips in the direction of Rowan, Annie, Evie, then said, "Oh, snap!"

"I'd ask you join me on a walk, but I think it'd be a little crowded."

Lena glanced at their tirelessly attentive audience and chuckled. From the moment they'd arrived, Lena and Duncan had been inspected, evaluated, and speculated upon by nearly every woman serving at the food tent—Lena's mother included.

Whatever thoughts were going on in Imelda Silva's head, Lena was sure she'd hear all about them.

"I had no idea we'd be subjected to this much scrutiny." Duncan had made the same observation in a variety of ways through the evening. Each time, he'd looked uncomfortable.

Lena knew bringing a date to such a public function—for the prying eyes of all of Bayberry Island to see—had been a major deal for Duncan. She had watched him struggle. Half the time he was enjoying himself. Half the time he was glancing over his shoulder.

They were sitting at one of the banquet tables, a flickering candle between them. Everyone else who'd been seated at their table had moved to the dance floor.

"I'm not much of a dancer." He sounded apologetic.

Lena nearly swooned. This new courteous and gentlemanly Duncan Flynn was almost too much for a girl to take. She was not the shallow type by any stretch of the definition, but Lena could admit the truth: Duncan would be hot even if he behaved like the biggest tool in the world. He was far hotter as a sweet and kind gentleman, even if it was in spite of himself, and tonight, as he focused on her with genuine interest, Lena had to work to keep her composure.

For the occasion, Duncan had shaved and combed back his hair, and his smooth, olive-brown skin glowed against the white of his shirt. And those jeans? She had become dizzy at the sight of him standing there in her studio with flowers in his hand, the dark denim hugging the hard contours of his slim hips and muscled thighs. Sure, Duncan had looked sexy in his tight Island Day police department polo shirt, but tonight he was a sizzling-hot piece of man candy, and all she could think about was when she would taste him again. Lena fanned herself.

"But if you'd like to, we can try."

She smiled at Duncan, placed her hand in his, and nodded. "Let's throw caution to the wind, Lieutenant."

The music selection that night had been up and down the spectrum in an attempt to appeal to every demographic at the clambake. The unfortunate result was that a big-band number might be followed by heavy metal, which might lead into country and then rap. So when Lena stepped on the dance floor with Duncan, she expected fate to have a sense of humor.

They burst out laughing as soon as the speakers came to life. It was the classic rhythm-and-blues tune "Sea of Love."

"So *do* you remember when we first met?" Lena asked.

"I do now," he said.

Duncan was a much better dancer than he'd let on, and Lena enjoyed the sensation of easing in to his body as he moved. She rested her head against his chest and closed her eyes. At first she thought to herself, *It's been a long, long time since any man has felt this good.* Then she realized that no man ever had.

"You smell good," Duncan said. "I've noticed it before. Do you wear a perfume?"

She smiled, feeling her cheek press against his chest. "Yes. It's called linseed oil and cerulean blue."

He chuckled. "Oh, it's more than that."

"Okay—its linseed oil, cerulean blue, and Lena Silva."

"That's what I'm talkin' about."

They swayed to the music, and eventually Lena raised her head to smile at him. She caught him with the curtain open, and his eyes revealed a depth of feeling Lena hadn't expected. He collected himself, however, and gave her a polite smile.

"What's on your mind?"

Duncan took his eyes from hers and gazed over her head, toward the ocean. "Did you know that one of your paintings was in my room when I first got back? Over the fireplace mantel?"

"Really? Which one?"

He looked down at her. "You didn't know it was there?"

She thought that an odd question, but answered it honestly. "Duncan, even before Ash and Rowan renovated the house, my paintings were all over the bed-and-breakfast. Tourists would see them on the walls and buy them on the spot, and I gave a cut to Rowan."

Duncan seemed to mull that over.

"And then, when the renovations were finishing up, Ash wanted to buy thirty-two paintings for permanent display throughout the house and guest rooms."

"Wow."

"Well, aren't you going to tell me which one was in your room?"

Duncan looked down at her, his eyes suddenly heavy and unmistakably sexual. Lena went still inside, wondering what just happened and where this conversation was headed.

"It was just one little dark-haired mermaid on the sea floor. She was on her tummy, her head turned and resting on her bent arms. Her eyes were partly closed, and she had the smile of a woman who wanted a whole lot more of the somethin'-somethin' she'd just had."

Lena laughed, a little uncomfortably. "Okay. I know the one."

"I had to take it down and put it in the attic. She would not give me any peace."

"Oh, *really*?"

"But the next day another mermaid painting was in her place. After I took that one down, another appeared. I think my mother wanted to make sure I had a sexy mermaid roommate at all times."

Lena chuckled. "Mona and her mermaids."

"That first mermaid was you." Duncan dipped his head to get closer. "Come on, now—admit it. That was you up there making it impossible for me to sleep."

"What?" She leaned away from him, only to feel his hands tighten around her waist. He wasn't letting her pull away. "Not intentionally, Duncan. I suppose some of me slips into all of my paintings. But I never intend anything to be a self-portrait, and I sure didn't arrange for it to be in your room."

"Whatever you say, Miss Silva." He pulled her close again, encouraging her to rest her head on his chest, and sang along with the music, asking her to come with him to the sea.

Chapter Seventeen

"Thank you, Duncan. I had such a good time to-night."

He knew how the evening should end. This was when he should get out of the car and open her door. He should walk her to the porch, give her a friendly peck good night, and make sure she got inside safely.

That was what any sane man in his position would do. Any sane and decent man planning to leave the island as soon as possible would not think about taking Lena Silva into his arms and kissing her until she melted in surrender against him. A decent man wouldn't still be fighting off the mental image of her appearing from the waves or the powerful vision of her bare flesh as she became lost in her painting. A sane man wouldn't keep thinking of how she felt pressed against his chest and how magical it was to breathe in the scent of her skin and hair.

It was settled then: Duncan was a crazy and selfish bastard. He said, "Since we couldn't walk on the public beach, how about we end the night with a stroll on a private one?"

Her face spread wide in a smile. "That sounds lovely."

He took her hand as they walked through the over-grown property toward the beach steps. As shocking as it was to him, this kind of intimacy with Lena felt natural. He couldn't even recall the last time he'd walked around holding a woman's hand, but with Lena he felt like he'd been doing it all his life.

"Moondance Beach." Duncan said those words once they rose over the dune. Immediately, he regretted every time he had made fun of the name she'd chosen for this piece of land. Tonight he saw why the name was perfect. The moon danced on the water, giving an ethereal glow to everything around them—the sand, the sea grass, Lena's skin.

Duncan looked down and smiled at her. It was like they were about to step into a magical fairyland.

They took off their shoes and walked, arms swinging freely. For a few minutes they talked about nothing in particular, but then Lena dropped the bomb.

"How did it go in Virginia? My mom told me you were going back to the joint base at Little Creek–Fort Story to talk with your higher-ups."

Duncan gave a nod. He knew Lena would bring up the topic sooner or later, but weren't women supposed to kick back and enjoy moonlit walks on the beach? And what was with her use of the formal name for the home of SEAL Team 2?

Lena explained before he could ask. "I've always tried to get the latest news about you through my mom, Rowan, and Mona. I did some research on your team and what it does. But you've managed to remain a mystery man. Nobody ever knows exactly where you are or what you're doing."

Duncan didn't reply, but he noticed how strange it was that he really didn't mind Lena asking him about his job. For some reason, he was less touchy about it with her.

"When I heard what happened, I . . ." Lena didn't finish her sentence. She looked out over the dune and kept walking.

"Are you asking me to tell you what happened the night I was injured?"

Her head snapped around, and she nodded quickly. "I don't want to push you."

He chuckled. "You couldn't if you wanted to."

He told her. Duncan shared with Lena the basic series of events, leaving out all of the gore and most of his survivor's guilt. He got through it, though he did hear how detached his voice sounded as he talked about his friends dying.

Lena was quiet for several minutes. She had slowed her walk and seemed to be lost in her own thoughts. Suddenly, she said, "You know it's not your fault."

Fuck. This was the last thing he wanted to do—talk about his level of culpability the night of the ambush. Honestly, he'd been hoping maybe Lena would suggest they go skinny-dipping.

It took him a minute to gather his thoughts. She cared about him, obviously, but she didn't have a clue about his world. But he also knew she would stay clueless unless he shared some of it with her. It would take real effort not to sound like he was lecturing her.

"Most people have the wrong idea about what it means to be a SEAL. We're not action heroes, and it's not all about surviving Hell Week and living a real-life *Zero Dark Thirty*. My only job—the only thing I became a SEAL to do—was to have the six of every man on my team."

Lena frowned. "The six?"

"Yeah. The expression 'I've got your six' is the same as saying 'I've got your back.' My job was to watch over my teammates and make sure nothing happened to them. It's what being a SEAL is about—building a team that operates as a single unit, a single living organism. Each part is responsible for the whole. And I failed the other members of my squad that night. They died and I didn't."

Lena didn't speak. She just kept her eyes trained on Duncan, letting him speak. He appreciated that.

"As far as it being my fault—I realize I did not go out there intending to get my teammates killed. Unfortunately, the intent doesn't matter if the end result is death."

"You tried your best."

"I failed them."

"Duncan, you were severely injured and you did the impossible to get to them."

"They were already dead."

"But you didn't kill them."

Duncan thought it was sweet that Lena wanted to defend his honor, but she was out of her league. "You don't understand, Lena. Let it drop."

She stopped walking and stood directly in front of him. "I do understand the burden of believing you let someone down."

Duncan decided to humor her. "How so?"

She crossed her arms over her stomach, as if she were cold. The faint wind rippled her hair. "Six years ago, I was selected to study in New York with a gifted painter named Jacqueline Broussard. She was eighty at the time, still brilliant and beautiful and funny. She had an impeccable eye for color. Jacqueline passed down her knowledge of mixing custom pigments, which probably sounds silly to you, but it was a gift she bestowed to me—an inheritance. Out of all the students she'd had, she chose me to carry her method forward. Honestly, she was the most beautiful human being I've ever known, and I let her down."

He was genuinely intrigued. "What happened?"

Duncan thought he saw Lena shiver before she spoke.

"I took her to a doctor's appointment in Manhattan one day, and since it was going to be several hours, she told me to go back to the studio and continue with my work in progress until she called me. She knew that I was right in the middle of a painting. So I did. But I lost track of time, and I didn't hear my phone—"

"Sounds familiar."

Lena smiled sadly at him. "She decided to go home on her own and hailed a taxi. As she was walking up the front steps of the loft, she had a stroke and died—half on the steps and half on the sidewalk. She was minutes away from safety and comfort. She died alone. I broke my promise."

Duncan touched her bare upper arms. "I'm sorry, Lena."

She nodded.

"I hope this doesn't sound insensitive, but she likely would have died even if you were with her. It sounds like she had a long and wonderful life. But with sudden strokes like that, you probably couldn't have done anything to stop her passing, even if you'd been right there at her side. It's not your fault."

She raised her face and her eyes flashed. "Then why is it *your* fault?"

"Say what?"

"Duncan, you left out a few details of your story. From what I understand, a burning car fell on you. Your side was on fire and your leg was broken in several places—yet you still managed to push that freaking car off of you and walk on your broken bones to try to help your friends."

"What's your point?"

Lena laughed. "My point is, Lieutenant, that you aren't a machine. You're a man, a mortal human being, and your friends were killed because something went horribly wrong, and you were not the cause of it." She tipped her head. "Think about it, Duncan. If I am not to blame for Jacqueline, then you sure as hell aren't to blame for the deaths of your teammates."

She turned and began walking again, and he fell into step with her. The fact that Duncan had no reply amazed him. Yes, Lena was a compact package of female, but she was a force all her own.

Duncan felt something begin to unknot in his heart, loosen enough to accommodate an unusual concept. He dared to want Lena. He dared to wonder if there might be a place in his life for her. But as abruptly as the opening appeared, reality sealed it shut again.

"Lena, I don't have a normal job. I'm not a normal man."

She laughed. "Amen to that! Fortunately, I'm not a normal woman and I don't have a normal job, so none of that freaks me out."

He looked sideways at her, stunned by how beautiful she looked bathed in moonlight. But she shivered again. "If I had a jacket or a sweater, I'd give it to you. I could take off my shirt . . ." Duncan began to unbutton his cotton dress shirt.

Lena stopped him by touching his arm. "It's okay. You don't have to go all Chippendales on me."

"Ha. Well, if you won't let me be a male stripper, then just let me be a gentleman." Duncan wrapped his arm around her shoulders and pulled her close to his side. "Is this okay?"

Her voice was a whisper. "It's very okay."

They strolled together like that for several minutes, not talking, their feet kicking the surf in unison. Duncan reveled in the feel of Lena's small body tucked up next to his. Soon he broke the silence.

"You know, Lena, I've been wanting to ask you something."

"Now's a good time."

Duncan smiled. "About that night in the Safe Haven kitchen . . ."

"Go ahead."

"When you pushed me off—which you had every right to do, don't get me wrong—you said, 'This is not the way.' What did you mean by that?"

She slipped her arm around his waist, as if assuring him that tonight she would not push him away. "I didn't want our first kiss to be like that. I had hoped that if we ever got to the point where we'd want to kiss each other, it would be after spending time together, getting to know the adult people we've become, you know . . ." She looked up at him and gave him a half smile. "Exactly what we're doing now. Talking. Enjoying the process. Enjoying each other."

"Hmm. I hate to be a stickler about this, but technically, that wasn't our first kiss."

She giggled. "Our first *grown-up* kiss, then."

Duncan pulled her tighter. "And it was pretty damn grown-up."

"It certainly was."

"And kind of wild."

"Kind of."

"But I still think there's room for improvement."

"Oh, really?" She looked up at him with a teasing grin.

"Sure—the pacing, the technique, the *artistry* of the execution."

"Oh, so you're some kind of sensual *artiste*?"

"Damn right, and my canvas is your lips."

Lena bent over and started guffawing. Duncan laughed, too, harder than he'd laughed in many months. The last person he'd laughed like this with was Justin, just days before he died. Not until this instant had Duncan realized how much he'd missed this kind of laughter.

Lena pulled away from his embrace, walking backward in the surf, facing him. "You're pretty funny, Duncan. You're a lot funnier now than when you were a kid."

"No kidding? Well, you've changed some yourself."

She batted her eyelashes. "Do tell."

Duncan took in the whole picture Lena presented— an open and happy face, gorgeous eyes, a perfectly sleek body, and that great laugh—and he realized that he had been enjoying their conversation so much that he'd forgotten he was chatting with the most drop-dead gorgeous woman he'd ever known. But he decided to start his list with something other than the physical.

"For starters, you were much quieter back then."

"And now I talk too much?"

"Not *too* much, but a lot more than you used to. And you're not nearly as shy."

"Huh."

"The shyness has morphed into something else, a

mysterious quality. You're interesting. You're not like anyone else I've ever known." He suddenly realized he was babbling. It wasn't like him. Duncan stopped walking and refocused. "I guess what I'm trying to say is that I find you to be a fascinating woman, Adelena Silva."

"What else is different about me?" she asked.

Duncan shook his head, smiling to himself. "I think this goes without saying, but physically, you have changed dramatically. I remembered you as this scrawny little thing, mousy, and kind of a nerd."

"No way!" She pretended to be shocked.

"My point is you're a woman now, all filled out and ..." He stopped himself. "You're smart and talented and you've made a wonderful life for yourself. I am happy for you, Lena. I'm blown away by what you've become."

She took a step closer to him, looked up, and took his hands in hers.

"And what about you, Duncan? I am in awe of what you've done with your life—the dedication and discipline. We may not have kept in touch over the years, but I've always kept you in my thoughts and prayed that you were safe."

He nodded. "Thank you."

"And I am immensely grateful that you are still alive. I know the world has so much more in store for you."

"I appreciate that."

"So unless you have to be somewhere else right now ..."

"What are you ...?"

Lena began wiggling and tugging on the hem of her sundress until the skirt was waaay up over her knees. "What do you say we work on our artistry?" Without warning, Lena jumped up. She threw her arms around Duncan's neck and her legs around his waist.

"Whoa! Hey!" He caught her under her bottom and staggered back a step or two, laughing the whole time. "Is this what it means to have a woman throw herself at you?"

Lena's face was so close to his that he felt her warm breath on his cheek. Slowly, teasingly, she dropped her half-smiling mouth to his. He welcomed her, pulled her closer. Instantly, it was there—the same power, the same drive and desire that had been present in the kitchen. But this time Lena had provided the spark. Lena was making it very clear that this was what she wanted.

The kiss spiraled into something hot and needy, and Lena did not retreat from the demands he made. She opened for him. She kissed him back. She clutched him between her thighs. Lena brought her hands to either side of Duncan's face and cradled him with tenderness, all while she devoured him.

Eventually, Lena loosened her grip on his waist and began to slide down the front of his body. He let her go, not sure if it meant they were done or just beginning. When her toes touched the sand and she gazed up at him, he nearly exploded. There they were, the eyes from his dream—*come back to me, lover; I want you here with me; I'm waiting . . .*

"I think I might need some help with my zipper," she said. "Would you mind?" She turned slowly, lifted her hair from her neck, and waited.

The fingers Duncan brought to that zipper were trembling with need—and uncertainty. *What the hell am I doing?* If he made love to Lena, it would only add another layer of messiness on top of an already complicated situation. As it was, Lena would be hurt when he shipped out, and they hadn't made love. What would happen after she gave herself to him? How much more painful would his leaving be for her?

He whispered in her ear, "Are you sure?" Lena nodded, so Duncan tugged on the zipper and watched the yellow cotton fabric part down the center of her straight, smooth back. Guided only by the moonlight, he traced his finger down her spine, watching her flesh react. She was thin, but not skinny. He could see the barest glimpse of muscle at her shoulders. He saw the swell of her ass just below the open zipper. No panties.

No way was he getting out of this alive.

"Lena—"

"Very sure," she said, glancing over her shoulder.

Duncan caressed her delicate shoulders and slowly pushed the thin dress straps down her upper arms, past her elbows, down her forearms and hands. Lena stepped out of the dress and remained facing away from him. She reached for her hair and let it sway loose down the middle of her back, a simple gesture packed with so much sensual energy that it made him weak in the knees.

Lena was once again naked on Moondance Beach, but this time he hadn't accidentally stumbled upon her. She was baring herself to him, giving herself to him.

"I want you, Duncan."

Still facing away, Lena stepped backward and pressed her hot, bare flesh against the front of his clothed body, as if making the decision for him. Duncan had to admit that in Lena's presence, he was no longer proficient in the practice of mind over matter. He seemed defenseless when it came to Adelena Silva.

He brushed his fingertips down the sides of her neck

and across her shoulders. He reached from behind to cup her breasts and heard his own sigh of pleasure—damn but she felt perfect. He traced the ridges of her ribs and covered her small, flat tummy with his hands. He stayed there, frozen, feeling her heat radiate into his skin, giving her one last chance to deny him.

"End this now, Lena," he said. "I'm a selfish bastard, and once I get my orders I'll be leaving on the first thing smokin' off this island. Tell me to stop."

Slowly—slowly and intentionally—she pushed against the front of his jeans and moved her bottom in a seductive rhythm. And with that, the pin was pulled.

"All that matters is that right now you're with me. And right now I don't want you to stop."

He turned Lena around and held her hands in his. Yes. This was the image that had burned into his brain that night—the delicate and feminine, perfectly formed petite curves of a woman with dark hair, dark eyes, and the teasing shape of that neat triangle between her legs. She looked tiny and vulnerable, but he already knew the power she would soon wield over him.

Lena's fingers were at his shirt buttons. She was no-nonsense about it, but didn't rush, her soft hands sliding hot over his chest, across his abs, down the length of his arms. She made small moaning sounds as she touched him, and he wondered if she was even aware she was doing it.

She raised her eyes to him, and Duncan saw a look of awe on her face. "You are magnificent," she said. "Perfect."

"Far from it, I'm afraid."

She shook her head. "Let me admire you, Duncan.

Let me take joy in seeing you for the first time. You are more beautiful than I could have imagined."

Her fingers fluttered down the burn scars on his right side. "These are like waves on the ocean," she said, not hesitating or pulling away. She made no other comments on his scars and did not ask any more questions. It was as if she was learning him, understanding him, and taking him in—flaws included. The idea of that caused his throat to narrow. The exchange was almost too deep, too intimate.

She reached for his belt, and his brain snapped to attention. Without a wasted movement, she unbuckled his belt, unbuttoned the waistband of his jeans, and opened the fly. Immediately, he felt the heat of her little hands pushing inside the waistband of his boxer briefs—and ripping everything down to his ankles.

Lena raised those dark, seductive eyes to his cock, and it was on. She cradled his balls in one hand and wrapped the other as tightly around him as she could manage. Her touch was gentle but not ticklish. It was just like in the dream—the caress was clearly her gift to him. She was just as bent on giving as receiving.

"You are magnificent—absolutely everywhere."

Duncan had to speak up before the lust fried his last functioning brain cell. "Lena, I don't have a condom. I had no idea—"

"Are you healthy?"

"I've had every lab test known to modern medicine since the ambush. Absolutely."

"I'm healthy, too," she said. "I haven't been with a man in two years."

"Whaa—" As interesting as that statement had been,

Duncan's mind went blank the instant her mouth opened and the tip of his cock slipped inside. He lifted his chin to the sky and let out a groan of surprise and gratitude. The sensation was magical, beautiful, lusty . . . and he loved every second of it. Until he realized that Lena had to be on her knees in the sand.

"You don't have to—"

She chuckled with her lips snug around him, and the vibration just about sent him shooting to the stars.

She played with him using her tongue and lips and teeth.

"Talk about an artiste," he mumbled. She continued to bring him an insane amount of pleasure until he couldn't take it anymore. He reached for her, pulled her up, and took her in his arms. His body knew how to embrace her, exactly how she would fit against him, and Duncan dove in. He needed her. He had to have her. He couldn't wait another second.

While they had been otherwise occupied, the tide had begun to move in. Water began to rise to Duncan's ankles. With his mouth planted firmly on hers, Duncan followed his instincts. He carried his lady of the waves into the dark water, devouring her with his mouth, sensing her shape and weight in his arms. She was so light he could carry her forever.

The water rose up to meet them, gentle waves lapping at their naked skin. Duncan realized it was inexplicably warm, as if the water had changed temperature just for them. Sure, he'd had his share of skinny-dipping sex over the years, but nothing had come anywhere close to the intensity of this moment. He had the distinct sensation that he was carrying Lena over a threshold.

Suddenly, she slipped out of his grasp and disappeared. Duncan stood on the sandbar with his eyes focused on the surface of the dark water. Was she toying with him? She couldn't possibly be in distress, could she? When Lena reappeared, she was nearly ten yards away.

He laughed. "Is this a challenge? A contest?"

Lena giggled and dove underwater again, her pointed toes disappearing without a splash in the roll of a gentle wave. Well, of course she was a good swimmer, Duncan reasoned. Any woman who swims in the Atlantic naked and alone in the middle of the night had to be comfortable with her skills.

Duncan had a few skills of his own. He used his training to go still and wait until he could pinpoint her movement. In a perfect maneuver, he dived under and cut her off mid–dolphin kick, then pulled her up to the surface.

"Hey!" she said, pushing water from her face. She began laughing.

"I thought you wanted me to catch you," he said, scooping her around the waist and pulling her to him. "So you'd better consider yourself caught."

Lena's expression morphed from delight to desire as their bodies rose and fell with the rhythm of the sea. They didn't speak for a few moments, but simply allowed the ocean to rock them, eye to eye, skin on skin.

Without a word, Lena brought her open legs around Duncan's waist. "Make love to me," she whispered in his ear, dragging her lips down the side of his neck. "Don't make me wait any longer."

Lena surrendered to the things she had always loved most—the ocean and Duncan Flynn. He gave her more than just his body; he gave her his spirit, too. When he was inside her, rocking her, taking her in rhythm with the waves, Lena felt the whole world shift on its axis. She suddenly knew—she had not been a fool for waiting.

Duncan Flynn was wild and greedy as he controlled her, moving her up and down on him, lowering her hair into the water as he deepened his thrust. When he kissed her, it bordered on rough, his lips and tongue and teeth consuming her. She felt it—it was just as much a release and a relief for him as it was for her.

"Oh, God, Lena." Duncan raised his face to the moon as he took her over and over again. From her own fog of bliss she saw the changes wash over his face. He was open. He was free. He had allowed himself to meld with her in the most ancient way possible.

The sea supported them and caressed them. They became part of the sea as they became part of each other. And when Duncan cried out and emptied himself inside her, he joined with the salty, life-giving essence of the ocean. With Lena, he returned to his origins.

They were happy and relaxed afterward, Duncan chasing her up the beach stairs and into the house. They shared a warm shower, raided the refrigerator, and eventually made it to her bed. Duncan made love to her through the night. She broke apart in his arms more times than she could count.

At one point, just as she began to drift off for another few minutes of sleep, she swore she heard a familiar tune in Duncan's deep whisper, asking her to come with him to the sea of love.

Chapter Eighteen

Seventeen years ago ...

"Hey, kid."

Lena winced when Duncan's hand tapped down on her head. She hated it every time he did that to her, which was often. These days, in the middle of Duncan's senior year, it was the only way he acknowledged that Lena was alive and drawing oxygen. He never noticed her at school. But at the Safe Haven, he would pat her head if they passed in the downstairs hallway or sat near each other at meals, like this morning. And every time he patted her head, she felt a kindergartner, a trained seal, or a stray dog.

Sometimes she thought it would be better if he didn't see her at all, anywhere.

Lena felt two sets of eyes on her. She knew without checking that her mother and Mona were studying her with sympathy, and even though she hadn't had a single bite of cereal yet, she was ready to excuse herself from the table.

But leaving wouldn't be an option on that particular

morning. Helium balloons were still tied to the dining room light sconces, and twisted crepe paper hung from the chandeliers. Frasier's booming laugh echoed off the walls and Duncan was the man of the hour. Clearly, breakfast was on its way to being a continuance of last night's big celebration.

Two days ago, Duncan had been accepted to the U.S. Naval Academy. Half the island had been invited to the Safe Haven last night to share in the excitement. Everyone kept saying, "Oh, look! A local boy on his way to becoming a hero!"

Yay.

Since Duncan had been planning for this since he was twelve, Lena had long ago checked the map to see how far Annapolis, Maryland, was from Bayberry Island, Massachusetts. The news wasn't good. To travel by car and car ferry it was four hundred ninety-one miles. On a boat it would be three hundred eighty-seven nautical miles from the entrance of the Chesapeake Bay to the public dock at Bayberry Island.

By land or sea, it sucked.

"Hey, Lena, could you pass the orange juice?" Duncan reached across the table and held out his hand. He barely looked her in the eye.

"Sure."

Duncan's fingers accidentally brushed against hers during the transfer, and Lena stifled a gasp. She kept her head down, shoveled in her Grape-Nuts, and pretended not to listen to the breakfast-table conversation.

"By God, I knew you'd do it, son."

"Thanks, Da."

Frasier raised his coffee cup. "This will be the first time in the history of the Flynns that a man will take to the sea for something other than catching fish!" Frasier laughed at his own joke. No one else did, probably because they'd heard it at least five times the night before.

"When's your orientation?" Clancy asked his brother.

"Plebe Summer starts in July."

"Wait. You have to waste all of next summer just to get oriented?"

Duncan shook his head. "The Navy isn't for slackers, little brother. From here on out, it's serious business."

Duncan's voice was so deep now. He had changed so much in the last three years. In fact, the whole world had changed in the last three years—since the day he had kissed her.

Duncan was a foot taller now, and one hundred ninety-two pounds. She knew because he talked about it all the time. His personal best for a bench press was two hundred thirty-two pounds. His fastest individual time for a 5K Postal distance swimming event was one hour, four minutes, and fifty-two seconds. His grade point average going into his senior year was a 3.95. He'd been free of bronchitis for five years and nine months, and though he had extra tests done on his lungs because of childhood asthma, he had cleared the Navy's medical assessment with flying colors.

Of course Duncan Flynn had made it into the Naval Academy. He had worked hard for it and deserved it.

Lena caught Rowan smiling at her, and she smiled back.

"How are you doing, Lena?"

"Good. Good. You?"

That was pretty much how their conversations went.

Lena would sneak a peek at Duncan every once in a while. In the morning sun he looked like a superhero, all golden and muscly. He spent a lot of time keeping his thick, black hair perfect. His teeth were that way naturally. She knew she would never—ever—know anyone like him.

But oh, God. This last summer had been the worst of Lena's life. Not only had Duncan forgotten about their kiss, but he'd forgotten their friendship. It was the way the high school food chain worked, she supposed. Duncan was the big shark on campus, while Lena was a pitiful hermit crab swept in by the tide. She'd watched Duncan spend the summer as a lifeguard on Safe Haven Beach, and that meant that from June to August, all the tourist girls made complete fools of themselves in an effort to attract his attention. The prettiest ones got what they wanted.

Lena read a lot of books over the summer. She taught a children's art class down at the tourist center and started a series of watercolors. Annie Parker's parents said she had talent and bought one of her paintings for fifty dollars! Lena started her college fund with it. The highlight of her summer was that she got her braces off.

"Lena, can you pass the butter?"

Her entire body buzzed with nervousness. Duncan had spoken to her for the second time in a single morning, which was unprecedented! She raised her eyes from her Grape-Nuts, and it happened—he looked at her. He really, really looked at Lena. His eyes were open and focused. It was just a flash, and he looked away almost immediately, but Lena swore he was trying to tell her something.

Like that would ever happen.

Fifteen minutes later, she was coming out of her room, not paying close attention to what she was doing. She walked right into a wall.

A wall of Duncan.

"Hey, kid," he said again.

"Whaaa—" Lena's brain scrambled. Why was he at her end of the third-floor hallway? What was he doing? She took a step back, thinking maybe he was trying to get by.

"I wanted to say thanks."

Lena looked behind her to make sure there wasn't someone else in the vicinity. It was the only complete sentence Duncan had spoken to her in three years.

"For what?" She hoisted her backpack into place and smoothed down her new acid-washed cropped jean jacket.

"You were a good friend to me when we were little."

Lena could not believe he'd just said that, but what happened next completely weirded her out. Duncan began closing the snaps on her jacket. Lena was so freaked that she just stood there, looking down at his fingers as they moved from the bottom hem to the collar.

Why would he do that? Was this a joke? Maybe just another way to put Lena in her place? It reminded her of a mom making sure her little one was bundled up to go sledding.

Duncan left the last snap open. He brought his fingertips to her chin and raised her face.

Now she knew. She had not imagined it down in the dining room. Duncan did have something he wanted to say to her. It was in his eyes.

He opened his mouth to speak. A wrinkle appeared between his eyebrows, almost as if he was worried.

All of a sudden, a loud voice came roaring up from the second floor. "Let's roll, Captain Crunch!" Clancy sounded irritated. "Stop playing with your hair. Ma's gonna drive us to school. It's started snowing! Hurry up!"

He froze. Lena waited.

"Duncan, let's go, dude!"

The moment was over. The need to speak had passed. Duncan patted her on the head and said, "See ya, kid."

Chapter Nineteen

It looked like a college fraternity had exploded in the lobby of the Bayberry Island Police Station. A half-dozen hungover kids were slumped on the benches and propped up against the wall. The decibel level coming from the lockup indicated there were plenty more in storage. Poor Chip Bradford was beside himself.

"Everything okay?"

The assistant chief looked up from the desk with red-rimmed eyes. "Does everything *look* okay to you?"

Duncan had to laugh. He had grown up with Chip, and that was the first time he'd ever heard him say something that was not completely earnest and/or helpful.

"What happened?"

He shook his head and whispered, "A bunch of rich kids from Boston rented a yacht and put together their own booze cruise. They docked illegally at the marine yard last night, and a fight broke out. A million *at least* in property damage to the boat. We've got eight facing charges, and guess who one of them is."

Duncan shook his head.

"The governor's kid."

"Ouch."

"Clancy tried to call you last night to help out with processing. He couldn't get ahold of you."

"Right." Duncan made a visual sweep of the room, just to be sure nobody was in the mood to cause trouble. "I made an early night of it."

Chip gave him a crooked smile. "That's not the scuttlebutt."

The only person Duncan knew who ever used that term was Polly Estherhausen, and she did so ironically. Duncan tipped his chin past the gate. "So is he around?"

"He should be, but let me warn you—"

"Not in a good mood?"

Chip shook his head with emphasis. "On top of everything else, we've got a serious situation with the weather. Clancy has to decide by today if he's going to move the Mermaid Ball from the public dock to the museum lobby."

"That's rough. Hey. . ." Duncan tried to sound as if an idea had just occurred to him. "Is that dog still around? Did you ever find her?"

"Ondine?"

"Yeah. That one."

Chip laughed. "We did. We handed her over to a tourist family, but she jumped out of the mom's arms and ran off the ferryboat yesterday and came right back here. The family said she failed to bond with them."

"Bond?"

"Yeah. I guess Ondine didn't like them. She peed on the dad's shoe, which I'm sure didn't help with the bonding process."

"Huh. Interesting." Duncan casually looked around, hoping she might come skittering down the hallway. "So where is she? Did you stick her in the lockup for failure to bond?"

Chip looked puzzled, clearly not finding the humor in Duncan's comment. "We would never do that. She's with the chief."

"Gotcha. Thanks, Chip." Duncan headed back to Clancy's office, and this time he was more respectful of his brother's privacy. Duncan knocked loudly, stepped away from the door, and waited.

Evie answered, smiling when she saw him. She threw the door open. "Hey! It's the mambo king himself! We're having breakfast. Want some?"

Clancy sat at his desk, working on a bagel with cream cheese, paperwork stacked nearly to his chin.

"No, thanks very much, Evie. I was just wondering—"

He got an answer immediately. Little Ondine, the shoe sprayer, jumped straight into his arms and began licking his face and wiggling her butt. When he pulled his head out of range, she started in on his neck.

"Man, she's really into you." Clancy wiped his mouth with a napkin. "It's kind of creepy."

Duncan laughed, checking the front of his shirt to make sure he hadn't been another victim, and set her down on the floor. She immediately leaned sideways against his ankle and straightened, like a sentry on duty.

"You know . . ." Evie moved to Duncan's side. "I bet Rowan would let you keep her."

"Baby, he can't have a dog," Clancy said. "He's going back to active duty."

"I've decided to take her."

Evie and Clancy froze for a moment. Then they exchanged glances.

"Not for me, technically. But I think I know a good permanent home for her. But only under one condition."

Clancy and Evie stared.

"You guys will have to agree to watch her about a week out of every month while . . . her owner travels on business."

A slow, knowing smile spread over his sister-in-law's face.

Clancy said, "Hold up. Does Lena know you're bringing her a—"

"I'll get her food and leash." Evie was almost out the door when she added, "Clancy, grab her dog bed, please."

Once his wife left the room, Clancy rose from his desk chair. Not surprisingly, he took a moment to put his suspect at ease before beginning the interrogation.

"You coming to the Flynn Family Fucking Fantastic Festival-Week Funfest tonight?"

Duncan burst out laughing. "Of course I am. I wouldn't miss our annual cookout for the world."

"Because Ma would kick your ass?"

"Precisely."

"You know Da's going to show up, right?"

"I figured."

Clancy sighed. "They're still behaving like children."

Duncan agreed. "It's painful to watch."

"That tropical system is really moving. Depending on the model, we could get nothing, some wind gusts, or the full brunt of a cyclone. Our rain tents won't be able to stand up to that."

"Yeah. Chip said you've got to make some decisions."

Clancy nodded. "So." He rested his hands on the desktop and leaned toward Duncan.

"Yeah?"

"What the hell are you doing, man?" He kept his voice low, but the look in his eye was hard-core. "Ma called me first thing this morning, followed almost immediately by Rowan. And Evie was just telling me you had a Duncan Do-Right thing going on at the clambake."

He didn't say anything.

"What are you *doing*?"

"I'm getting Lena a dog to keep her company. She's in that huge place all by herself."

"And you two are dating now?"

"Don't be ridiculous. She's an old friend. She's a part of our extended family."

"Ooo-kay. Sure. You're a man who happens to be a friend, so you're just her man-friend."

"Come on, Clancy. Cut me some slack. She's a wonderful woman and she's fun to be with. That's all. She knows I'm leaving."

"And when will that be, exactly?"

"Like I said, I go back in October for my medical screening. I'll get my ship date after I'm cleared."

Clancy looked down at Ondine. "You know, once you take this ball of dryer lint off my hands, you can't bring her back. If Lena doesn't want her, then you have to find another home. Got it?"

"Hooya, Chief."

Clancy shook his head. "I hope you know what you're doing, man."

Duncan felt exactly the same way.

"I'm in my studio!"

Duncan had called to say he was coming over, and Lena had actually answered her phone, so she was far more prepared for his visit than the last time—and far more dressed. She carefully covered her canvas with a cloth drape and turned to greet him at the studio door.

She was nervous and excited. Something was happening between the two of them and it was one hundred percent incredible. Lena had no idea where it was headed, of course, and she was doing her best to let go of any expectations. She continually reminded herself of Jacqueline's advice—there was nothing she could do to hurry things along. The truth was, she believed things were unfolding at just the right tempo. She was certain that all those years of loving Duncan were not wasted.

Lena heard Duncan's footfalls on the staircase and his progress on the wood floors of the hallway. When he finally appeared in the studio doorway, Lena was surprised by what she saw.

"Who in the world is this?"

The cutest little puppy wiggled from Duncan's arms and raced over to Lena. She bent down and picked her up and was immediately bathed in a rapid-fire succession of dog kisses.

"What a cutie! What's her name?" Lena asked Duncan while trying to dodge the onslaught.

"Her name is Ondine."

"On what?"

With that, the little dog jumped from Lena's arms and ran at full speed across the studio, toward the wall of windows. She sailed through the air, landed on the chaise, and circled a few times before plopping down with a big sigh. Lena was astounded.

"I didn't know you had a dog!" She turned to find Duncan just a few inches away. Lena studied his face to see a combination of emotions at play—humor, affection, and maybe a twinge of guilt.

"Actually," he said, caressing her upper arms with his hands. He gave her a quick kiss hello. "She's your dog."

Lena shook her head in disbelief. "Mine?"

"I know I should have checked with you. I hope you don't hate dogs."

"I love dogs, but—"

"I thought you needed someone here to watch over you. You get so wrapped up in your work. I want you to be safe."

Lena felt a smile spread over her whole face. She smiled so wide her cheeks hurt. "You mean she's going to have my six?"

"Exactly." Duncan cupped her face in his hands and gave her a proper greeting.

Lena felt herself relax. Her body leaned in to the kiss, feeling its warmth and depth of feeling spread through her. When Duncan raised his lips from hers, he left his eyes closed for a moment, as if he, too, was unwinding into the full sensation.

Suddenly, they heard a high-pitched yip. Lena turned to see the dog with her paws on the windowsill, intent on watching seagulls dive-bomb into the water. She and Duncan walked over to her.

"Did you say her name was Ondine?"

"As in the water nymph from mythology."

Lena laughed and looked up at him. "What else do you know about water nymphs, Lieutenant Flynn?"

"That would be it."

Lena turned her attention to the dog again. She had stopped barking at the seagulls and was now seated on the chaise, her cream-colored fur looking clean against the old velvet of Jacqueline's divan.

"Duncan, as much as I appreciate your bringing me a

new friend, I don't know if I can keep her. What will I do with her when I'm out of town?"

"I thought of that," he said, reaching around Lena to press her back against his body. It felt so good she let her head lean back on his chest. "Clancy and Evie said they will take her whenever you have to go on a trip. They've already got two dogs, and Christina could play with her."

"You've got everything figured out, I see."

"Do you want her?"

Lena studied the dog, who couldn't have been more than fifteen pounds. She was obviously a mutt but still a pretty little thing, quite feminine. Lena figured there would be no harm in seeing how it went. "I don't have anything for her to eat."

"I brought dog food, a leash, and a dog bed, all courtesy of the Bayberry Island Police Department."

Lena looked over her shoulder and frowned.

"She was a stray. She showed up at the station's back door soaked in rain. They haven't been able to find the right home for her."

Just then Ondine turned around to face them. Her little dark eyes sparkled and her tail began to wag so hard it blurred. She padded over to the edge of the chaise and waited patiently for Lena to reach out for her. Then she jumped right into her arms.

The three of them stood like that by the windows for a few moments, Duncan holding Lena close, Ondine snuggled into Lena's arms.

"Do you have any plans tonight?" Duncan asked, his voice soft in her ear.

"You mean besides my dog?"

Duncan laughed. "I will take her if it doesn't work out. I won't stick you with her."

Lena managed to twist her way out of Duncan's embrace and turned to face him. In that moment there was as much gentleness as ruggedness in his handsome face. He seemed peaceful and contented.

"What are you looking at?"

"You," she said.

"I probably need to shave." He raised his hand to the scruff that had already grown on his chin.

Lena shook her head. "Don't do it on my account. I like it." She wiggled her eyebrows. "It makes you look like a badass."

Duncan laughed. The sound filled her studio and left her no choice but to join in. Ondine began to bark.

"So." Duncan slipped his arm around her waist. "Are you busy tonight?"

"Oh, Duncan, I'm afraid I am."

His face tightened. "Oh. No problem."

"Aren't you going to ask me where I'm going?"

One of his eyebrows arched on his forehead. "Where, pray tell, are you going?"

"To the Flynn family cookout. Your mother invited me early this morning."

A shadow passed over Duncan's face. "Are you kidding me?"

"I've been invited every year that I've been back on Bayberry. It's not because we went to the clambake together."

"But I've never seen you there."

"I've always politely declined Mona's invitation."

A smile tugged at the corner of Duncan's mouth. "But this year is different?"

Lena raised her mouth to his. "Boy, is it ever," she said.

Chapter Twenty

Duncan pulled into a crushed-shell drive off Idlewilde Lane and parked in front of his mother's cottage. It was a one-story cedar-shingled home surrounded by scraggly boxwoods and a variety of rosebushes, all of which were in need of a good cutting back. Duncan would stop by tomorrow and take care of it for her.

Lena was next to him in the passenger seat, looking incredibly beautiful in a simple light blue summer dress and dainty sandals. From what he had observed, she made even the simplest outfit stunning. They had a third wheel with them that evening. Ondine was in Lena's lap, gazing out the window as if she were royalty riding in a carriage.

"You sure your mom's okay with me bringing the dog?"

"I'm sure."

"I didn't think I should leave her there all alone just hours after she arrived."

"I totally agree."

He watched her bite her lip.

"Are you nervous about being here tonight, Lena?"

She gazed over at him, her eyes big and dark. "Maybe a little. It's been a long, long time since I sat down for a meal with the entire Flynn clan. I'm out of practice."

Duncan paused. Something about the way she'd said that felt like a jab. And out of nowhere, a memory slid into his consciousness. Lena at the Safe Haven breakfast table, eyes down, not interacting with anyone, while he, the seventeen-year-old idiot that he was, behaved like an asshole.

Just then the terrible truth hit Duncan. He had abandoned Lena back then. He had turned his back to the friendship she'd offered him, and he'd hurt her. Duncan had been nothing less than a bastard toward her, and yet here she was with him.

How could she have forgiven him?

"Lena—?"

Just then Clancy pulled up in his department-issued Jeep, beeping the horn. Christina jumped out of the back, and Evelyn exited gracefully, already smiling and waving.

Duncan swallowed the bitter guilt he felt rising into his mouth and returned Clancy's wave. Why was all this old garbage hitting him now?

"So they gave you a pass from the lunatic asylum?" he asked his brother.

Clancy nodded. "Just three hours, but I'll take it. Chip's handling the reenactment, and thank God that's our least rowdy event."

Duncan had to laugh. Of all the festival-week spectacles, he made a point of avoiding the reenactment. It was a stage play depicting the fateful day Rutherford Flynn and his entire fishing fleet were rescued by a mermaid. Not exactly the Cirque du Soleil.

Just then Christina came running. "Uncle Duncle!" She jumped straight up and down like a pogo stick, trying to look in the window of Lena's SUV. "They've got the puppy! They've got the puppy!"

Duncan walked around the vehicle and opened the door for Lena. Christina was going crazy with excitement and turned to Clancy with disbelief in her eyes. "Look, Daddy! They brought John Dean!" She looked up to Lena. "Can I walk him? Can I?"

"It's a she, sweetie, and her name is *On*dine." Lena set the dog down and handed the leash to Christina. The little girl took off down the path into Mona's backyard, Ondine traveling as fast as her short legs could carry her. Christina announced to the rest of the family, "John Dean is here! John Dean is here!"

Still chuckling, Duncan made his way with everyone down the side of the house toward an old wooden arbor heavy with roses, Lena and Evelyn leading the way.

Clancy turned toward Duncan. "How's it going? Is she a keeper?"

Duncan lowered his chin and scowled at him.

"Ondine," Clancy clarified. "The dog."

"Ah." Duncan's neck muscles unknotted. "For now. It was kind of funny how she just waltzed into Lena's studio and made herself at home. Maybe they were meant for each other or something."

"Stranger things have happened."

"What did you decide about the Mermaid Ball?"

Clancy shook his head. "The festival committee absolutely hates holding it indoors—they say it ruins the magic. I told them forty-mile-an-hour winds could ruin more than magic."

Duncan chuckled. "So what did you decide?"

"I've looked at all the models. I called the National Weather Service on the mainland. Nobody knows the trajectory for sure, so I went ahead and cleared the event for outdoors." Clancy rubbed his face nervously. "I had to make the call because it takes forty-eight hours to set up. God, I hope I didn't screw the pooch."

As soon as their little group passed beneath the arbor, Duncan saw his mother had gone all out for the event, as usual. The large old table was covered with a white cloth and decorated with strategically placed seashells and glass jars of wildflowers. In a new twist, a drape of fishing net hung from the old sycamore above, loaded down with its catch of the day: construction-paper fish, corals, and mermaids.

"Christina worked on those all afternoon," Evie told Lena. "It kept her busy while we cooked."

Duncan saw Lena stiffen just before she gasped, "I forgot to bring something!"

"No worries." Evie leaned in close. "Your date dropped off his specialty earlier today."

Lena whipped her head around. "You have a specialty?"

"Yep. I got the keg."

Rowan, Annie, and Serena greeted everyone at the arbor gate. Nat and Ash shouted their hellos from the far end of the yard, where they were building the bonfire. Even while Duncan received hugs from his sister and her best friend, a sick feeling had begun to settle in the pit of his stomach. He glanced at Clancy.

It was obvious his brother was thinking the same thing.

Last year at this event, right in front of the bonfire and the entire family, the brothers had nearly come to blows. Duncan had confessed that he'd kept Evie and

Clancy apart when they were teenagers, that he'd thrown away a love letter she'd mailed to Clancy after Evie had returned home from festival week. Because of Duncan's actions, it had taken the couple eighteen years to find each other again.

The words exchanged that night had been ugly. Clancy had called Duncan a "jealous son of a bitch" and said that being a Navy SEAL didn't give him dibs on courage. How had his little brother put it? *Being strong enough to love someone, strong enough to risk everything by loving someone—that is manning up, bro.*

Looking in his brother's eyes right then, Duncan was slammed by so much regret that it left him speechless. He had been cruel to Lena. He had been cruel to Clancy and Evie.

He wondered if that was the real reason he preferred to keep his distance from Bayberry Island—his own shame.

"Duncan." Clancy looked him square in the eye. "It's water under the bridge, man. All is forgiven. Seriously." With that, Clancy gave him a firm, steady hug and slapped him on the back. "Now, you need to tap the keg. I get one beer before I go back on duty, and I think right now's a good time to drink it."

The gathering descended into chaos soon after. Christina and "John Dean" zigzagged through the grass. Serena had a meltdown. Evie dropped her famous quinoa and fresh mint salad onto the lawn. "I can run home and make another," she offered.

A unanimous "no" assured her it wasn't necessary. While Duncan helped Evie clean up the mess, Ondine stopped by for a sniff. She turned up her nose at the side dish and wandered off.

Eventually, Mona lit the candles and asked everyone to take their seats around an outrageous display of food. A big old soup tureen overflowed with a homemade bouillabaisse of clams, prawns, mussels, and fresh cod. There was freshly baked bread, cranberry relish, roasted leg of lamb, lobster, spinach salad, and crispy new potatoes with rosemary. The only thing missing from the table was Da.

Frasier had dutifully attended every family festival-week cookout since he and Ma separated. Their close proximity was usually a silent one, though a verbal barb or two was sometimes exchanged. Tonight was the first time he hadn't bothered to show up.

Mona sighed, clearly deciding to move on with the evening, Frasier or no. She raised her wineglass. "I would like to make a toast to all of us, young and old and in between. Our family grows in number and in joy with each passing year, and for that I am deeply grate—"

Mona stopped in midsentence. Duncan had a very bad feeling, and his intuition proved correct when he turned around.

"Granda!" Christina yelled.

"Oh, *hell* no," Rowan whispered.

Ondine's sharp little bark split the air.

There stood Frasier, hands in the pockets of his neatly pressed dress trousers, with Sally at his side.

Clancy jumped up so fast that he knocked over his precious beer. "Da, are you insane?"

A painful silence settled over the group until Nat asked, "More wine, anyone?"

"Wait." Frasier approached the table the way a man might walk to his execution. Both he and Sally seemed strangely repentant. "There is something everyone needs to hear, so I would appreciate it if you all just sat down"—that was directed toward Clancy—"and hold your comments." That was for Rowan. "I need three minutes. That's all I ask of you."

Lena turned toward Duncan, clearly baffled.

"Your guess is as good as mine," he whispered.

At that point, Sally stepped forward. She wore an off-white pantsuit that made her look more like Hillary Clinton than Dolly Parton. "Hi, everyone," she said. "Hello, Mona. This won't take long."

Clancy looked sideways at Duncan, who shook his head, silently suggesting his little brother let things unfold.

Frasier cleared his throat. "Yes, well." He gave Sally a nod.

"I am not here tonight as Frasier's date." She was addressing Mona in particular. "I'm here because I want to make amends and do whatever I can to convince you to take your husband back."

Every woman at the table gasped. Nat poured himself more wine. Duncan checked on his mother, but if she were preparing to strangle the shit out of Sally, it didn't show. Ma was a class act.

"I was diagnosed with cancer two weeks ago."

Murmurs of sympathy went around the table. Mona said, "I am truly sorry to hear that, Sally."

Though she held her back straight and her chin high, it was obvious that Sally struggled to keep her composure. "It's stage two. The doctors say I have a sixty percent chance of survival, and so I'm going to think on the positive."

"Oh, Sally." Mona sighed. "Please let me know if there's anything we can do."

Ma's kindness released Sally's tears. She nodded. "That's not what I came to tell you, Mona."

"All right."

"See, when something like that happens to you, your perspective changes. I suddenly realized the things I thought were so damn important were just bullshit."

"Uh-oh," Christina said.

Sally looked horrified. "I am *so* sorry," she said to Clancy and Evie.

Frasier patted Sally's shoulder in an awkward show of support. Sally took a big breath and continued.

"Mona, I was so jealous of you I couldn't see straight. I've wasted so much of my life trying to one-up you, and the only reason I broke from the mermaids and started the fairies was to cause you grief. I mean, otherwise what's the point in a bunch of middle-aged women running around the island dressed in tutus and gauzy wings?"

"Many of us have wondered that very thing," Nat said.

"Shh!" Annie scowled at him.

"And that whole nasty battle about development on the island . . ." Sally looked at Ash. "The only reason I championed the resort and casino was to get back at Mona. I wanted to see her suffer."

"Whoa." Rowan made the only comment.

Christina began picking hunks of bread from the basket and feeding them to Ondine, who was lounging under her chair. Serena hurled her spoon into the bushes. Duncan felt Lena reach for his hand under the table, and he squeezed it in reassurance. Because really, what were the possible outcomes here? This standoff would either resolve calmly or it would break out into a mass riot of hair-pulling and food-throwing, and Duncan had more faith in the Flynns than that.

Sally grabbed a tissue out of the pocket of her jacket, dabbing at her eyes and nose. "Look. I'm here this evening to tell you that Frasier is a good man. He's been very decent to me, a true friend. But the truth is—I'm nothing but a catch-and-release thing for him." Sally inclined her head toward Mona. "Don't you think for one second that Frasier Flynn has *ever* loved anyone but you."

Mona rose from her chair at the far end of the table. She neatly folded her napkin and dropped it in her plate.

Sally went on. "From here on out, I will be focusing all my energy on getting better and spending as much time with my own family as I can." She glanced at Frasier, as if to assure him she was wrapping up. "Anyway. You are a beautiful family, and I am sorry for any harm I've caused. This is where Frasier belongs." She paused a moment before she turned to go.

Clancy popped up from his seat once more. "Let me drive you back to town."

Sally shook her head. "I drove myself. I wish all of you the best."

All eyes were on Sally as she walked through the yard and under the arbor. Mona slowly returned to her seat. Frasier remained where he was, his feet planted so rigidly in the grass that he looked like an oversized garden gnome. No one made a move or said a word. This was Ma's call and they all knew it.

"Sit down, Frasier," she said.

Da scrambled to his chair at the opposite end of the table, his eyes wide and hopeful.

Ma said, "We'll have to see how things go. That's all I can offer you at the moment."

"That's enough," Da replied.

As always, good food soothed the collective soul of

the Flynns, and within minutes everyone was eating, talking, and laughing. Before too long, Frasier even had Mona giggling as he regaled them all with the story of her first official visit to the island as his girlfriend.

"Do you remember? We walked in on my mother and her friends having a Mermaid Society meeting in the dining room. You got a look at their mermaid costumes for the first time, and I thought you were going to pass out."

"I feel your pain," Nat said to Mona.

She just giggled some more. In a pensive voice she said, "You know, it's astounding what a person can learn to consider normal over time."

The meal went on without additional drama, although Serena was so busy that Rowan hardly got a bite to eat.

"I'll take her for a while," Duncan said. He retrieved his niece and returned to his seat. She blinked at him with those big blue eyes.

Frasier cleared his throat. "Well, Lena, it sure is a pleasure having you with us this evening," Frasier said. "I'm glad Duncan could persuade you to finally make an appearance."

She smiled politely. "It's very nice to be here. It's been lovely."

"I imagine my boy's quite good at persuasion," Frasier added, laughing.

Lena didn't answer. Duncan sliced his finger across his throat to get his father to stop talking.

Christina cocked her head. "Why did you do that to your neck, Uncle Duncle?"

Duncan helped clear the table before dessert was served and found that popping in and out of the kitchen provided some eye-opening reconnaissance. Though he'd heard a hundred times about Lena's shyness, she seemed to fit right in with Rowan, Annie, and Evelyn, as they put away leftovers and put serving platters in the sink to soak. In fact, Duncan noticed that Evelyn had taken a special liking to Lena, maybe because Annie and Rowan already came packaged as a pair. Women seemed to be much more attuned to that sort of thing than men.

When he saw his sister pull Lena aside and whisper to her, Duncan pretended not to notice. He caught mention of some kind of meeting the next day, but because of Evie and Annie's laughter, he couldn't catch the details. A meeting? What kind of meeting? Did women just get together for no reason except that they were female? Whatever it was, Lena nodded and agreed to attend.

While placing coffee cups and saucers around the table a few moments later, a thought hit Duncan so hard he stood straight and stared at nothing. That kitchen business with Lena was far too cozy. It was almost as if the other women had just crowned Lena as Duncan's "significant other" and had welcomed her into their clique with that understanding. That was wrong. It made too many assumptions and went way over the line.

Duncan enjoyed the bread pudding with salted caramel sauce as much as anyone, but, unfortunately, he had to fight off a vague sense of confinement the rest of the evening. His mind kept spinning—what was happening with his feelings for Lena? What was he doing to himself by spending time with her? What was he doing to *her*?

He wondered if he'd already made an irreparable number of errors.

Clancy had to go back to work, but everyone else roasted marshmallows around the fire. Duncan noticed his father had maneuvered a lawn chair next to Ma, who pretended not to notice. Ol' Frasier was still a smooth operator, it seemed.

Duncan sat next to Lena, who had somehow ended up at the bottom of a triple-decker pile. Christina was sprawled out on her lap, and Ondine was sprawled out on Christina's. That dog was a real piece of work. She had immediately claimed everyone as part of her pack that evening and had traveled from lap to lap, absolutely sure she would be welcomed. She'd been right.

Duncan had been given Serena to hold. It was becoming a pattern. She was obviously sleepy, and her little cheek was pressed to his chest, but she couldn't manage to conk out. Every once in a while Serena would raise her head and look up, as if checking on him, which made him smile. Granted, Duncan had spent zero time with babies before Serena came on the scene, but he really did think she was something special. It suddenly occurred to him that she probably wouldn't remember any of this time with him. She'd have no memory of the summer after her uncle was injured and before he went back to active duty.

And how grown-up would this baby girl be the next time Duncan managed to spend more than three days in a row on Bayberry? She'd be ten? Fourteen? He would be a stranger to her. He would probably miss her whole childhood.

The thought of that left a lump of sadness in his chest.

Eventually, the night came to a close. Duncan handed Serena to Rowan and Lena peeled Christina off her lap. Everyone said their good nights, and he drove Lena and Ondine back to Moondance Beach. Duncan knew he was being far too quiet, but he was too distracted for chitchat.

He pulled into Lena's garage, and though Lena and the dog climbed down from the vehicle, Duncan didn't move. He just sat there, staring at his hands on the steering wheel, wishing he were anywhere else.

"I'm taking her for a walk. Want to come along?"

This was one of those "interpersonal" moments Duncan sucked at. He had so much boiling over inside him at that moment and no idea how to get it all out without hurting Lena. The only thing he was sure of: he had hurt Lena enough.

"Duncan? Is everything all right?"

Boy, that was a loaded question.

Chapter Twenty-one

The change in Duncan happened so suddenly and so thoroughly that Lena was blindsided. He'd seemed to be enjoying himself all evening and then, for no obvious reason, he'd shut down. So far, she hadn't been able to crack him open again.

They walked along the windy beach with Ondine. What a funny little creature she was, completely self-assured and strutting around like a canine princess. She had none of the nervousness that could be associated with an abused or neglected pet, which made Lena quite curious about her origins. Clancy told her no one had any idea where she was from or how she'd come to the island. "She is a woman of mystery," he'd said.

Mystery or not, Ondine was Lena's dog now. There was no doubt about it. The fact that she'd been a gift from Duncan made her all the more special.

Lena didn't want to push him, so she gave Duncan some space as they walked. She thought the subdued night sky was in sync with Duncan's mood, whatever that might be. She was only just beginning to learn to interpret his subtle signals, and she suspected there was more going on under his reserved surface. No doubt hiding his emotions was a skill he had perfected as a Navy SEAL, but it had been there when he was a boy, too. It was part of how he was made and part of why Duncan had always posed a challenge to her.

They continued to walk in silence, Lena in no hurry to change that. She wasn't a fan of talking just to provide noise.

"I have a lot on my mind, Lena. I don't mean to brood. I hate brooders—I've always thought moping around was such a passive-aggressive thing to do."

She smiled to herself in the dim light of the moon and waited for him to elaborate. He didn't, so she said, "If you'd ever like to share, I'm here."

"And if I don't?"

"I'm still here." She looked at him over her shoulder. "But, to be honest, I hate brooding, too."

He touched her shoulder. When she turned to face him, Lena saw the strangest look in Duncan's eyes. She couldn't name the precise disturbance, but a storm was definitely coming. Without a word, he pulled her tight to the front of his body, and she hugged him back—hard. Lena wasn't sure if he needed her or if he knew she needed him, but it didn't matter. The hug would prevent him from drifting farther away, at least temporarily.

"I was such a jerk when I was young," he said. Lena remained still, sensing that he preferred to talk while she was hidden away in his arms. "I threw you away when you were the only real friend I ever had."

She turned her cheek to his chest.

"I am so sorry, Lena."

"I've already forgiven you, Duncan. A long time ago."

She heard his heart beat like he was sprinting. She waited patiently.

"I have no intention of staying on Bayberry. I can't see myself leaving the Navy. It's not in my plan."

She pressed hard against him and backed away a step, the wind picking up around them. "I never asked you to."

"Lena," Duncan's face was twisted with confusion. "You're the most incredible woman I've ever known. I'm drawn to you like I've never been drawn to a woman in my life, but I think I'm making a horrible mistake. I don't want a relationship right now."

She nodded soberly. "What *do* you want?"

"You." He raised a hand and brushed his fingertips down the side of her face. "I want you. I want to spend time with you. I want to make love to you and laugh with you for as long as we're here together—but I know in the end it won't be fair to you."

She smiled. "How about you let me decide what's fair? I'm a grown woman."

He dropped his hand from her face. "I realize that."

"I am perfectly capable of deciding how much I'm willing to give to a man. I've been taking care of myself for a very long time."

Duncan blinked in surprise, as if the thought had never occurred to him. "Of course. I didn't mean to imply . . . I'm only trying to protect you."

Lena laughed, though she felt her fists ball up at her sides. "Protect me? From what? From *you*?" She looked away, thinking, *It's a little late for that.*

She saw Ondine sitting in the sand right at their feet, as if she were eavesdropping. Lena picked her up. "You know, it's getting pretty windy. I want to go back to the house."

The air seemed to escape from Duncan's body. His brow became deeply creased, and he lowered his head.

"We can continue this conversation inside if you'd like."

But Duncan didn't move. Instead, he said, "What was that painting about?" Duncan's question came out of nowhere, and his voice sounded hollow. He raised his head to look her square in the eye. "You know the one I'm talking about—the one you were working on when I barged in on you. Please give me a truthful answer."

What? Lena felt herself go still inside. She would rather he'd seen the charcoal nude than *that* painting! But of course he'd seen it—he didn't miss anything.

"I only ask because it was so unlike your other work. It was real dark stuff."

She shook her head and looked out over the dune. "That was never supposed to be seen by anyone, Duncan. I never planned to exhibit it or sell it—it was just for me. Sometimes I paint to work through negative emotion. It's like keeping a diary, I guess."

Duncan slid his hand along her upper arm. The feel of his touch was warm and comforting, but at that moment she wasn't interested in being comforted.

"Is the painting about me? The ambush?"

Lena gasped. She stared at him in the dim moonlight, amazed he'd been able to make the connection. "Why do you think that, Duncan?"

"Easy." He shrugged. "There were eight bloody bodies in the water and there were eight men in my insertion team. The ocean setting looked bombed out. And the image contained such violence and . . . *grief*." Duncan nodded, as if he were just now putting the pieces together for himself. "You may have painted it, Lena, but I lived it, and I know it can't be a coincidence."

Her body went rigid.

"And while we're at it, you knew I was on your beach five nights in a row, waiting for you to come out of the surf, didn't you?" Duncan pointed his thumb over his shoulder. "I bet you observed me from your studio."

Lena's mouth fell open. Duncan was using everything in his arsenal to blame her for his own anger. To find an excuse for it.

"You walked around me that night I fell asleep, didn't you? You came to make sure I was all right." He pointed down the beach. "Those were your footprints in the sand, weren't they?"

Lena nodded slowly. "My goodness, you do have a lot on your mind, Duncan. But you haven't shared with me the only thing that matters."

"And what's that?"

"Why you are so angry." She adjusted Ondine in her arms. "Are you angry because I care for you as much as I do? Are you pissed off that it caused me pain to hear you were nearly killed? What is it that got under your skin at your mother's tonight?"

A shadow fell over his face, and Lena glanced up to see the moon completely disappear behind a dark cloud. Duncan had no reply, and though Lena waited for a long moment, she saw nothing but a statue standing in front of her. He may have spoken several languages, but he wasn't anywhere near fluent in the language of the heart.

"All right," she whispered. "I'm going in." Lena headed for the beach steps, figuring that if Duncan wanted to follow, that would be wonderful. And if he didn't, she would find a way to make peace with it.

She got halfway up the stairs and heard him call out to her.

"Lena!"

With Ondine in her arms, she turned, the wind whipping her hair into her face.

"This is insane." He raised his arms in a gesture of frustration. Even in the low light she could see the torment in his face. "We hadn't said a word to each other since we were kids and then—*boom!*—we're all up in each other's lives in a matter of days. And now I'm crazy about you. What the *hell* is going on?"

Lena did not smile, but her heart lifted. Duncan had asked her, and she would answer him. "Come inside." She held out her hand. "I'll tell you what I know."

The last thing he wanted to do when he got inside Lena's house was *talk*. That girl's strength had turned him on so much that he was on the verge of making an idiot of himself. Seeing her hold her position on the sand like that, the wind whipping her hair, telling him she didn't need his protection and could take care of herself—that was the most god-awful sexy thing he'd ever seen in his life. No woman had ever stood up to him like that. It had been the last straw—it had cracked open his heart.

"Lena." A stunningly beautiful wild woman stood in the kitchen before him. She was barefoot and breathing hard. Her hair was windblown and her dark eyes seared into him. He wanted her with a fierceness that made no sense, that burned so hot it liquefied all his plans, all his strategies, and all his reasoning.

He said nothing more. Instead he walked in to her,

kept her upright, and pressed her against the wall. He devoured her with his mouth and hands, gripping at her dress, sliding his hands up the insides of her hot thighs. This woman was a seductress. A magician. She had power over him that wasn't natural. And at that moment, Duncan knew he would do whatever she wanted him to do, for however long she wanted him to do it.

Her fingers were in his hair. She pulled him down to her. Lena tore at his shirt, her small fingers insistent and greedy. Just like her mouth. Like her thighs.

Duncan grabbed her under her ass and lifted her from the floor, her legs falling open in a sign of surrender. And that's when the most remarkable thought entered his brain: this was mutual surrender. He'd never felt anything like it. He was yielding to her as much as she yielded to him, and the power in it was astounding.

He carried Lena through the cavernous downstairs and up the staircase, relieved to see Ondine scurry up the steps ahead of them. Once on the second floor, Ondine peeled off for the studio, and Duncan headed to the bedroom.

Lena was whimpering as she kissed him, hands on his neck, her small but luscious body crushed against his. As they reached the bed, Duncan realized they were both out of control and in complete agreement about it.

He tossed her on the bed and pressed her down into the mattress, hands inside her dress now, caressing her breasts and hard nipples, feeling her hands up inside his shirt, burning his already hot skin.

"This is crazy," she mumbled, kissing his throat and chest.

"Fuckin' nuts," Duncan said, peeling the dress away from her body. He rose above her, supporting his weight on his hands. Duncan let his gaze travel from her beautiful face to her firm breasts, down her tight belly, to the succulent place she had opened for him between her legs.

"You're the most beautiful thing I've ever seen," he said.

Just then tears slipped from Lena's eyes and rolled across her temples to the sheets. Duncan was astounded by the intensity of Lena's reaction.

"Are you all right, baby?"

She nodded.

"I need to be inside you," he whispered.

She reached up and touched his mouth with her delicate fingers. He opened his lips, kissing them, licking them, biting them. "Yes," she whispered. "I have to have you, too."

He slid into her. She was tight and slick and so warm he worried he would explode before he took her where she needed to go. They locked eyes and hands and moved together in need and passion, twisted, turned, sought out each other in an endless changing sea of sex. His mind drifted, his body and heart flowed into hers. And suddenly, it was like nothing he'd ever known. She was his. She had always been his, and he could not enter her deep enough. This beautiful woman closed her eyes and cried his name.

"Duncan!"

He wanted this for her. He wanted her to know a place without limits, where she could fall apart beneath him and know he was there to catch her. He wanted this beautiful woman to break free, fly so high that her only tether was her love for him and his love for her.

They climaxed together, and the instant was so beautiful it danced on the edge of pain. He called out her name as he emptied his soul into hers.

"Lena," he cried. "Lena! My God, I love you so much."

The ceiling fan whirred, and the cool ocean air slipped in through a bedroom screen. The in-and-out breathing of the ocean soothed them. Lena snuggled up against Duncan's chest, one leg thrown over his body. Her fingers fiddled with his chest hair.

Duncan stared at the fan—*'round and 'round and 'round* ... He'd just told Lena he loved her. It was a miracle. He'd just told a woman he loved her, and he'd meant it. It was a new and terrifying sensation.

Ondine decided the coast was clear and hopped up on Lena's bed. The dog found a comfortable position and turned her head away, as if their nakedness were too much for her to take.

"Holy moly," Lena said.

"Baby Jesus on the B train."

She giggled. "Would you like some water?"

Duncan shook his head, pulling her tighter. "Don't move, Lena. Stay here a little longer." He kissed her silky hair and breathed her in, detecting a perfect mix of salt water, woman, and sex. His mind wandered off to his buddy Jax, the only married guy in their platoon. When Jax would talk about his wife, his whole face would change. The hard edges would soften and his lips would curl up in the most useless, inexcusable, pussy-whipped smile that ever appeared on a Navy SEAL's face. Duncan would rib him mercilessly about it.

But right then Duncan was certain that if he had a mirror, he would look an awful lot like his late friend Jax.

"Duncan?"

"Hmmm?"

'Round and 'round and 'round ...

"You asked me something important when we were on the beach. I have an answer for you."

"Okay, baby." He smiled.

'Round and 'round and 'round ...

"You said something about how we hadn't spoken since we were kids but now here we were ... how did you say it?"

"All up in each other." Duncan laughed.

"Kind of prophetic, wouldn't you say?"

"Prophetic and fantastic." He reached around and played with the ends of her hair.

"Well, there's something you should know."

And with that, his Zen-like, post-sex stupor was blown the fuck up. He'd just heard a hint of fear in Lena's voice, and now she was sitting up in bed and pulling the covers around her.

Duncan stayed where he was, trying to focus on the view. She was so damn beautiful. Soft and sensual and uninhibited ...

"I have loved you my whole life, Duncan Flynn."

He stared at her. "What do you mean?"

"I mean ..." She pushed the hair from her face. Her expression was far too serious for pillow talk. "I had a vision. It was on the day you did the pencil drawing, the day you kissed me."

Duncan nodded, hoping to God this was not headed in the woo-woo direction he suspected. "A vision?"

"Remember when you said the kiss felt 'unearthly'?"

It was time for Duncan to sit up, too. He shoved himself against the headboard, rubbed his face in his hands, and tried to appear nonjudgmental. Yes, he had in fact said that, and now he deeply regretted it. "I remember."

"Well, I believe it really was. I think it was some sort of . . . I don't know how to explain it exactly . . . a powerful *sign* for us to see together. I know this is going to sound really strange . . ."

It already does. Duncan touched her hand and smiled, while inside he felt like he was going to be sick.

"As soon as you kissed me, I knew you were my destiny. I have loved you ever since that moment, and I've waited for you to come to me. Through all these years I've *never given up.*"

Duncan couldn't swallow. He stared at that annoying ceiling fan, and after a frozen second or two, he said, "Excuse me. Be right back."

He escaped into Lena's bathroom and shut the door. Duncan looked at himself in the mirror and almost started laughing—what an idiot he'd been! He couldn't imagine a worse turn of events. *An otherworldly destiny?* Oh, holy shit, he was trapped in one of his mother's mermaid meetings!

The mermaid.

God, how he hated that bitch.

Duncan slipped back into the room and grabbed his clothes. He put his boxer briefs and pants on first, then his shirt. Next he slipped on his shoes. All the while Lena sat there, with her legs tucked under her and the covers wrapped around her, looking like a lost puppy. The actual lost puppy was in her lap.

"Lena." He sat on the edge of the bed and leaned over to kiss her. Her lips felt cool. "Look, I have to ask you something."

She nodded, her eyes wide with regret.

"Sweetie, do you believe in the mermaid?"

She cocked her head and looked at him quizzically. "Are you asking me if I believe there are unseen forces at work in our lives? Are you asking me if I believe there's room for magic in this world? Then the answer is 'yes, absolutely.'"

"No." He shook his head incredulously. "My question was quite simple: do you ... believe ... in the mermaid?"

Her eyes flashed in defiance. "Do I believe mermaids live in the sea? Or do I believe in the mermaid legend of Bayberry Island?"

Duncan laughed. "Seriously? Is there a difference?"

"That's not for me to say."

"Ooo-kay. Let me rephrase that." He briefly squeezed his eyes shut to regain his focus. "Lena, do you think the mermaid statue in Fountain Square brought you and me together? Did she determine our 'destiny'?"

Lena's face fell in sadness. "You asked why our connection has been so intense, so fast. I answered you to the best of my ability. And now you're ridiculing me for being honest."

Duncan shook his head. "Look, I'm sorry. This is way out of my comfort zone. It pushes all my buttons, and I can't even sit here and have a conversation like this—it's just too crazy."

He headed toward the bedroom door.

"Aren't you going to ask me if *I'm* a mermaid?"

Duncan's head spun around. Lena stared at him with wild eyes.

"Sure, Lena. Are you a mermaid?"

"You really want me to answer that?"

That was it for him—he'd had enough. Duncan could see the conversation veering off into whether the moon was an alien hovercraft and the mating habits of Bigfoot.

"I'm sorry, Lena. You have no idea how sorry I am. But I can't do this."

It was a long-assed walk back to the Safe Haven on a cool and windy night, but Duncan had survived far worse—at least in terms of weather. The way his heart felt, however, was something new—it was ripped to fucking shreds. One minute he was desperately in love, and the next minute he was discussing the finer points of mermaidery.

He should never have come home.

Duncan walked past the Safe Haven and into town. He wasn't ready to bump into Ash or Rowan and have them ask about Lena. What the hell would he say? *"She's a swell girl—and she believes in mermaids! Just like the girl who married dear old Dad!"*

He ended up near Fountain Square, and because it was late and a little too windy for optimum comfort, there were no tourists to be seen. Duncan sat on the bench and clasped his hands between his knees.

No wonder he'd left Bayberry and never looked back. This place was created by, and for, crazy people. Looking back, he saw that Lena had done a bang-up job masking her true feelings in those media interviews. No doubt sales would suffer if the world knew she was cuckoo bananas.

Shit. He was crying. He was a thirty-four-year-old Navy SEAL scheduled to receive a Purple Heart, yet he was sitting on a bench, in the dark, at the mermaid fountain, crying because his heart was broken.

The worst part was that he had no frame of reference for going forward. Duncan really loved Lena. He *loved* her. But he could never build something with her because she lived in a world of unicorns and rainbows and mermaids, for shit's sake! In the end it didn't matter how wonderful she was or how much he loved her. It wasn't enough.

How had he even gotten here? When he'd returned to Bayberry this summer, the last thing Duncan had wanted was a woman. Then suddenly he did want a woman, and not just any woman. He wanted Adelena Silva. He wanted her with everything in him.

The wind picked up, blowing directly into his face.

"She is yours and you are hers."

Duncan suddenly felt as if he'd been slapped. The dream! Making love to Lena tonight was a near reenactment of that devastating dream he'd had in June, almost sensation by sensation. The only difference was that in the dream he could not call out his lover's name—because he did not know it. He knew it tonight.

And that deep sensation of loss, of something slipping through his fingers . . . That dream was an exact version of how he felt right that instant. He'd lost something precious. It had disappeared into thin air. He'd been left hollowed out.

The wind rushed him. *"She is yours and you are hers."*

Wait—that voice hadn't been in his head. He really had just heard something. Duncan stood, scanning the area, but saw no one. Which was impossible. Because he'd clearly just heard a voice.

And he did it. Dammit, he couldn't stop himself. His eyes traveled up to the bronze sea hag, the source of hundreds of years of ridiculousness.

She rose above him, round and feminine, holding herself with purpose as she looked out to sea. A half smile played on those bronze lips. Her neck arched gracefully and her hair flowed over a shoulder and across some spectacular cleavage. Her mermaid tail flipped up coyly, yet she refused to make eye contact. Oh, she was impressive, all right. Sixteen feet of mythic femininity, flirty and aloof. It was no wonder some people anointed her with an authority she didn't deserve.

"Thanks for nothing," he told her.

Duncan jogged back to the Safe Haven and went directly to his room. He flipped on the light and noticed an envelope sitting in the middle of his bed. When he saw the cursive handwriting on the front, he grabbed it and immediately tore it open.

Dear Duncan,

We received your letter last month and wanted to tell you how much it meant to us. We know you grieve the loss of Justin as we do. Nestor and I (this is Beth writing) keep you in our thoughts and prayers every day. You were the brother Justin never had. Did you know that? Because he grew up with three older sisters, your friendship was a priceless gift. I remember how you two pushed each other and never allowed the other to give up, but did you know that Justin also looked up to you and admired you? Well, he did.

After thinking a long while about what you wrote, I had to respond. You may not want to hear what I have to say, but know it comes from my heart—a mother's heart. I hope that you are in a frame of mind to hear it.

You wrote that you must live a life that honors Justin, Simon, Jax, Terrence, Paul, Mike, and Scotty. You said that going back to active duty is the only way you know how to do that. But I have to tell you, Duncan, because we love you like you were one of our own: there is another way. Please allow me to explain what I mean.

We met your parents and your brother and sister at Walter Reed. They are wonderful people. I can see where you got your sense of humor and love of life. Nestor and I have been blessed in so many ways, and the primary blessing has been our children and the family we have created together. It was clear to us that your family is similarly blessed.

Justin is gone forever. He was an honorable and brave U.S. Navy SEAL, and he, like you, reached the pinnacle in service to his country. But he never had the chance to fully experience life.

Should you decide to return to active duty, please do not do so because of a vague notion that you are serving in Justin's honor. He had ample opportunity to wage war and he did so, but he never had a chance to love, which—in my humble opinion—is the pinnacle of being human. Justin ran out of time.

You are a marvel, Duncan, a man of determination and purpose. But if you truly want to live in a way that honors our Justin, do the things he didn't live long enough to do. Slow down and open your heart to the people near you. Let them know who you are. Step back from the constant drive to succeed just long enough to experience joy. Find a way to compassionately serve your fellow warriors. Forgive even when it seems impossible. And, most im-

portant, if you ever find a woman who touches your spirit and is worthy of your love, don't retreat from the challenge. Do the bravest thing any man can do and love her in return.

We support you in whatever you choose and are here for you always. Please be happy. Life is precious.

Love,
Nestor and Beth

Chapter Twenty-two

It was all Lena could do to drag herself to the Safe Haven, but she'd promised Rowan she would come. For reasons she didn't yet understand, the get-together sounded like serious business for Duncan's sister.

Lena dressed in a khaki skirt and cotton blouse and pulled her hair up in a ponytail. Though it was something she rarely attempted, she dabbed some concealer under her eyes to hide the fact that she'd been crying for twelve hours. Unfortunately, she'd had better results painting other people's eyes on a canvas than her own in real life.

As she drove to the bed-and-breakfast, Lena convinced herself that she would make it through the day. She told herself that sharing a few laughs with other women would be good for her soul. And if she should happen to run into Duncan, she would survive. She always had.

But God, she ached inside. She felt lost. And she feared in her heart that she'd lost Duncan forever.

Rowan and Ash's apartment in the Safe Haven was comfortable and welcoming and certainly less high Victorian than the rest of the bed-and-breakfast. The space was dominated by a large family room overlooking Safe Haven Beach and an open-concept kitchen and dining area. A seating area had neutral overstuffed chairs, couches, and ottomans grouped on a round area rug. Painted tables were scattered throughout, as were colorful lamps and fresh flowers. Framed photos lined the fireplace mantel and walls, and it took Lena just a glance to see that the pictures were from Rowan's life, Ash's life, and the life they were building together.

Annie and Evelyn were already there, and Christina was lying on her belly on the rug, busy with crayons and paper.

"Lena! Come on in!" With Serena on her hip, Rowan cleared pillows and toys from the sofa and made room for her to sit.

Evie asked, "Would you like some tea? Red wine?"

Lena noted that though there were two bottles of wine and four wineglasses on the coffee table, there wasn't a teapot in sight. "Um, wine?"

"Good answer!" Annie said, laughing.

Christina asked if John Dean had come along. "Not today," Lena said. "She's taking a nap." *Probably on my clean sheets,* she thought.

Lena immediately felt at ease. The women had been so fun and kind last evening that Lena felt ridiculous for ever believing Rowan and Annie were standoffish. The truth was quite the opposite. And Evelyn, the most recent addition to the island, was smart, witty, and caring. Lena had to admit that for a woman more accustomed to solitude than a girls' night out, she enjoyed their company immensely.

Why, exactly, they were gathered today was still unclear to Lena. When Rowan asked her to come by to talk

about the future of the Bayberry Island Mermaid Society, Lena thought she had misheard her.

"My mother is shutting down the organization," Rowan
said. "I need help brainstorming about how I can make
the process easier for her."

So there they were, gathered in Rowan's home, the
subdued light of a cloudy day reaching through the windows and resting on their faces.

"Thank you for coming," Rowan said, a twinge of
guilt in her voice.

Lena suddenly feared she'd been summoned on false
pretenses. She set down her wineglass, praying that this
was not about her relationship with Duncan, because
whatever questions they had, she had no answers for.
Maybe she never would.

"Lena, we're going to take over the merms." Rowan
made the announcement with no lead-in whatsoever.
"We want you to do it with us."

She cocked her head to the side. "Take over? Like a
coup?"

Annie laughed loudly. "Wouldn't that be fun? I've always wanted to go mano a mano with Polly Estherhausen."

"I'm not sure I'm following you," Lena said.

Serena was drowsing off in her mother's arms, so
Rowan softened her voice. "Ma has been leading the
group for forty years, but she just can't do it any longer.
No one else wants to do it, either. In fact, I would say no
one wants to bother with the group at all."

Lena was surprised. "But I thought there's always
been a Mermaid Society, that it was a tradition here."

"It is," Rowan said. "But it's a tradition that's hit a
dead end unless we can find a way to resurrect it."

"They've been trying to get Rowan and me to join for

at least fifteen years," Annie said. "They always pictured us as the 'next generation.'"

"Kinda like Star Trek?" Evie asked.

Annie snorted.

"I've always been seen as the de-facto future president," Rowan explained. "It's a job that's been held by a Flynn daughter or daughter-in-law for one hundred twenty-four years, and my number was up."

Lena didn't want to appear rude, but she had always thought the Mermaid Society slightly absurd. It was one thing to ride on a joyful parade float once a year dressed like a mermaid, but it was quite another to wear a spandex fantail to the grocery store.

Suddenly, a gust of wind beat at the side of the house, and they all jumped in surprise.

"The Mermaid Ball's going to be interesting tonight," Evie said. "Clancy's been freaking out because of the weather reports."

"We've been rained on before," Rowan said. "As long as there's not a power outage, we can work with it. But, boy, would I love to make it through one summer without the lights going out."

"Are you coming to the ball, Lena?"

She stared at Annie. "Who? *Me*?" Lena had never been to a Mermaid Ball.

"Yes, you." Annie smiled. "Are you going with Duncan?"

"Ah, no. I doubt that." Lena plastered a smile on her face. "Anyway, I need to get some work done tonight."

Rowan reached over and touched her hand. "Please come, Lena. I think it would be nice if all of us were there together. Maybe even make an announcement if we feel ready to."

Lena quickly changed the topic. "So you've already made up your minds? You're going to do it?"

Rowan and Annie glanced at each other. "That's what we're here to discuss. I felt horrible when I saw how broken up Ma and the other merms were, but not horrible enough to throw my common sense out the window."

"So we thought we might agree to join if we were able to make some changes," Annie said. "You know, dial back the cray-cray a little bit. I'm sorry, but I just don't want to be a sixty-year-old lady wandering around in coconut boobs and snow boots like Izzy McCracken. Nothing says 'out of my freakin mind' like that outfit."

Everyone laughed.

"So you think if you kept the general spirit of the group, they wouldn't mind if you made a few changes?"

Rowan winced. "I don't know, Lena. I haven't really talked to them about it. I wanted to have some ideas in place before I approached them."

"But what *is* the spirit of the group? Why does it even exist?" Evie poured herself more wine. "I know what the legend says, and I've seen enough to know that the merms are silly but harmless. So what is it that you've always run from?"

"I think the society started out with good intentions," Annie said. "They wanted to keep the original legend alive and encourage people to find love, and there's nothing wrong with that. But it's just derailed into a bunch of nonsense, and not all of it is harmless if you ask me. But I'll let our natural-born Flynn tell you about that."

Lena sat back and listened as Rowan talked about how she'd sit on the stairs as a child and eavesdrop on Mermaid Society meetings being held in the dining room. Her confession made Lena smile, since she'd sometimes listened from her apartment off the kitchen. Rowan described what she'd learned about the rituals performed on solstices and equinoxes. "It's just some repeat-after-me stuff about their respect for the Mermaid Queen."

Evie scrunched up her face. "That sounds a little too Druidy for my tastes."

"I dated a Druid once," Annie said. "He always smelled like pinesap."

"I think we're veering off topic, Annie," Evie said.

She raised her wineglass. "Carry on."

Rowan also described how they performed "interventions," where members would ask the mermaid to help two people find love—without the couple's knowledge or permission.

"I could never butt into people's lives like that," Evie said, shaking her head. "Even if it's not real."

"But," Rowan continued, "that's not the worst. The thing that really chaps my ass is their stupid book."

Lena listened as Rowan detailed how the Mermaid Society kept a log of major developments in the love lives of islanders and visitors. She remembered hearing mention of it, too.

Evie gasped. "You're *kidding* me!"

Rowan shook her head. "They go out and collect evidence of what happened to so-and-so in order to decide if it was a bona fide mermaid miracle or something more mundane like hormones, or too many daiquiris, or whatever."

Evie's eyes got huge. "It sounds like the Pope deciding who to canonize."

"Exactly," Annie said. They clinked wineglasses.

Lena decided to speak up. "I eavesdropped sometimes myself."

Rowan's lips parted. She looked surprised. "You did?"

"Sure. And one night I heard them arguing about whether to 'sanction' the love story of a woman who ran away with one of the party planners for her wedding."

"Oh, my God!" Annie laughed. "That girl is a legend—she hooked up with the equipment rental guy after her groom missed the mainland ferry and didn't show up for hours. She married the rental guy, moved to the Cape, and had seven kids."

Evie looked disturbed. "They keep all these love stories in an actual book?"

Rowan nodded. "I've never seen it, but I've heard them talk about it many times."

Everyone got quiet. Eventually Lena said, "Well, without all that stuff none of us would want to do, what's left? Why have a Mermaid Society at all?"

Rowan looked thoughtful. "There's the original legend, which is really nothing but a reminder that miracles occur in our lives every day. Then there's one hundred and fifty years of island history. And an unbroken tradition passed down through the women of my family." Rowan kissed the top of Serena's head.

"She's named after the original mermaid," Lena said.

"She is—she's the namesake of my great-great-grandmother." Rowan looked around the room. "So I guess if I let the mermaid tradition die, then Serena wouldn't get to put her stamp on it in the future."

"What should we do?" Annie asked. "Are we going to try to resurrect the Bayberry Island Mermaid Society? Drag it kicking and screaming into the twenty-first century?"

Suddenly, Christina hopped up from the floor. She'd been coloring so quietly that everyone had forgotten she was in the room. There were tears rolling down her cheeks. "I want to be a mermaid when I grow up. So does Serena. Please don't take it away from us."

The women sat in stunned silence for a moment. Eventually, Annie said, "Maybe we should put it up for a vote."

Rowan reached out to her niece and pulled her close. Christina cuddled into her side. "All righty, then. All those in favor of keeping the Bayberry Island Mermaid Society around for a few more years—in some form— please raise your hands," Rowan said.

It passed unanimously—four women and one little girl were in favor.

Rowan looked at the others and said, "I know what our first order of business should be."

Everyone waited.

"Mona and Frasier Flynn, my mother and father. Talk about two people who are in desperate need of a miracle."

"Then let's ask for one. What harm could it do?" Annie raised her glass, and everyone joined her. "Here's to miracles."

"To miracles," they repeated.

Mona stood in her front door, watching Duncan trim back her roses. If she didn't know better, she'd think he was trying to exterminate them along with all plant life in the immediate vicinity.

He had switched out the pruning shears for the electric hedge trimmer about a half hour before, saying the shears required maximum effort for minimal results.

Now piles and piles of blooms, thorns, and branches littered the yard. The arbor was next on his list, he had told her, followed by the boxwoods. Mona said a little prayer that her flora would survive the one-man invasion that was her son.

Mona could not see his eyes behind the safety goggles, but she could tell by the stiffness in his shoulders and neck that he was hurting terribly.

So he cut and cut and cut. Mona readjusted her earplugs.

Duncan had arrived at her front door, unannounced, the worries of the world etched on his handsome face. He said that during the cookout he'd noticed her outdoor plants had become overgrown, and he was there to fix the problem for her. Mona walked with him out to the shed and made sure he had everything he needed.

"Would you like some lemonade?"

"No thanks, Ma."

She looked him up and down. He had obviously been running—for a good long while. His shorts and shirt were soaked with sweat and rivulets ran down his shins. Duncan was healed physically. That was clear to see. The pain he carried that day was heartache.

Mona knew better than to push her eldest child. She left him to his work, setting large glasses of water on the edge of the front porch like one might leave food for a feral cat of unknown temperament. When he'd gulp one down, she'd refill it. And that was the only conversation they'd managed to have since he'd arrived.

Mona knew his pain was because of Lena. Hadn't she known this storm was a possibility? There was no way that Duncan could fall in love without it causing great conflict inside him. He had his life all planned out, and his brush with death hadn't caused him to adjust his course. Love, home, and family did not have a place in his world, and he would fight anything that tempted him in that direction. He saw the need for connection as a weakness, and he was terrified of ever being weak again.

And Lena had done far more than tempt him. From what Mona could tell, Lena had captured his heart.

Once Duncan was done with the front yard, he sheared away at the arbor. Though Mona knew a good trim was necessary to promote new and continued growth, she winced at the sight of all those blooms hitting the ground. When he finished the arbor, it took just fifteen minutes to trim back the boxwoods. When all was said and done, they appeared puny but far less traumatized than the roses.

He tidied up, dumped all the trimmings into the mulch pile behind the shed, then cleaned and put away the equipment. Mona watched him make his way through the side yard with his shoulders rounded and his head down, which was unlike him.

"Duncan."

He looked up. Because she'd caught him unaware, she saw the depth of his sadness and confusion, and it just about broke her heart.

"Are you all right?"

He nodded. "Fine."

"You can tell me anything. Your secrets are safe with me."

He chuckled, shaking his head. "You know, Ma, I'm learning I'm just not cut out for deep conversation. It never seems to end well for me."

"Do you love her?"

Mona wasn't sure what kind of reaction she expected from her son, but it certainly wasn't the one she got. Duncan nodded slowly, his face twisted in agony.

"Oh, honey."

"I don't know what I'm doing, Ma. Suddenly my whole life seems up in the air—what I want, what is most important to me, where my duty lies. I'm questioning everything."

Mona tried to hide her shock. Unless she was reading something into his words, Duncan had, for the first time, expressed doubt about returning to active duty. Before she could comment, he began speaking again.

"And the way this whole thing happened with Lena is too much for me to accept"—Duncan knocked on his own forehead—"in here. It doesn't make any sense."

Mona smiled at her son. "Love doesn't always make sense up there." She pointed to her heart. "Only here."

He shook his head and looked away.

Mona stepped closer to him, placing her hand on his large forearm. Sometimes it seemed like only yesterday that this big, burly man had been a sickly little boy. But never had she seen him as low as he was at that moment.

"Does she love you?"

He nodded again.

"Then a way *will* reveal itself. You simply have to have faith."

Duncan laughed, pulling her in for a quick and sweaty hug. "Thanks, Ma. You just hit the nail on the head—I don't have that amorphous kind of faith everybody talks about. It's not how I'm wired. And Lena, she's—" He cut himself off. "You know, at first I thought she was a flake, all dreamy and artsy and off in her own la-la land. And, Ma, I swear to God, at one point the thought even crossed my mind that she was an *actual mermaid*. How crazy is that?"

Mona felt her eyes widen.

"But it turns out she and I are alike in a lot of ways."

Mona didn't dare interrupt. This was more than Duncan had ever shared with her on any subject at all, let alone his thoughts on love. She was afraid to breathe.

"Lena's hardworking and determined. She pushes through the boundaries most people assume are impassable. She's beautiful and smart and funny, and I've never known anyone like her. But she's . . ."

"She's what?"

Duncan took a big breath. "Lena sees and feels things I do not. She goes places I can't go. Lena believes in mystical forces and signs and destiny, you know, the kind of gibberish I've always heard from you."

Mona laughed.

"It's just not going to work between us."

She carefully weighed her response. Duncan was teetering on the edge of discovery, but he had to do it his own way, at his own pace. "Different doesn't always mean incompatible."

He turned away and looked out toward the cliffs. "There's absolutely no way, Ma. Even if I could love her, I couldn't be in a relationship with her—I'm already in a relationship with the U.S. Navy's Special Warfare Command, and she's one hell of a jealous lover."

"Oh, my!" Mona melodramatically placed the back of her hand on her forehead as if she were on the edge of fainting. "Who are you and what have you done with my son?"

He scowled at her. "Say what?"

"I won't listen to this—what did you call it? *Gibber-*

ish?" Mona rested her hands on her hips. "Since when are you a quitter? Since when does Duncan Flynn walk away from a challenge and give up before he's even started?"

His eyes flashed.

"Now." Mona led him out of the yard and knew she had to change the subject before he could refresh his argument. He had heard her, and the barb was set, even if it did take a while to reel him in. "I have a very big favor to ask you."

He squinted at her. His apprehension made her laugh.

"I want you to be my escort to the Mermaid Ball tonight."

Both of Duncan's eyebrows arched. He stared at her without a word.

"How many Mermaid Balls have I insisted you attend since you graduated from high school?"

"Zero."

"And how much longer will you be with your family here on the island?"

"Not long."

"Good, then you see where I'm headed with this." She slid her arm inside his and walked with him. "It's formal attire, just an FYI."

"Oh, come on, Ma."

"Good thing your dress whites are hanging pressed and clean in your closet."

Chapter Twenty-three

Duncan's date for the evening wore a colorful sequined tail, coral jewelry, and a modest coconut and sequined bikini top with matching jacket. By the time they arrived, the crowd had already begun to assemble under the fairy lights. The public dock had been transformed into a wonderland of gauzy decorations, portable fountains, floral arrangements, and even a disco ball. Two giant rain tents had been hoisted up over the dock, one for the dance floor and bandstand and the other for tables, chairs, and food and drink. The evening was warm, with an occasional gust of wind, but so far the weather was holding up.

Clancy, however, was not.

Duncan watched him juggle his cell phone, radio, and pager, pacing in front of the bandstand—pointing to Main Street and sending Chip off in a panic. He looked like a man on the edge. When Duncan caught his little brother's eye, Clancy waved him over.

He hung up from the call and said, "Whoa. Lookin' good, Lieutenant. Where's your date?"

Duncan pointed. "Over there. By the potted ferns."

Clancy frowned. "That's Ma."

"Yep. She's my date, and she's one of the loveliest mermaids at the ball."

Clancy lolled his head around in exaggerated disbelief. "So where's Lena?"

"I don't have the slightest idea."

"Oh, for fuck's sake." He pulled Duncan by the sleeve of his dress whites and took him around behind the huge bandstand speakers. "What happened?"

"It's really none of your business, but I'll give you the executive summary: it's not going to work out. Our lifestyles don't mesh."

Clancy shut one eye and glared at Duncan with the other. "Hold up. It is my business if I see you about to make a colossal mistake, and brother, what you just said is bullshit."

"I better go back to Ma."

"Bull. *Shit.*" His brother pointed two fingers toward his own eyeballs, then at Duncan's, and back and forth several times. It was quite dramatic. "Look me in the eye and tell me you're not falling in love with Lena."

"Can't do that."

"Then what *happened*?"

Duncan laughed. "You wouldn't understand."

"Why's that?"

"Because Evie, your wife, is a very levelheaded woman. She lives in the real world. Lena is as airy-fairy as they come, and I can't deal with it. Call me what you want—a prick, a bastard, a dickhead—but love only goes so far after your girl tells you she believes in mermaids."

For a moment, Clancy's mouth froze in the shape of a small O.

"Yeah."

"Wait." Clancy thought for a minute. "Lena told you she believes in mermaids?"

"Not directly. But she implied as much. And then she implied that she might be one herself."

"Okay. Well, *that's* different."

"Yeah. Crazy different."

"So you just threw her overboard?"

Duncan sighed. "We had an adult discussion and then I left. Can I get back to Ma now?"

Clancy began laughing. "Look, I got so much crap to deal with tonight—the Weather Service just changed their forecast and we're going to get hit. It might hold off until after the dance is over, but it just as easily might not. So we'll have to talk about this later."

"I think we've pretty much covered it." Duncan turned around to look for his mother, but she wasn't where he'd last seen her. He wandered around, said hello to a few people, then picked up an ice tea from Rusty, who was bartending.

"Woo-wee, Lieutenant Flynn! Aren't you all shined up for the occasion?"

"Cheers, Rusty." He raised his plastic cup. "Have you seen my mother?"

"As a matter of fact, I have." He pointed beyond the food and beverage tent to the promenade of the public dock. "She just walked over thataway with the mayor."

Duncan jerked his head back in surprise. "The mayor ... of Bayberry? My father?"

"Yes, sir. They just strolled by hand in hand. Couldn't have been more than two minutes ago."

Duncan thanked Rusty for the intel and headed in that direction. There were plenty of strolling couples on the promenade—mermaids and sea captains, mermaids and pirates, mermaids and mermen, mermen and mermen—but he didn't see his parents. Duncan found a bench near a decorative birch tree and decided to pop a squat.

He thought about what his brother had just said. It was true that Lena hadn't come right out and claimed she believed in mermaids. Or that she was one. But Lena had made roundabout indications to that effect. *Hadn't she*?

He raised his eyes to the cloudy evening sky and sighed. What exactly had she said?

Just then Duncan heard a familiar voice. "Oh, Frasier! Why in the world did you wait twenty-five years to tell me this?"

"I . . I didn't know myself until recently."

Duncan turned his head just enough to see his father, in his Mermaid Ball tuxedo, down on one knee in front of his mother. She was crying.

Duncan didn't move.

"I knew you'd given up on me, Mona. I could see it in your eyes—you saw me as a failure as a man for what I'd done."

"Frasier, that's not true! I never blamed you for the collapse of the business. I never said you were a failure."

"But you *thought* it." Frasier sniffed, and his lip trembled. "You took charge of the family like I was incapable of the job."

"Oh, Frasier. You silly man." Mona grabbed Frasier's face and pulled it to hers and kissed the daylights out of him. "You gave up on *yourself*," she said. "Only *you* believed you were a failure—no one else did. It was all in your head. And because of that, you shut everyone out. You shut me out and locked yourself away from me! I took charge of the family because you'd given up on us!"

"Oh, God, Mona. I did. I know I did. I felt so much shame that I just curled in on myself."

"I couldn't get to you!" Mona began crying harder. "Sweetheart, I tried for years and years and you slammed the door in my face! My God, you are such a stubborn bastard!" She gripped his father's big body to hers, and for the first time ever, Duncan saw his father cry. He cried like a baby into Mona's coconuts.

"I could lose a thousand companies before I would ever want to lose you again," Frasier said. "I can't live without you any longer. You are my joy. You always have been."

"You don't have to live without me. I miss you so much."

"Forgive me, Mona. Take me back."

"I already have forgiven you, and of course I will take you back."

Duncan turned away. He shouldn't have witnessed that, but he supposed his parents couldn't be overly concerned about their privacy if they decided to have a gut-wrenching talk in the middle of the promenade. But now he'd leave them alone.

He rose from the bench, wondering if he might have more in common with his da than he'd ever imagined. Shame and guilt. Shut off and locked away. Feeling unworthy.

A tidal wave of emotion washed over him, and he knew if he didn't pull himself together, he was in danger of an outburst like the one he'd had during the night swim or after the dream. He shoved his hands into the pockets of his dress-white trousers and wandered through the crowd. Laughter spilled out from each little group of people. The band was assembling on the stage. Chip ran by, and when he saw Duncan, he looked relieved.

"Have you seen the mayor? We can't kick things off until the mayor takes the stage and does his official welcome."

Duncan smiled. "The mayor is indisposed at the moment, Chip." Duncan patted his shoulder. "Where's Clancy?"

"He told me he was too busy and to find the mayor."

"I'll take care of it."

Duncan walked up the risers leading to the stage and had a few words with the lead singer. She turned on the mike, and Duncan adjusted the height to reach his mouth. He tapped it to make sure it was operational.

"Good evening, ladies and gentlemen. I am U.S. Navy Lieutenant Duncan Flynn, and on behalf of my father, Mayor Frasier Flynn, I would like to welcome everyone to the . . ." Duncan quickly scanned the area for one of those huge event banners he'd seen displayed near the public dock. He found one. In the process, he also found Lena. She was standing toward the back of the tent with Rowan, Annie, and Evie, and all of them were dressed like mermaids.

Duncan's heart nearly stopped.

Lena stared at him like he'd returned from the dead.

The wind picked up.

Duncan regained his focus. "The . . . uh . . . one hundred and fourth annual Bayberry Island Mermaid Ball! Have fun tonight, and enjoy the rest of the festival."

Duncan lowered the mike for the singer and stepped off the stage, making a beeline to Lena. He didn't care how it went. How much worse could it get between them? He knew only that he might have made a mistake cutting himself off from her, and he was man enough to admit it.

She kept her dark eyes on him as he slipped through the crowd. The closer Duncan got to Lena, the stronger her magnetic tug became, drawing him nearer, pulling him in. Adelena Silva was so splendid she nearly blinded him.

She was a vision in all black against creamy skin. The mermaid skirt was a shimmering blue-black, all its thousands of tiny iridescent scales appearing slick with water. He had no idea how a fabric could produce such an illusion, but he appreciated the engineering involved, especially since the skirt clung to every dip and swell of her flesh. Only at her dainty ankles did the skirt part, revealing a pair of simple black sandals with heels.

There was no zipper in that thing. He had no idea how she'd even gotten into it.

Her breasts were tucked into two large black scallop shells tied around her neck and at her ribs with what looked like a satin cord. Her hair was loose and sleek, draped over one shoulder, her black eyes sparkled, and her skin glowed.

He was stupefied.

"Hey, sailor," Annie said.

Duncan snapped out of his trance. "Oh. Hi. You all look drop-dead gorgeous tonight."

Evie giggled. "We were just saying the same thing about you."

Duncan was confused. For an instant he couldn't remember why he had come over here.

"You look very handsome tonight, Duncan." Rowan kissed her brother's cheek, but before she pulled away, she whispered in his ear, "Don't you dare let her get away."

The band started playing, and out of the loudspeakers

came a melancholy big-band song. Duncan turned and met Lena's eyes. "May I have this dance?"

He could see Lena's pulse thumping in her neck. Her bosom rose and fell. But she didn't answer.

"Ladies, please excuse us." He took her hand.

When he'd stepped up on that stage, Lena had gasped. She wasn't alone. Half the women under the tent had some visceral reaction to the sight of a brawny six-foot-two Naval officer dressed in white from head to toe, dotted with gold buttons, and topped off with a stiff white hat with a black brim and gold braid.

"I think I'm going to faint," an older woman said.

"Hubba-hubba."

Rowan elbowed Annie for the outburst.

"Hey, I'm sorry," she said. "But if ever a man deserved a *hubba-hubba*, it's your brother at this moment."

"What's he doing up there?" Evie asked.

They soon found out. Lena nearly lost her balance when Duncan looked out into the crowd and his eyes connected with hers. She may have whimpered. And when he walked right up to her and asked her to dance, every molecule in her body told her to say yes, but her mind listed the one hundred reasons why she should say no. The most important reason of all: Duncan had turned his back on her.

The whole situation had a familiar stench to it.

But he'd made the decision for her, and Duncan was now escorting her to the dance floor, the singer crooning about the purple dust of twilight and love's refrain.

The wind kicked up again.

"Thank you for dancing with me."

Lena kept her eyes anywhere but on his face. "What do you want, Duncan?"

"I want to apologize. Lena, you have to understand how shocked I was. Here I am, really starting to believe that we've got something special . . ."

Her head snapped up. Duncan looked on the verge of tears.

". . . and you dropped the bomb on me—otherworldly signs and destiny and magic. It was all the crap I hated most as a kid. It's what I ran away from when I left Bayberry."

She listened.

"I'm not usually the kind of man to fall in love like . . ."

"Like what?"

"Like I have with you. I swear, if I didn't know better, I'd think you put some kind of spell on me, like you were a sorceress."

Her brain began to buzz. The music became muffled. She reared back.

"What I mean is it's almost like you have some kind of power over me. It overrides my rational thought."

"So loving me is irrational?"

"No! Lena, please, I'm not good at this."

Suddenly, they both turned to see Mona and Frasier dancing cheek to cheek not far from them. Mona winked and Frasier looked like he knew he was the luckiest guy on earth.

She was so happy for them. But it suddenly occurred to her how delicate love was. How hard it was to keep alive. How nearly impossible it was to find.

"Duncan, what are you saying? I think maybe I should just go."

"No! I'm trying to apologize. What I'm saying is I don't understand your world. You see things differently than I do. But you're sweet and talented and beautiful and kind and wonderful, and even though falling in love was not in my plan, you've completely bewitched me."

Lena shoved her way out of his embrace. "So I'm a witch now, too?"

Duncan looked lost. "What? No! I'm just saying that your world is foreign to me."

"My witchy world?"

Duncan looked crestfallen. "Lena, I never wanted to hurt you."

"But you did. And you're hurting me now, too." By then she was blind with pain. She stormed off the dance floor, leaving Duncan standing there like a white pillar candle in a puddle of sequins. She headed straight to her car.

What a horrible mistake. She shouldn't have come. It was the worst decision of her life.

On the way home, the wind really started in. Only minutes after she'd passed through the automatic garage door and threw her keys on the kitchen island, the power went out. Ondine was under her feet. Lena grabbed a candle from the dining room and a fireplace match from the great room, then stomped upstairs. She stripped out of the mermaid skirt and shells and put on a pair of shorts and a T-shirt, then went into her studio.

Lena cracked open a nearby window for air and placed the candle on the floor next to the chaise. Ondine settled in between her legs. And by candlelight she sketched and cried. She looked out on the wind-tossed water. Lena cried until she had no more tears left in her, no more breath, no more strength.

*   *   *

All hell broke loose at the Mermaid Ball. The wind had shorted out some of the electrical lines snaking from the bandstand, which started a good-sized fire by a line of garbage cans. Immediately after, the whole island lost power. Every one of Bayberry's pumper trucks had pulled onto the scene, lights flashing and sirens going. It seemed like overkill to Duncan, but what did he know?

Clearly, he didn't know shit.

Clancy had his hands full orchestrating the teardown. About two dozen men — rental company employees, police officers, and tourists — were holding on to tent poles, attempting to keep the huge canvases from going airborne before they could be disassembled. Most of the attendees had run for cover in one of the Main Street shops or inside the ferry terminal. When it started to rain, it came down hard and sharp, and the wind gusted to at least fifty knots by Duncan's estimates.

Banners began to rip. Tables, chairs, and decorations were knocked over and skidded along the dock. Tablecloths and trash went flying. Clancy yelled for Duncan to help him dismantle the largest of the temporary fountains, which had already started to topple over. As if the rain hadn't soaked him enough, Clancy got a direct shot from the disconnected hoses, which left him drenched in water.

A flash of lightning struck a transformer, and sparks went spraying over the bandstand. And just as Duncan ran over to help, the most horrific feeling of doom cut through him. He went still. His back shot ramrod straight and all his senses went on alert. He scanned the area to figure out the source of the danger, but that's when he realized the rush of foreboding had nothing to do with the chaos at the public dock.

Something was wrong with Lena.

"I've gotta go!" he screamed to Clancy.

"What's going on?"

"I'm not sure—hate to do this to you, but I have to leave!"

Duncan turned toward the public parking deck to get his mother's car and found that the fire trucks had blocked any exit. He began running up Main Street to see if he could catch a ride with someone to the north end of the island, but the traffic was moving far slower than he could run.

Duncan cut through the three side streets to get to Safe Haven Beach, and took off. Almost immediately he realized his heavy, wet uniform was restricting his movement, so he paused long enough to rip off his dress shoes, socks, and his clothes except for his undershirt and trousers.

And then Duncan began to run, churning through the sand, his mind fixed on his only objective: getting to Moondance Beach. He did the math in his head. He had five miles of beach to cover, and his best four-mile timed run was just over twenty-three minutes in Bates 922 combat boots, a time considered stellar by Navy standards but not nearly fast enough now. But what choice did he have with the traffic?

He dug his heels into the sand and pushed himself, careful to avoid the violent and steadily rising surf.

If his feeling of impending doom had been strong back at the public dock, it was nearly choking him now. Something was horribly wrong with Lena. He knew it. His knowledge was irrational, unrelated to any kind of recognizable evidence, but it was real. And it wasn't the first time he'd felt this. The night of the ambush, seconds before the explosion, he knew what was coming. That sick feeling ... he *knew*.

Duncan pushed himself harder and faster, not questioning the accuracy of his instinct. He was sure he was running for Lena's life.

She woke up to the sound of Ondine yapping and the taste of smoke in her mouth. Lena shot up to a sitting position and jumped up in the air. The chaise was on fire! The flames were licking across her arms! The pounding of her heart in her ears nearly drowned out Ondine's hysterical barking. She took a second to try to clear her mind. She'd fallen asleep.

The candle.

Just then the smoke alarm went off.

She grabbed Ondine and ran with her across the studio, tossing her to safety in the hallway. With only the light of the flames to guide her, Lena raced into the brush room to find the fire extinguisher. She began to panic. Where had she put it? When had she seen it last? Why wasn't she more prepared for something like this?

She flailed around blindly. She ran her hands along shelves and counter space, knocking over God knows what in the process. She got on her hands and knees and checked under the sink a second time, finally finding it shoved in the back behind a large jug of dish soap. She grabbed it. She couldn't see well. She'd never used one before! She held it up to catch more light, and with shaking fingers she wrestled with the unlocking pin. It pulled free.

Ondine barked louder. The fire alarm pierced her eardrums.

Lena turned, ran from the brush room, and was stopped

in her tracks by a wall of smoke and heat. What had happened? Oh, God! The whole studio had gone up while she was looking for the goddamn fire extinguisher! She heard a loud popping sound, and she watched as flames engulfed her wall of stored canvases.

The solvents! They were everywhere. On everything. Oh, God, no . . .

Duncan's pencil drawing! Her painting!

Fire licked up the walls and across the floor. It moved in endless liquid waves, eating away at everything it touched. Tears ran down her face as she tried to aim the extinguisher at anything and everything. It was useless.

She felt a rush of air and realized the window she'd cracked had been pulled open by the wind, now howling outside . . . and inside.

This was all her fault. It was a perfect storm of stupidity—wind, flame, solvents . . . She'd just burned down her beautiful studio! Her beautiful home!

There was no more time. She had to get out.

Just then she heard the sound of breaking glass. Lena looked up in time to see the skylight crack. She gasped in horror—this could *not* be happening! She watched the glass come loose in large, ugly shards. It was coming down on top of her . . .

Lena reacted without thought. She dived under the worktable in the middle of the room, thinking it would at least protect her from the falling glass.

She hit the ground with a thud. Everything went black.

He was flying in the darkness. In the zone. Running faster than he'd ever run in his life. His mind was trained on Lena.

Duncan got about a quarter mile from the chain-link fence marking the entrance to Moondance Beach when he saw the flames.

He put his head down and ripped into the sand, feeling his body move like a machine, perfect rhythm, combat breathing. Power. Speed. Focus.

Duncan barely slowed down, flying over the fence, then digging into the sand to the dune steps. He took them two at a time, breathing in the smoke now, hearing the crackle and pop of a huge fire. He took half a second to assess the situation—the exterior shingles were engulfed. In an upstairs corner he could see some of the building's framing, black bones against the orange flames. It was the studio. The fire had started in the studio.

He raced across the property, jumped on the back deck, and reached the kitchen door. Locked. He kicked it down with his bare feet.

"Lena!"

He quickly scanned the downstairs, all the while sensing the dread in his gut—she was upstairs. In the worst of it.

"Lena!" He screamed her name over and over again, running through the smoke. As he reached the foot of the staircase, Duncan did two things.

First, he took a second to locate his mental trigger, the reason he would push himself to do whatever had to be done in the next few moments, no matter how impossible. His trigger was Lena. Holding her in his arms again. Hearing her husky laugh. Seeing the spark in those dark eyes. He loved her, and he would have one more chance to tell her that. There was no other option.

And then, because he had no idea what awaited him

upstairs, he screamed out her name one last time and took a giant breath of air, aware it might be his last.

Duncan pounded up the staircase. On the second floor, he was met by thick smoke, fierce heat. He turned toward the studio, hoping to God he hadn't made the wrong choice, when he heard Ondine's piercing little bark. It was the most beautiful sound he'd ever heard.

He pushed through the smoke, a surreal, dim fog, through the double doors. His eyes went low, and he saw her. She was on the floor, half under the worktable and half under the huge easel, which had trapped the lower part of her body. There was no time to think. There was no air. Glass everywhere. In one seamless movement Duncan lunged forward, ripped the easel from her body, and threw it aside. He grabbed her—but he couldn't tell if she was alive. She was limp. In a glance, he saw her leg was covered in blood and lying at an odd angle. And in that last second he heard a whimper and reached out into the black smoke toward it. Grabbing the dog's collar, Duncan charged down the hall, down the steps, and kicked down the front door.

Once he had cleared the structure, he stopped to breathe—exhaled, inhaled—then carried Lena and the dog far away from the building, near the gate, as the wind whipped around them like crazy, the flames shooting into the sky.

Duncan lowered himself to the ground, cradling Lena in his arms. He reached into his pants pocket for his cell phone, turned on the speaker, and placed it on the ground.

"Lena. Can you hear me?"

She was breathing, but there was a streak of gray saliva around her lips. She had breathed in a lot of smoke.

The phone came to life. "Nine one one, what's your emergency? Police, fire, or—"

"Ambulance and fire. North Shoreline Road. Bayberry. House fire with serious injury, compound fracture, and smoke inhalation. One ambulance. Hurry."

"Sir, what is your name? Sir? Do you have a—"

Duncan gently propped Lena in his lap. He made a second quick scan of her body, immediately reaching around to his side to tear at his undershirt. In a one-handed burst of fury, he ripped off a strip about eight inches long—it would have to do—and gingerly tied it tightly around her lower leg. It would slow the bleeding. He knew the reality of the situation. The entire Bayberry Fire Department was busy at the dock, and that meant help would not be coming quickly.

Thank God not all the blood soaking into the ground was from Lena. Some of it was his—his feet were raw hamburger from running across broken glass.

"Lena. Sweetheart, can you hear me?"

She didn't respond.

He stared at her wide-eyed. *This cannot be happening. She cannot be gone.*

"Lena!" he cried, shaking her.

And just when he thought his mind would explode from the pain of her silence, her eyelids fluttered. Her lips parted and she whispered, "Duncan."

Oh, Jesus. She was alive. "Lena, I'm here."

"Duncan," she whispered again.

He put his face next to hers. He kissed her cheeks and forehead and tried so very hard not to jar her body or squeeze her, but the joy he felt was overwhelming.

"It happened so fast . . ."

"Shhh. Baby. It's all right. You're hurt, but you're going to be fine. I promise."

"Is Ondine . . . ?"

"I've got her. She's right here."

The dog toddled up to Lena and began licking her hand. Duncan looked down at the poor thing to see her fur was singed and black, but otherwise she didn't seem injured. He scratched her behind the ears.

"Bravo Zulu, Ondine," he said.

Lena began to cry. He felt her shake and tremble. He held her close, covering her body with his.

"I love you, Lena. So much." Duncan's tears fell on her face, rinsing the soot away in narrow streaks. "I'm sorry. I'm so sorry. I will never doubt you again. I get it now—sometimes you just *know*. Like just now I knew something had happened to you. I can't explain it . . ."

"Shhh," she said, cutting off his rambling. "I love you, Duncan. Thank you for not giving up on me."

Epilogue

One year later ...

Lena lay on a blanket in the sand and watched the high evening clouds float along, pastel wisps of red and orange making their way across the horizon line. Though beautiful, she knew the passing clouds were an illusion. The sky was still—*they* were the ones in motion down here on earth, spinning through time, the tides and seasons always in a state of change.

A warm breeze ruffled their hair and clothing. Ondine continued to chase seagulls up and down the surf. And Lena reveled in her husband's touch. One of his hands gently stroked her hair while the other protected her enormous belly.

Sometimes Lena cried when she recalled last year's fire and the chaos and pain it had caused. But mostly she looked back on herself a year ago with bittersweet amusement. Right here on this beach, she'd dug her heels into the sand and informed Duncan that she could take care of herself. She didn't need his protection. Thank you very much.

As it turned out, she'd missed the mark on both counts. In the moment when all was lost, she had needed Duncan. She hadn't been able to do it by herself. And he had been there—to take care of her and protect her. He still was.

"I love you, Adelena Silva-Flynn." Duncan's voice was low and gentle as he leaned down to kiss her forehead. "Are you getting tired? We can go in if you'd like."

"Naw, I'm great. I've got at least ten good minutes left in me."

They laughed. Lena was due with their daughter any day now, and she had become grumpy, uncomfortable, and exhausted from not being able to sleep. Duncan had cleared his schedule for the next month so that he could be with her for the birth and then stay at home with his girls.

It was not something Lena had asked him to do, but after the fire Duncan had resigned from the Navy. He'd accepted a job as director of a national nonprofit that brought together his two passions, wounded warriors and competitive water sports. Duncan had resigned while Lena was still in the hospital recovering from her injuries, which had allowed him to stay in Boston to be at her side.

Sanders took care of everything else—all the insurance hassles and all of Lena's finances. "Just get better," he'd told her.

The first time she'd asked Duncan about his decision not to return to active duty, he'd explained his thinking this way: "I listened to others. I listened to my heart. And I realized I could still serve in honor of my friends. It's just a different kind of service to my country and to those I love. I think my friends would approve."

So, in this last year, not only had Duncan started a new career, but he had acted as general contractor in the rebuilding of their home. He'd also provided expert personal coaching for Lena as she got back on her feet—literally.

Her right leg had been broken in two places, and she now sported a screw in her ankle and knee, with a metal rod at her tibia. Though it wasn't planned, Lena had become pregnant just three months after the fire, while still in the thick of physical therapy with the always-energetic and competent Brandy. Lena and Duncan now affectionately referred to her as "the Perky-nator." Just not to her face.

Duncan and Lena had moved into the Safe Haven while the house was being rebuilt. He'd created a studio space for her and had encouraged her to get back to work, even gifting her with a stool and a beret. Lena had decided not to use oils and solvents during her pregnancy, sticking with acrylics, egg tempura, and watercolor, a change that had brought out new dimensions in her paintings.

"Are you up for a swim?" Duncan asked.

"Always."

For some men it could prove challenging to maneuver a very pregnant woman from a prone to standing position in the sand. Not for Duncan Flynn. He simply reached down, scooped his arms under Lena's knees and back, and stood up. Slowly and carefully, he carried Lena to the rolling surf, walking with her until the salt water lifted her away from Duncan's arms. Lena drifted, floating on her back, feeling the familiar rocking motion provided by the mother of all life and the forceful kicks coming from inside her own body.

"Looks like we've got company again."

She raised her head from the water and turned to where Duncan pointed. A group of fantails playfully splashed in the waves not ten yards away, their sleek shapes slipping through the water in unison. They seemed particularly joyous, Lena thought. It was almost like a celebration.

"They're unusually active this evening."

She nodded, swimming toward Duncan. Lena eased into his embrace and kissed his warm lips. "The ocean is full of surprises, you know." She smiled up at his handsome face.

"You don't say?"

"It's true." Lena brushed her fingertip down his scruffy cheek and sighed with contentment. "All kinds of unusual things happen here at Moondance Beach. Who knows what you'll experience in the years to come?"

"Hmm." Duncan dipped his lips to hers once more, cupping the back of her head in his hand as he kissed her lovingly. When he pulled away, Lena saw that his eyes were full of mischief.

"Lena?"

"Yes?"

"What are the chances that our daughter will be a . . . you know . . . a natural swimmer?"

Lena laughed. "That goes without saying! Her daddy is a SEAL!"

Lena and Duncan laughed, holding each other as they watched the graceful creatures swim out to deep water.

Read on for a look at the first spellbinding
book in the Bayberry Island series

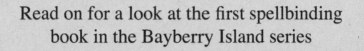

Sea of Love

Available now from

headline
ETERNAL

"Is it true what they say about the mermaid statue?"

"Yeah, like, can she really hook us up with some hot guys while we're here?"

Rowan Flynn's eyelid began to twitch. She gently closed the cash drawer and smiled at her latest arrivals, grateful they couldn't read her thoughts. But holy hell—this had to be the hundredth mermaid question of the day! At this rate she'd never make it through festival week without completely losing her mind.

"And, like, where's the nearest liquor store?"

But wait ... what if this were the opportunity she'd been waiting for, the perfect time to knock some sense into the tourists? Maybe these girls—two typical, clueless, party-hungry twentysomethings checking into her family's godforsaken, falling-down bed-and-breakfast—would be better off knowing the awful, horrible truth about the Bayberry Island mermaid legend. And love in general.

The thought made her giddy.

Rowan was prepared for this opportunity. She'd rehearsed her mermaid smackdown a thousand times. The words were locked, loaded, and ready to *zing!* from her mouth and slap these chicks right on their empty, tanned foreheads, perhaps saving them from years of heartache and delusion.

Yo! Wake up! she could say. *Of course there's no truth to the legend. Trust me—the mermaid can't bring you true love. It's a frickin' fountain carved from a lifeless, soulless hunk of bronze, sitting in a town square in the middle of a useless island stuck between Nantucket and Martha's Vineyard, where . . .*

"Uh, like, hell-*oh*-oh?"

The girls stared at Rowan. They waited for her answer with optimistic, wide eyes. She just couldn't do it. What right did she have to stomp all over their fantasies? How could she crush the romantic tendencies nature had hard-wired into their feminine souls? How could she jack up their weeklong vacation?

Besides, her mother would kill her if she flipped out in front of paying guests. The Flynns relied on the B and B to keep them afloat—a predicament that was 100 percent Rowan's fault.

So she handed her guests the keys to the Tea Rose Room, put on her happy-hotelier face, and offered up the standard line of crap. "Well, as we locals like to say, there's no limit to the mermaid's magical powers—but only if you *believe.*"

"Awesome." The dark-haired woman snatched the keys from Rowan and glanced at her friend. "Because I *believe* we need to get laid this week!"

The girls laughed so hard they practically tripped over themselves getting to the grand staircase. Rowan cocked her head and watched them guffaw their way to the landing, banging their rolling suitcases against the already banged-up oak steps. For about the tenth time that day, she imagined how horrified her loony great-great-grandfather would be at the state of this place. Rutherford Flynn's mansion was once considered an architectural wonder, a symbol of the family patriarch's huge ego, legendary business acumen, enormous wallet, and enduring passion for his wife—a woman he swore was a mermaid.

"Oh! Like, ma'am, we forgot to ask. Where's our room?"

Ma'am? Rowan was only thirty, just a few years older than these girls! Since when was she a damn *ma'am*?

Oh. That's right. She'd become a *ma'am* the day she'd left the real world to become the spinster innkeeper of Bayberry Island.

"Turn right at the top of the stairs." Rowan heard the forced cheerfulness disappear from her voice. "It's the second room on the left. Enjoy your stay, ladies."

"We are so going to try!"

As the giggling and suitcase dragging continued directly overhead, Rowan propped her elbows on the old wood of the front desk and let her face fall into her hands. So she was a ma'am now, a ma'am with three check-ins arriving on the evening ferry. She was a ma'am with one clogged toilet on the third floor, twenty-two guests for breakfast tomorrow, four temporary maids who spoke as many languages, and eight hellish days until the island's annual Mermaid Festival had run its course. Oh, and one more detail: the business was twenty-seven thousand dollars in the hole for the year, losses that absolutely *had* to be made up in the coming week or bankruptcy was a distinct possibility. Which also was this ma'am's fault, thank you very much.

And every second Rowan stayed on the island playing pimp to the mermaid legend was a reminder of the lethal error she'd made while visiting her family exactly three years before. She'd dropped her guard with that fish bitch just long enough to leave her vulnerable to heartbreak, betrayal, and the theft of what little remained of the Flynn family fortune. It was hard to believe, but Rowan had been happy before then. She'd studied organizational psychology and had a career she loved, working as an executive recruiter in the higher-education field. She had a great apartment in Boston and a busy social life. So what if she hadn't found her true love? She'd been in no rush.

But she'd returned for the Mermaid Festival that year and met a B and B guest named Frederick Theissen. He was so charming, handsome, and witty that before she could say, "Hold on a jiff while I check your references," Rowan had fallen insanely in love with a complete stranger determined to whisk her away to New York. Her mother and her cronies insisted it was the legend at work and that Frederick was her destiny.

As it turned out, her charming, handsome, and witty stranger might have loved her, but he also happened to be a Wall Street con man who used her to steal what remained of her family's money. Destiny sucked.

Of course, her mother wasn't entirely to blame for her downfall. Rowan should have known better. But she still had the right to despise anything and everything related to the frickin' mermaid until the day she died.

The familiar *putt-putt* of a car engine caught her attention, and Rowan raised her head to look out the beveled glass of the heavily carved front doors. She watched the VW Bug plastered with iridescent fish scales come to a stop in the semicircle driveway. Since it was festival week, the car was decked out for maximum gawking effect, with its headlights covered in huge plastic seashells and a giant-assed mermaid tail sticking out from the trunk. Her mother got out of the car and strolled through the door.

"Hi, honey! Everything going smoothly? How many more are due on the last ferry?"

Rowan gave Mona the once-over and smiled. Like the car, her mother was in her festival finery, in her case the formal costume of the president of the Bayberry Island Mermaid Society. Mona's flowing blond wig was parted in the center and fell down her back. She wore shells on her boobs, sea glass drop earrings, and a spandex skirt of mother-of-pearl scales that hugged her hips, thighs, and legs. The skirt's hem fanned out into a mermaid flipper that provided just enough ankle room for her to walk around like Morticia Addams. Unlike Morticia, however, Rowan's mother wore a pair of coral-embellished flip-flops.

"Hi, Ma." Rowan checked the B and B reservation list. "Two doubles and a quad—parents and two kids."

"Will you put the family in the Seahorse Suite?"

"No. I've already got a family in there. I'm putting the new arrivals in the Dolphin Suite."

Her mother approached the front desk, leaned in close, and whispered, "What's the status of the commode?"

"I'm hoping it'll get fixed before they check in."

One of Mona's eyebrows arched high, and she tapped a finger on the front desk. "You'd better do more than hope, my dear. The Safe Haven Bed-and-Breakfast has a reputation to uphold."

Rowan held her tongue. Some might argue the establishment's only reputation was that it had seen better days and was owned by the island's first family of cray-cray.

"But why worry?" Mona waved an arm around dramatically, a move that caused one of her shells to shift slightly north of decent. "The evening ferry might not even make it here. Did you hear the forecast?"

This was a rhetorical question, Rowan suspected, but she could tell by the tone of her mother's voice that the news wasn't good. "Last I heard, it was just some rain."

Mona shook her head, her blond tresses swinging. "Ten-foot swells. Wind gusts up to forty-five knots. Lightning. The coast guard's already issued a small-craft advisory. And the island council is meeting with Clancy right now to decide if they should take down the outdoor festival decorations—a public safety concern, you know. We wouldn't want that giant starfish flying around the boardwalk like back in 1995. Nearly killed that poor man from Arkansas."

"Absolutely." Rowan pretended to tidy some papers on the desk as she forced her chuckle into submission. They both knew the real public safety risk was that council members could come to blows deciding whether to undecorate for what might be just a quick-moving summer squall. She didn't pity her older brother Clancy. Tempers were known to flare up during festival week, a make-or-break seven days for anyone trying to eke out a living on this island, which was nearly everyone. And that didn't count the latest twist. A Boston developer's plans to build a swanky marina, golf course, and casino hotel had split the locals into two warring factions. About half of the island's residents preferred to keep Bayberry's quaint New England vibe. The other half wanted increased tourism revenue, even if it meant crowds, traffic, noise, and pollution. And the Flynns were at the center of the dispute, since their land sat smack dab in the middle of the mile-long cove and was essential to the development plans. Much to the dismay of every other property owner on the cove, both Mona and Frasier were listed as owners, and Mona forbade Rowan's father to sell the land. This meant that one little, middle-aged, spandex-clad mermaid was holding a major real estate developer, every other cove landowner, and half the population of the island hostage.

Rowan had come to view the conflict as a kind of civil war, and like the more historically significant one, the conflict had pitted family member against family member, neighbor against neighbor. The weapon of choice around here wasn't cannon or musket, though. It was endless squabbling, ruthless name-calling, and an occasional episode of hair pulling or tire slashing.

Rowan might not be thrilled about running from Manhattan with her life in shambles, but one thing could be said for her place of birth. It wasn't dull.

"Well, Ma, I'm sure Clancy will handle the situation with tact and diplomacy. He always does."

"That is so true." As Mona's gaze wandered off past the French doors and into the parlor, a faint smile settled on her lips. Rowan was well aware that her mother was enamored with her two grown sons—Clancy, a former Boston patrol officer who was now the island's chief of police, and Duncan, a Navy SEAL deployed somewhere in the Middle East. As the baby of the family, Rowan had grown up accepting that her mother was unabashedly proud of her two smart, handsome, and capable boys. Of course Mona had always loved Rowan, too—but *enamored*? Not so much. Exasperated was more like it, especially starting in about fifth grade, when Rowan began talking about how she couldn't wait to escape the island and start her real life.

"This *is* your real life," her mother would say. "Every day you're alive is real. And if you can't be really alive here on Bayberry Island, you'll never be really alive, no matter where you go."

God, how that used to piss Rowan off. It still did.

Mona adjusted her shell bra and returned her attention to her daughter. "I told Clancy to come over here after the meeting and help you with the storm shutters. God knows your father is useless when it comes to that sort of thing, if he cared enough to check on the house in the first place."

Rowan ignored the jab. She'd adopted a hands-off policy when it came to her parents' ongoing power struggles, including their opposing positions on the development plans. "Only a few shutters are in good enough condition to make a difference, and besides, Clancy's got more important things to do right now."

Mona didn't like that response, apparently. Her brow crinkled up. "Who's going to help you, then? Has a handsome and single handyman managed to check in without me noticing?"

"Not possible, Ma."

"It's not possible that such a man would want to visit Bayberry Island?"

"No—it's not possible you wouldn't have noticed."

"True enough." Mona giggled. "It *is* my job, you know."

Rowan's eyes got big, and all she could think was, *Dear God, not this again.* Her mother was the retired principal of the island's only school, but she'd just alluded to her other "job"—that of Mermaid Society president and keeper of all things legend related. It was a wide net that Mona and her posse used to fish around in other people's love lives.

Her mother glanced down at Rowan and put her hands on her scale-covered hips. "You look like you have something facetious to say."

"Nope. Not me, Ma. I'm totally cool with the legend. Love is a many-splendored thing ... all you need is love ... back that ass up and all that shit."

Mona gasped. "*Rowan Moira Flynn!*"

Just then, the *tap-tap* of quick footsteps moved through the huge formal dining room and headed toward the foyer, which was enough to divert Mona's attention.

"Imelda!"

The petite older woman clutched her chest in surprise, then cut loose with a long string of Portuguese-laced obscenities. "You're gonna give me a heart attack one day, Mona."

"I was just happy to see you."

Imelda Silva, who had once been the family's private housekeeper and was now the B and B's cook, shook her head and marched through the foyer on her way to the staircase. "I've been working for your family for twenty-some years. You and I both know you're not happy to see me. You just want me to do something for that fruity mermaid group of yours and the answer is still *não*! I'd rather fix the toilet in the Dolphin Suite! And you, Rowan." Imelda pointed an accusatory finger in her direction. "Stay out of the butter pecan ice cream. It's the topping for tomorrow's waffles."

Mona looked hurt as she watched Imelda trudge up the grand staircase. "What is *wrong* with everybody this year?" She sighed loudly. "Everywhere I turn, it's just one bad attitude after another! What happened to the joy and delight of the biggest week of the whole summer season? Why aren't people filled with excitement?"

"We're tired."

"Ha!" Mona narrowed her eyes at Rowan. "We are the people of Bayberry Island, my dear, caretakers of the mermaid, the sea goddess of love. This week is nothing short of sacred to us, to our way of life. We have no time to be tired." She paused for dramatic effect. "Mark my words, honey. If we don't perk the hell up around here, we're completely screwed."

Sea of
Love

Bayberry Island
Home to an infamous mermaid
statue which legend says grants true love...

When Rowan Flynn returns home to escape her
heartbreak she vows never to love again.
But will her fortunes be changed?

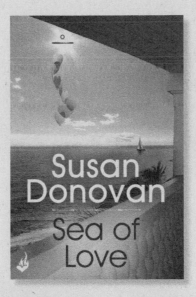

The Sweetest Summer

Bayberry Island
Home to an infamous mermaid
statue which legend says grants true love...

A beautiful blast from Police Chief Clancy Flynn's
past walks back into Bayberry with a crime on her head.
Will he follow his heart?

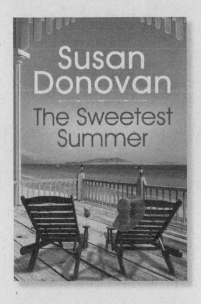

headline
ETERNAL

FIND YOUR HEART'S DESIRE...